BUCCANEER'S
MURDER

BUCCANEER'S MURDER

Roger Keevil

also by Roger Keevil

THE INSPECTOR CONSTABLE MURDER MYSTERIES

Murderer's Fête
Murder Unearthed
Death Sails In The Sunset
Murder Comes To Call
Murder Most Frequent
The Odds On Murder
No Bar To Murder
The Murder Cabinet
The Game Of Murder

THE COPPER & CO MURDER MYSTERIES

Honeymooner's Murder
Murder At Witch's Holt

BUCCANEER'S MURDER

a Copper & Co. murder mystery

by
Roger Keevil

Cover design by Christopher Brooke

This book is dedicated to the optimists

Chapter 1
Friday

"Well, that's a very satisfactory outcome," remarked Detective Inspector Dave Copper.

"Too right, boss," agreed his colleague Detective Sergeant Pete Radley, as the pair descended the steps of the grand nineteenth-century edifice that was the Westchester Crown Court complex. "Don't you love it when a plan comes together?"

"Especially when it takes a whole lot of very unsavoury characters off the streets," said Copper. "One way or another."

"And you'd have potted even more," grinned Radley, "if they hadn't had a falling-out among thieves and started shooting one another."

"That's gangs for you," said the inspector. In his late thirties, above medium height and with a stocky frame, the responsibilities of rank sat lightly on him, although the tousled hair, together with the laugh-lines around his eyes, were a reminder of the irreverent sergeant who once provided a constant foil to his former superior Inspector Andy Constable, now elevated in attendance to the higher echelons of government. "Even so," continued Copper, "murder is murder, and the law does not approve. But on the other hand, if we hadn't been called in to investigate the killings, it would never have led us into a situation where we could round up the whole crew and put a stop to the damage they were doing."

"Well, whichever way you slice it, the A.C.C. looks as if she's having a field day." Radley, curly-haired, a few years younger and a touch chubbier, thanks to a perpetual struggle against the lure of the doughnut, pointed to the far corner of the foot of the steps, where a senior officer, resplendent in dress uniform, could be seen making a statement in front of a television camera crew, while a gaggle of reporters surrounded them, phones outstretched in an attempt to garner footage or quotes for their respective media outlets. "Bet she's going to hoover up as much credit for herself as she can."

"And she's entirely welcome to it," responded Copper. "That's what Assistant Chief Constables are for. The cameras love a bit of silver braid, and it leaves the rest of us to get on with the real job with a reasonable degree of anonymity. I don't know which fiction writer came up with the idea of a celebrity detective, but I'm glad it didn't spill over into real life. I don't want camera crews on my doorstep."

"So what now, boss?" Radley consulted his watch. "It's only just on midday. I don't know about you, but I was a bit surprised when the jury came back so quickly with a straight 'guilty' for the whole mob. And the dear old judge didn't hang about in sending them all down for a good long time, did he?"

"Maybe he had plans for the weekend and wanted to get away in a hurry," smiled Copper. "Or at the very least, he was getting peckish and fancied an early lunch." He thought for a moment. "Actually, that's not an entirely stupid idea."

The sergeant looked up in surprise. "What's this then, boss? You're standing me lunch?"

Copper laughed. "Sorry, Peter. No such luck. I'm afraid you're going to have to put up with gristle pies in the canteen back at the station. I'm planning on pulling the privilege of rank. You can get back over to home base and tell the others all about our very happy result – that's if they haven't been glued to the live news feed of the A.C.C. doing her stuff – while I head over to County H.Q. here and see if I can't lure my dear wife away from her duties for a spot of celebratory lunch. After all, the credit's just as much the Forensic Department's as ours.

8

And who knows? As it's Friday, we might decide to take the rest of the day off."

"So I get the mucky end of the stick as usual," groaned Radley in mock complaint. "Dumped in favour of Una, eh? Can't see the attraction, myself."

"Don't gripe, sergeant," responded Copper. "I didn't mention what I expected you to do after you'd reported in back at the station, did I? I'd be amazed if there's much going on to keep you at your desk for the remainder of the afternoon. And as I shan't be there to keep an eye on you ..."

"Oh. Right." The grin returned to Radley's face. "Er ... drop you at H.Q. then, shall I, boss? As you'll be getting a lift home with Una?"

"An excellent suggestion," smiled Copper in return. "And I will see you on Monday."

*

As Sergeant Una Singleton emerged from the imposing front entrance of Westchester's modern police headquarters, her husband bounded up the steps to deposit a resounding kiss on her cheek.

"Excellent timing, love," said Dave Copper, a broad smile on his face.

"You're in alarmingly chipper mood," responded his wife with an answering smile. Slim and attractive, with long blonde hair caught back in an uncomplicated style, and clear grey eyes whose sometimes piercing gaze rarely missed even the tiniest detail in her work as a forensics officer, she combined calm efficiency with a ready sparkle. "What happened to that grumpy old bear who left our house after breakfast?"

"That grumpy old bear has just had one of the best results of his professional career," replied Copper. "The jury steamed back this morning in double-quick time, much to everybody's surprise, with a full set of ringing guilty verdicts on the entire mob, and His Honour the judge then promptly sent the whole lot down for satisfactorily long stretches without pausing for breath. And the upshot is that, instead of hanging around depressing court waiting rooms, cooling my heels and fearing that some idiot would find an excuse to let the evil-doers go free, I find myself unexpectedly available for the afternoon. Hence the invitation to lunch."

"Not that I'm complaining," said Una. "This version of my favourite detective is much more to my liking."

"Glad to hear it, love."

"Obviously the judge must have had some kind words for your efforts," surmised Una.

"Not just me, love," replied a still-grinning Copper. "You and your team came in for your fair share of credit from the bench. Which is why I thought you deserved a treat. Lunch on me. The only question is, can you get away with skiving off for the rest of the day?"

"No problem," said Una. "Sooz is covering for me."

"So Suzanne is happy to lie in a good cause?" enquired the inspector.

"No word of a lie will be uttered," countered Una. "If anyone asks, Sooz will simply say that, as a result of this morning's court proceedings, I am being debriefed on the case by a senior detective. And that, Inspector Copper, will be that. So where do you propose to take me for this official working lunch?" she twinkled.

"The thought struck me that we might have a celebratory glass of wine or two with the meal," suggested her husband. "So with that in mind, how about dropping your car back home and then taking a stroll up the village to the Dammett Well Inn? Jerry Porter's cooking is probably better than anything we'll find in any of the places around here, and then we can saunter back home and complete the debriefing session in comfort." He raised a roguish eyebrow.

"You, Mr. Copper," retorted his wife in mock

reproof, "should be ashamed of yourself. If I didn't know better ..."

"What makes you think you do?" laughed Copper. "Come on – dig out your car keys. I'm developing a serious appetite."

*

As Bob de Waters gently eased the nose of *Red Buccaneer II* through the jaws of the harbour of St. Malo, his eye fell upon the dinghy containing the official from the port authorities, already approaching from the quayside. And he thought he could tell, even at this distance, that the yacht was having her usual effect on those who saw her for the first time.

Although not one of the larger super-yachts – under thirty metres, considerably less than some of her more gigantic sisters who clustered in the bay of Monte Carlo during the peak of the social season – *Buck*, as all the crew called her, unfailingly drew the eye wherever she went. It was not the racy lines of her profile – many of the newest motor yachts seemed to have more in common with the design features of the rockets portrayed in schoolboy comics of the 1950s, with exaggeratedly raked windows, go-faster fins, and knife-like bows which looked as if they could cut through granite. While less than ten years old, *Buck* had more in common with the more traditional outlines of the pleasure craft of the wealthy of the 1930s, with a slightly more upright and less athletic stance. This was not to say that she looked old-fashioned. It was more that she stood out as a lady among a group of pushy young celebrities. But her unique feature, which attracted instant attention whenever she made an appearance, was her colouring. In a world where her sisters all wore liveries consisting of muted creams, deep marine blues, and smoky graphite greys, *Buck* burst on to the scene flaunting the brightest scarlet clothing. The forward half of her hull was emblazoned with a rippling representation of the Jolly Roger skull-and-crossbones flag, not in its traditional black-and-white version, but in a vivid red-and-white which was painted to give the effect that the flag, whipped by the wind, was beginning to shred into tatters on its trailing edge. The remainder of the hull, together with the vessel's upper works, was painted in stark white, relieved with occasional touches of red at strategic points. And, to accompany the usual British Red Duster at the stern and the courtesy French Tricolor displayed above the wheelhouse, the Red Roger, house flag of Pirate Holdings, flew proudly from the topmost mast.

Bob eased back even further on the throttle as the harbourmaster's dinghy came alongside, and watched as a rope was thrown by Taff, his deck hand – it would be stretching the language to give him the title of 'mate', the traditional word for the second rung on the ladder of command, given that there were just the two of them crewing the vessel above decks. The rope was expertly caught by the young man in charge of the dinghy, and the small boat was guided towards the stern of *Buck*, where it would be easiest for the port official to step aboard on to the swimming platform. Bob took a deep breath as the official started to make his way towards the wheelhouse. 'Time to dig out the French vocabulary again,' he thought to himself. 'I really ought to have this off pat by now, being the third port in four days. And that's not counting the times before. So why doesn't it ever get any easier?' He stitched a welcoming smile on to his face and held open the wheelhouse door.

*

Treymain Loader glanced out at the steepled skyline of St. Malo rising above the city's ramparts and did a quick mental calculation. Now that everyone had finished breakfast, it wouldn't take long to clear down and have everything put away. If there was one thing he couldn't abide, it was an untidy galley. Not, he smiled to himself, that you could really call his surroundings by the undignified title of 'galley'. The kitchen adjacent to the main saloon of *Red Buccaneer* gleamed with immaculate stainless steel and mirrored glass, and was furnished with the most lavish array of appliances that he had ever imagined could be found on a boat of this size. Although for the moment, they would not be called into use. Lunch was pretty much organised – he'd already done most of the *mise-en-place* with the items he'd picked up around the market in Granville yesterday, so the usual lunchtime cold buffet for anyone who hadn't gone ashore would be well supplied today with a good selection of Normandy cheeses and cold meats with accompanying salads, with a *Tarte Tatin* – what else? - to finish. Everything was sat ready in one of the capacious fridges, together with plentiful quantities of Sir's favourite champagne in the wine chiller. Just a few baguettes to pick up from the nearest *boulangerie*, and he'd be ready to roll. And for dinner? He grinned as inspiration struck. How about ... something involving scallops, with a Calvados sauce? He took a look at his watch. Surely he would have plenty of time to get across to Cancale and pick up some of the best ones the port was famous for. It couldn't be more than seven or eight miles away, and Sir wouldn't complain about springing for a taxi, no worries. Nice to work for an employer who didn't count the pennies, thought Trey. He finished polishing the last of the glasses and closed the cupboard with a small nod of satisfaction.

The position of steward aboard a luxurious private yacht like *Buck* was the last thing Trey could possibly have imagined during his boyhood in the small house on the outskirts of Bridgetown, Barbados where he grew up. Despite being a bright pupil at school, good employment was not always guaranteed on the Caribbean island, but Trey's willingness to learn, together with the excellent manners dinned into him by a loving but sometimes strict mother, obtained him a job as a waiter at one of the island's smartest tourist hotels. Trey soon found himself spending more time around the kitchens observing the chefs than waiting at tables, and eventually the head chef, in response to Trey's remorseless pestering, agreed to tutor him as an occasional assistant. The young man's talent blossomed, and he was soon taken into the kitchen brigade on a full-time basis. Then, one day, came the opportunity which changed everything. A wealthy industrialist staying at the hotel was particularly impressed with a dish which Trey had prepared, and insisted on conveying his compliments in person. During the conversation which followed, it emerged that the man was in the process of acquiring a new motor yacht, and would be needing a chef-cum-steward as part of the crew. With enthusiastic testimonials from the hotel's management, matters were soon arranged, and when *Buck*'s new owner returned to the Caribbean some weeks later to take command of his new vessel, Trey found himself in an undreamed-of situation, with virtually unlimited funds and the world before him. And in the past five years, he had never for a moment ceased to bless his good fortune.

After a brief check around the saloon to ensure that everything was in order, Trey climbed up to the wheelhouse. "I'm going ashore, Bob," he announced. "Doing a little shopping. Shouldn't be more than an hour or so. Back in plenty of time to serve lunch." And without waiting for a reply, he clattered down to his cabin below decks, changed out of his uniform of white shirt and shorts, gathered up his wallet, and made his way ashore.

*

It was a poem, read around the class in an unpromising English Literature lesson, which unexpectedly fired a yearning in the teenage Felicity

14

Witcher for a life at sea. As the images in John Masefield's 'Cargoes' formed in her mind, she found herself swept away in her imagination by thoughts of the romantic 'quinquireme of Nineveh', its hold laden with ivory and apes and peacocks. Even mention of the 'dirty British coaster with a salt-caked smoke-stack' was not enough to damp the fire. And so, in that moment, her course was set.

For a girl born and brought up in the landlocked English Midlands, a maritime career seemed the most unlikely path to take. But once Flix's mind had settled on her plans for the future, nothing would alter it, least of all the frequently-voiced scepticism of her parents, teachers, and friends. She pursued the option of the science subjects throughout the rest of her schooling. On leaving with a highly satisfactory set of exam results, she disregarded the route to university which many of her contemporaries took, in favour of a course in electrical and mechanical engineering at a college on the south coast which offered entry into the marine world. Her tutors and class-mates alike were charmed and impressed by her determination and quick intelligence, although it also had to be said that her striking good looks, with her tumble of blonde hair, large blue eyes, and petite figure, did her no harm at all in their eyes. At the end of her course, having been adopted as a kind of mascot by her otherwise entirely male fellows, all cheerfully content to refer to themselves as 'spanner-men', it was no surprise that her emergence as top student was greeted by universal acclaim and a seriously rowdy pub crawl.

With such testimonials under her belt, it was never in doubt that Flix would succeed in her ambition. Conquering the initial raised eyebrows whenever she applied for a job, she had a series of employments in fairly lowly engineering positions aboard local ferries and coastal cargo vessels, before a chance encounter with one of her former tutors led to a surprising offer. It seemed that a fellow-member of his yacht club was about to lose the engineer on his private motor yacht, and he was casting around for a replacement. Within hours, Flix's name had been enthusiastically put forward, and after a brief interview, the job was hers, at an eye-wateringly generous salary. And so Flix, at the age of twenty-seven, found herself sole mistress of the gleaming kingdom that was the engine compartment of *Red Buccaneer*.

Flix cast an eye over the bank of gauges in front of her, picked up the telephone handset alongside, and pushed a button. 'Hi, Bob. Flix ... Nice smooth ride this morning. Everyone happy up top? ... Good. Look, there's something I need to do before we sail this evening. It's the fuel ... No, no problem at all. It's just that I want to make sure we've got a full load on board before we leave tonight ... No, there's probably plenty to get us home under normal circumstances, but Sir said something about wanting to open her up on the homeward run from Guernsey to see what we can get out of her. He reckons *Buck* ought to be able to do more than the advertised eleven-and-a-half knots ..." Flix laughed. "Yes, I know that she's likely to drink a lot more than usual, but it's his money. And if we're anchoring off in St. Peter Port, it's not going to be so easy to refuel. So can we sort something out today? ... Great. I'm staying on board this morning, but I might pop ashore after lunch for a bit of shopping. What time are we due to sail? ... Oh, I'll be back long before then. See you later." She replaced the receiver, made her way along the narrow passage to her cabin, took off her cap, shook her hair loose, peeled off her overalls, and lay down on her bunk with a sigh.

*

Sir Lionel Butler towelled dry his thick mane of

silver hair as he stepped out from the owner's suite immediately aft of *Red Buccaneer*'s bridge on to his small private deck. Not tall, and with a frame which could at best be described as sturdy, his vigorous manner was frequently remarked upon by business associates, and was the despair of many of his sixty-eight-year-old contemporaries, especially those who had crumbled before his aggressive negotiating techniques. One of his most striking features was a pair of piercing dark eyes which seemed to have been designed never to miss the smallest detail of anything he surveyed.

Sir Lionel gave a small nod of approval as the vessel eased her way out of St. Malo's harbour, and then began to gather speed as she moved out of the restricted approach zone. 'Very smoothly done,' he thought, as he turned back into his suite and glanced up at the brass clock mounted on the wall above his bed. 'Plenty of time to get dressed before dinner. I might even wear that new shirt Dee bought me in Deauville. And according to Trey, he's got something special planned for main course.' A chuckle. 'He does like to be mysterious about some of his culinary creations. But he never disappoints. And I imagine he's also planned one of his usual clever cocktails to get everyone in the mood.' The smile faded. 'Well, let everyone enjoy it while they can They'll all soon have plenty else to think about. But not just yet, I think.'

He crossed to the wardrobe and opened it, to find that the shirt in question was hanging right in front of him, already crisply ironed. "Well done yet again, Trey," he murmured. "That young man is a wonder. Why on earth couldn't those sons of mine ..." He let the thought fade as he threw the towel on to the rail in the bathroom and reached for a bottle of cologne.

Chapter 2
Saturday

"But Ty, I still don't see why we had to come here instead of going to Jersey," pouted Jessica Butler. "I've got lots of lovely friends living in Jersey." She gave a little frown. "Or is it on Jersey?" A perplexed blink.

"Does it really matter?" responded her husband, with an almost imperceptible sigh.

"And I'm sure it's going to be boring. There'll be nothing to do."

"Well then, we'll have a good time doing nothing," said Tyrone Butler, a slight edge of determination in his smile. He'd had more than enough practice at handling his wife's whims and tantrums. "Anyway, Jezza, according to Dad, we'd never have been able to relax and enjoy ourselves, not with this Jersey Battle of Flowers thing they've had going on over there this week. The place is still bound to be packed, and I wouldn't mind betting that you'd have been pestered by fans all the time. You know what it's like when you get surrounded by a crowd."

Jessica smiled, a childish smile of self-satisfaction. "I can't help it if people recognise me when we're out." With a tall slim figure which just stopped short of being angular, huge dark eyes, and an almost waif-like air which the camera lens adored, Jessica Bell was one of the most sought-after models of the current generation. Spotted when dining in a smart London restaurant by a celebrated fashion designer who, without benefit of introduction, simply marched up to her table and, ignoring her much older companion completely, invited her to model for his new collection, Jezza was whisked away to find herself on catwalks and all over the press, the sensation of the season. The world of the glitterati enveloped her and, almost before she could draw breath, her social life had become a round of cocktails, premières, house parties and race meetings. And it was at the British Grand Prix that she was introduced to Tyrone Butler, lead driver for his father's Barbarossa Formula One racing team. The attraction was immediate and mutual, and the pair were married in months, to massive press coverage. "Anyway," continued Jezza, "you get people asking for selfies and autographs too."

"Not as many as you," retorted her husband. "Most people don't know who I am when I'm not sitting in the car. I might as well still have my helmet on." It was not strictly true. Even if not one of the most successful drivers of the pack, Tyrone's smouldering dark good looks and lean muscularity drew attention wherever he went. And if his erratic race results sometimes made some people wonder whether his presence was entirely justified among the top flight of drivers, they simply nodded sagely, gave thought to the enormous amount of money which his father had ploughed into the race business, and wisely kept their opinions to themselves.

Jessica shrugged prettily. "What can I do if all the fashion editors want to put me on their magazine covers? Anyway," she added, slightly waspishly, "you've never complained about being seen in public with me. That hasn't done your image any harm, has it?"

Tyrone swiftly moved to her, put his arm around her, and kissed her cheek. "Of course it hasn't, sweetheart," he soothed. "It's just one of the reasons I love you." He took a breath. "So, what would you like to do?"

Jessica made a moue. "I don't know. You choose. You're the one with all the ideas."

Her husband thought for a moment. "Tell you what. It's a beautiful day. Why don't we rent a car and go off and find a nice quiet beach, just the two of us? I can have you all to myself, for a change. You can top up the tan, and I can just sit there admiring you in that new bikini of yours. It'll be much better than swimming off the deck at the back here, with all this harbour traffic going past, and you won't have the two weird sisters curling their lips at you."

A giggle. "Your brothers did marry a pair of jealous frumps, didn't they?"

"What can I say? I definitely got the best deal." Another kiss, and then Tyrone broke away. "Right. Let's get sorted. Glamorous as it may be, you can't go ashore in nothing but that silk thing. I'll get out of your way."

"You need to," remarked Jessica, a touch grumpily. "There's no room to swing a cat in here. How come Robin gets the VIP cabin when we're both much more famous than he is?"

"Eldest son's privilege," replied Tyrone with a smile. He looked around the guest cabin the couple were occupying, with its fine wood panelling, elegant fitted furnishings, and stylish upholstery, with gleaming mirrors and a glimpse of the marble en-suite bathroom. "And anyway, you can't exactly call this 'roughing it'." He gave his wife a gentle tap on the behind. "You get dressed, and I'll see what I can do about finding a car to hire. There's bound to be something where I can put the top down and roar around showing you off to everyone." He pulled a phone from his pocket. "And I'll get Taff organised to run us ashore. I'll see you up in the saloon." The cabin door closed behind him.

*

In the identical but mirror-image suite next door on *Red Buccaneer*'s lower deck, Cordelia Butler was putting the finishing touches to her make-up. Despite Jessica's dismissive description, there was nothing frumpy about Cordelia. In fact, at the age of thirty-three, she exuded an air of stylish confidence which many older women might have envied. Her otherwise unpromising mousey-brown hair was worn up in an intricate chignon, held under the tutelage of an antique mother-of-pearl hair ornament, and her hazel eyes sparkled with intelligence. The blue-and-white dress she wore, printed with a subtle design of cornflowers, was obviously not the product of a chain store, and the pale blue linen jacket casually lying on the foot of the bed looked set to complete an outfit which almost succeeded in concealing its expensive nature.

"If you're coming, you ought to get a move on," she called, as she put away her mascara brush and surveyed the final result of her efforts. "You really should have done that before breakfast."

Her husband poked his head out from the bathroom, his face half-covered with shaving foam. "You know, Cordy, I don't think I can be bothered," replied Leo Butler. In his late thirties, with a head of thick dark blonde wavy hair and the dark brown eyes and regular features of a matinée idol, he was capable, when he wished, of emitting an aura of effortless charm which had often been crucial in persuading juries throughout his career at the bar. "Why don't you go on ahead without me?"

"Oh. Are you sure?"

"Positive," insisted Leo. "I've never been that much of a fan of Victor Hugo, and I can't imagine that a tour of his house is going to be anything other than miserable." He let out a short bark of self-congratulatory mirth. "And whatever the garden is like, it's going to be much more your thing than mine."

"I suppose so," agreed Cordelia reluctantly. As a fashionable garden designer under her maiden name of Cordelia Lyne, with two awards already for display gardens at the annual Chelsea Flower Show, she was much in demand among those of the wealthy and aristocratic who had the desire and resources to create

21

something impressive on their estates, calculated to provoke envy and irritation in equal measure among their neighbours and alleged friends. And so, wherever she went, it was always among her first priorities to visit great houses and gardens, notebook discreetly tucked away in her handbag, in case some feature should spark the inspiration for a novel design. To her, this week's break with its chance to visit a French château or two was a heaven-sent opportunity. "So what will you do?" she wondered.

"Oh, I suppose I'll just mooch ashore at some point," replied her husband casually. "I'll find something to do." He disappeared back into the bathroom.

"Did you ever get around to taking a look at that brief for your case on Monday?" asked Cordelia, as she slipped into her jacket and turned this way and that to survey the final result in the mirror. "I know you said you were going to bring the papers with you, but I haven't seen you with them."

"Oh for heaven's sake, Cordy, don't pester," came the rather irritated response from the bathroom. "This week was supposed to be a holiday. Mind you," Leo added in what he evidently thought was an undertone, "a week in the bosom of this family is anything but a holiday."

"But you can't go into court unprepared," protested Cordelia. "The judge will eat you."

"It'll be fine," stated Leo firmly. "He's an old sweetie anyway, and I've got the whole of tomorrow to look through everything on the way back. There's scarcely going to be anything in the way of rival entertainment, is there? 'Oh look, a seagull!' 'Oh look, a wave!' 'Oh look, another seagull!'"

"There's no need to be snappy."

"Sorry, darling." A contrite Leo emerged from the bathroom and wrapped his arms around his wife. "I'll do it all tomorrow, I promise. In the meantime, you go off and enjoy yourself."

An hour later, Cordelia was reflecting that perhaps her husband had been right all along. The house where Victor Hugo had written one of his most celebrated works, now part-museum and part-consulate owned by the French government, was neither as impressive nor as interesting as she had hoped. And the garden was frankly nondescript, a vista of lawn and shrubs which seemed to have seen no designer's hand. Cordy searched her mind to think where she had read somebody's words of approval. Evidently they were no critic. Thank goodness that she had taken the opportunity to visit Monet's gardens at Giverny on the day they had been docked at Deauville. Now those were clearly the result of one man's inspiration, although she feared that if she let slip in future the fact of her visit to some of her clients, she might be inundated with requests to recreate lily-filled ponds with rustic wooden bridges, all over the U.K. Not the most challenging or innovative prospect.

With a small sigh of regret, Cordelia made her way out of the house and down the hill towards the centre of St. Peter Port. Approaching the main street, she smiled as she noticed her husband seated at a table outside a cafe, in conversation with another man. As she approached, the man stood and, with a brief handshake, disappeared into the shopping crowds without a backward glance.

"Who was that, Leo?" she asked, as she took the just-vacated seat, provoking a slightly startled reaction from her husband.

"What? Sorry, darling. You made me jump. I didn't see you." A somewhat strained smile. "Did you have a nice time?"

"Not especially. So, who was he?"

"Him? Oh, just a chap I happened to meet at court once. Nobody you'd know. He lives in Jersey, and he'd just popped over for the day. Quite a surprise, running into him." A laugh. "Anyway, let's not bother about him. Why don't I order you a coffee – you look as if you could do with one, and I wouldn't mind another – and then you can tell me all about this morning. And after that, we'll find somewhere nice for me to treat you to lunch."

*

"What on earth is taking that boy so long?" growled an irritated Robin Butler as he stepped out on to the afterdeck for the umpteenth time and scanned the busy harbour. The oldest of the three brothers, he was the least impressive in stature, with a thickening body, a spreading paunch, and a thinning head of hair which all combined to make him appear older than his forty-two years.

"Oh, for goodness sake, stop pacing up and down, Rob," replied his wife Desdemona wearily. At the age of thirty-eight, Dee Butler still carried an air of serious gravitas, no doubt a hangover from her time as a barrister. Her habitual costume of a simple skirt and trim jacket in plain dark colours, often accompanied by a blouse with a froth of white at the neck, certainly did nothing to dispel the image, which was rather reinforced by the plain bobbed style in which she wore her dark brown hair, and her glasses with their heavy square rims. Her sole, and slightly surprising, concession to glamour was a heavy bracelet at her wrist, an intricately twisted modern design in a white metal, which to an untutored eye could well have been silver, but which was clearly platinum, the only fitting setting for the substantial diamonds which adorned it. "Just come and sit down and wait quietly. It's not as if we're in a mad hurry to go anywhere, is it?"

"No, I suppose not," admitted her husband grumpily, taking a seat alongside her on the saloon's sofa. "But I don't like waiting about. I just want to get ashore and stretch my legs. And I don't see why we should have to be the last ones off this blasted boat."

"Because everyone else beat us to it," pointed out Dee reasonably. "You should have got ready straight after breakfast. Anyway, Ty wanted to get off in his usual mad hurry – something about a car that was too good to miss – and Cordy said she was going to try to get ahead of the tourist crowds. You've seen all the tenders going to and fro from that cruise ship anchored over the way. 'Aida-something', isn't it? Aren't they a German company? So I expect half of their passengers will be forming long orderly queues outside that house she was heading for. But I'm sure Taff will be back with the dinghy before long."

"Well, I hope so."

"Why? I didn't think you had anything in particular planned."

"Er ... no. I haven't."

"What, then?"

"I thought I might take a stroll out to the castle," replied Robin, a touch defensively. "It looks as if it might be quite interesting. And it'll keep me out of the crowds. Judging by the number of packed tenders going ashore, the town is probably going to be bursting. I'd rather have some quiet time to myself. I've got some particularly gruesome meetings coming up at work next week, and today is probably going to be my last taste of freedom." A hint of a wry smile. 'No irony there,' he thought to himself.

Dee shrugged. "Well, that's up to you. Although I've never known you to have that much interest in history."

"There's a lot you don't know," said Robin, a touch obliquely. "Anyway, what about you?"

"Actually," said Dee, "I have thought of something." She held up her wrist. "I may see if I can find some earrings to go with this bracelet. I might as well take advantage of the fact that there's no V.A.T. on Guernsey."

"You'll still have to declare them to Customs when we get back into the U.K., though," pointed out Robin.

"Don't be childish, Rob," replied his wife with a quiet smile, giving him a sideways look.

And as Robin was about to respond, the pair were interrupted by the sound of hurried approaching footsteps. "I'm so sorry, Mr. Butler," gasped Taff, as he appeared up the steps from the stern and burst into the saloon. "I had to wait for ages to get alongside the quay because of all the other boats unloading from the cruise ship. But I can take you ashore now, if you still want to go."

"Of course we do," rasped Robin. "We're not sat here for the good of our health, are we? Ready, Dee?"

Dee cast her eyes heavenwards. "Right behind you, dearest," she said sweetly, with a gracious forgiving smile in the direction of Taff, who turned and led the way down to the afterdeck landing platform.

Chapter 3
Sunday

"Are you sure you don't mind, Sharon?" asked Pete Radley, poking his head round the living room door of the modest three-bedroomed semi.

His wife looked up from the child on her lap. "Of course I don't. Go and have your beer with the boys. We'll manage perfectly fine."

"Only I promised Matt I'd thrash him at darts after he hammered me last week." Pete still seemed reluctant to cash in on the permission. He advanced into the room, still in stockinged feet, and settled into the sofa next to his wife, putting an arm round her shoulders.

"I've told you, go. Lunch is all in the oven, and Tommy and I are going to have a lovely time with our new story book, aren't we?" The young mother smiled fondly at her toddler and tickled him, to be rewarded with a hiccup and a happy gurgle. "Just remember, we eat at half past one, so don't get carried away and forget the time."

"I won't, I promise. You two enjoy yourselves." Pete gave his wife a peck on the cheek, and then deposited a kiss on the top of his son's head. "And always remember, little man – there's no such thing as a Gruffalo."

"Out!" cried his wife with a laugh, as Pete disappeared through a rapidly closing door, just avoiding the flying cushion which followed him.

*

"I've brought you a lager," announced Una. "You look as if you could do with one."

Dave Copper threw down the spade in his hand and gratefully accepted the glass. "Thanks, love," he replied, after taking a long swallow. "You're a life-saver." He grinned at his wife. "Whose stupid idea was this, anyway?"

27

Una laughed. "I seem to remember a certain someone saying that we shouldn't be living in the country without growing at least some of our own food. I just happened to mention that I love home-grown veg like my dad used to bring home from his allotment. Especially new potatoes. And potatoes don't plant themselves."

"Well, I wish they would," retorted Copper. He surveyed the marked-out trench, still only one-third dug, in the garden of the couple's cottage, formerly the police house in the village of Dammett Worthy. "And why did nobody tell me that this village was built on the stickiest clay in the world, mixed with rocks they could have built Stonehenge with? No wonder Robbie Collins never did any gardening when he was living here. Are you sure you don't want a rockery instead?"

"It will all be worth it in the end," said Una. "Although I'm not sure that the hottest day of the year is the best time for you to be engaged in a major excavation. And is this the potato-planting season anyway?"

Copper shrugged good-humouredly. "Haven't a clue, love. You're supposed to be the one who does all the research. I just leap to obey when you issue your commands."

"That'll be the day," chuckled Una. "Look, I think you've done quite enough for the time being. You'll be as stiff as a board tomorrow if you don't stop now. So drink your lager and then come inside and take a shower, while I rustle up something irresistible in the kitchen for lunch."

"I can think of something irresistible in the kitchen," smiled Copper with a wink. "Shall I pop down when I'm fresh out of the shower?"

Una shook her head with a sigh of mock despair, turned, and made for the cottage, while Copper downed the rest of his lager, grabbed his discarded t-shirt, and scampered after her.

*

"Like this?" asked Jessica Butler breathlessly.

"That's right, miss," said Bob de Waters in his comfortable West Country burr. Odd, he thought. He always called Dee and Cordelia 'Mrs. Rob' and 'Mrs. Leo', but he couldn't think of Jessica as anything other than 'Miss'. Must be the air of youthful innocence about her. "Just keep your hands at ten to two, just like if you were driving a car, but don't look down at them. Keep watching the horizon straight above the bow, and leave *Buck* to do the rest."

"And I'm really driving him?" marvelled Jessica.

Bob smiled indulgently. "Yes you are, miss. And it's 'her', not 'him'."

Jezza frowned. "But why? I don't understand. *Red Buccaneer* is a man's name, surely."

"It's traditional, miss. All boats and ships are called 'she', even if they've got a male name. They have been for centuries. Don't ask me how it came about." He chuckled. "Even I'm not that old."

After a few moments, Jessica spoke up again. "And there's another thing I still don't understand. Why couldn't we have gone to Jersey yesterday instead of dull old Guernsey? I know Ty said that it was because it would have been too busy, but I'm sure that it would have been more fun. And I've got girlfriends who live there – we could have had a party."

"It wasn't just because the island would have been packed, miss," explained Bob, "although I wouldn't mind betting we'd have had trouble getting a berth, what with all the visitors. But to be honest, with the tides at the state they were, I didn't fancy facing the Minkies."

Jessica gave her trademark owlish blink of bewilderment. "What's a Minkie?"

29

"Sorry, miss. Sailors' slang. There's a great big reef of rocks just off Jersey, as big as the island itself. It's called Les Minquiers, but we all call it the Minkies. It's not too bad to get across at high tide, but on a falling tide, which it was when we came out of St. Malo, it can be a deathtrap. And I don't think Sir Lionel would have thanked me if I'd risked tearing the bottom of his boat out, just so you and your girlfriends could have a party. So Guernsey it had to be. Sorry."

"Oh, it wasn't really too bad. Ty hired this super red Lamborghini. It was left-hand drive, but he said so much the better, and he found us a lovely quiet beach at the top of the island. We actually went in the sea, which I never do at home, but it was so lovely and hot that I just had to." Jezza giggled. "Ty said he'd have put money on the fact that my new bikini would never get wet. And then I had a lovely sunbathe, and he wandered off somewhere until it was time to get back."

"What's this, then?" A deep voice from behind them made Bob and Jezza turn in surprise, as Sir Lionel Butler appeared at the rear of the wheelhouse. "Slacking on the job, captain?"

"Miss Jessica thought it might be fun to take the wheel for a bit, sir," replied Bob.

Sir Lionel moved forward and slid an arm around Jessica's waist. "So how is my baby doing?"

"Very well, sir," said Bob, after a moment's slightly uncertain pause, doubtful as to exactly what the yacht's owner meant, and ignoring Jessica's intake of breath, before deciding diplomatically that it was *Red Buccaneer*'s performance which was being queried. "You were right about her speed. Flix seems to have managed to tune her up a notch, and we're making over twelve knots. Mind you, it helps that we've got a virtually flat calm. So we should be into port around sixish by my reckoning."

"Excellent." Sir Lionel nodded in approval. "That fits in very well. I've just come off the phone to the clubhouse at the marina, and they've reserved a private room for the family to have dinner at eight. So you can tell the rest of the crew that, once we're ashore, the rest of the evening's their own. You've all worked very hard over the past week, which I appreciate, so you can take some time for yourselves. Go ashore. Let your hair down a little."

"That's very good of you, sir," smiled Bob. "I'll let them know. But in the meantime, miss, I suppose I ought to earn my wages and take the wheel again."

"Good idea," said Sir Lionel. "Come along, Jessica." His arm tightened around her. "If we had a yardarm, I'm sure the sun would be well over it. Let's you and I go and see if Trey can rustle us up one of his best cooling cocktails."

"Jezza?" Tyrone's voice sounded from the doorway. "I wondered where you'd got to."

His wife whirled round, startled. "Oh, Ty! I've been driving *Buck*," she said breathlessly. "But we're just coming down now."

"Good." Tyrone left as abruptly as he'd arrived.

*

"Lunch won't be long." As she looked in through the cabin door, Cordelia Butler took in the sight of her husband sprawled on the bed, surrounded by a sea of paperwork. "Oh Leo - are you still not finished going through those?"

"What does it look like?" retorted her husband. "This is ridiculous. That clerk of mine is going to get it in the neck when I see him. There's more contradictory evidence here than you can shake a stick at. Half the witness statements don't make sense, and the other half have got glaring gaps in the timeline. I'm never going to get it all under my belt by tomorrow. I wish I'd looked at

31

the file before we came away. I might even have decided to cry off and stay home. And I suppose," he added grumpily, "you're going to say that I should have known, and you told me so."

"I wouldn't dream of it, darling," said Cordelia. "I just wish I could do something to help. I don't want you rampaging about like a bear with a sore head because you've had a hard time in court." A thought struck her. "What about Dee? You used to work together. Can't she help you to straighten out some of the muddle?"

"No use at all," responded Leo sharply. "Totally different areas. I'm criminal, and she was corporate. Why do you think my brother snapped her up? Free legal advice at the breakfast table." He sighed. "No. I'll just plough on through it."

"Well, at least take a break. Come up and have some lunch. It looks as if Trey has done one of his lobster salads. And one glass of champagne to go with it won't hurt. You can come back to this after you've refuelled your brain."

With another sigh, Leo put down the document he was holding. "I suppose you're right. As ever." He swung his legs round and slipped into his discarded deck shoes. "So, who's up there? Or can I guess? I suppose Dad is doing his usual Admiral of the Fleet act."

"The last I saw of him," said Cordelia, "he was sitting in the hot tub sipping a champagne cocktail. With Jezza," she added.

"Hmmm. No fool like an old fool," muttered Leo under his breath. "And where's Ty?"

"Stretched out on a lounger with his earphones plugged in, apparently oblivious to everything, although I'm sure I saw him casting looks. And Dee is sitting in the saloon, looking very prim, and reading a copy of 'The Lady'. I don't think she is too fond of the sound of Jessica's giggling."

"Can't say I blame her. And Rob? Is he shedding his usual air of cheerfulness over the company?"

"I haven't seen him," said Cordelia. "He won't have gone far, will he? Now come along," she insisted, taking her husband by the hand. "Lunch!"

*

Red Buccaneer ghosted her way through the entrance of Porthampton's Sea Village marina, her engine now muted from its throaty cross-channel growl to a low burble, and in response to Bob de Waters' deft touches at the wheel, negotiated her way delicately past the other pontoons and eased gently into her home berth.

Lionel Butler, standing at Bob's shoulder, nodded approvingly, as Taff leapt lightly ashore and fastened the mooring lines to their bollards. "Very neatly done." He consulted the ostentatious chronometer on his wrist. "And perfectly on time too. You estimated that we'd get in at sixish, and it's just after five past. I call that a good job."

"I'm glad you're pleased, sir."

"Of course I am. I don't think that could have gone much better. Not as far as the sailing goes, anyway. Very nearly a perfect end to the week." The businessman's face lost a little of its cheerful bonhomie. "Not that it's quite over yet. We shall have to see ..." He tailed off, gazing unfocussed into the middle distance for a moment, before recalling himself to the present. "Anyway, you can ring down 'Finished with engines' to Felicity, or whatever it is you do, and I shall go and put my feet up for a little before everybody assembles for sundowners at seven." He turned and headed in the direction of his suite.

After a swift glance ashore, where Taff could be seen neatly coiling the loose ends of the mooring ropes into impeccable spirals, Bob made his way down to the engine compartment in the bowels of the boat. "Well, how was it for you?" he asked, as he entered the cramped space.

Flix Witcher looked up. "Absolutely fine," she smiled. "Is Sir pleased?"

"I might even say 'chuffed'," reported Bob. "According to him, 'a perfect end to the week'. I quote. So, no problems down here?"

"None whatsoever. No hint of overheating, which was the one thing I thought might happen if we pushed *Buck* too hard. No nasty noises. And at one point, I think we touched 12.7 knots, which is a whole knot over the declared maximum speed. So if Sir's chuffed, I'm chuffed."

"Great chuffiness all round then," chuckled Bob. "So we've earned our time off. Sir says the party's meeting for drinks at seven, and I know they've got a private dining room booked at the clubhouse for eight, so they'll be off just before then. That means we've got nearly two hours to unwind and get ourselves ready to hit the town." He ran a hand over his grizzled chin. "I may even have a shave in celebration." A laugh. "You wouldn't want to be seen in public with me looking like Popeye's pappy. Catch you later." He closed the door behind him and sidled his way to his own cubbyhole of a cabin.

*

"And that, I think, will do nicely," said Lionel Butler, putting down his glass. "Thank you, Trey. Delicious, as always."

"No worries, sir. Glad you liked it."

"And now I suppose you're all ready for your night off?"

"Rarin' to go, sir," smiled the steward.

Sir Lionel looked up at the clock on the bulkhead above the bar. "As should we be." He turned back to the rest of the party scattered around the saloon. "Come along, everybody. Dinner is reserved for eight. We should make a move."

As the family group stood on the pontoon, Sir Lionel looked up at the three crew members gathered together at the yacht's rail. "Well, I hope you enjoy yourselves. What have you got planned?"

"Oh, nothing too special, sir," replied Bob de Waters. "Flix has some mad idea of going to a club later and seems determined to drag this old sea-dog along with her, but before that we're just going over to the pizza restaurant across the marina for some supper."

"Nonsense!" declared Sir Lionel robustly. "You deserve better than a pizza. Leave it with me. I'll have a word with the yacht clubhouse restaurant manager, and he'll have a table waiting for you when you arrive. Order what you like. Wine too. It's all on me." A thought struck him. "Where's the boy?"

"Taff? He's staying on board to look after the boat, sir."

"Oh, we can't have that," replied Sir Lionel. "Why should he miss out? No, you go and tell him to smarten himself up, and I'll have Marina Security keep an eye on *Buccaneer*. They ought to do something to justify the amount I pay in mooring fees. Right, that's settled. Come along, everyone." He made his way up the pontoon's ramp in order to reach the quayside, the rest of the family following in his wake.

Chapter 4
Monday

"Don't bother to sit down," instructed Detective Inspector Dave Copper, replacing the phone receiver and coming to his feet, as his junior colleague backed his way through the door into their office, his hands occupied with a take-away coffee cup and a cardboard plate bowing under the weight of several doughnuts.

"Hell's bells, boss!" ejaculated Detective Sergeant Pete Radley. "You gave me the shock of my life. I'd thought, get in a bit early and nip to the canteen to pick up a couple of life's essentials, and then I can fuel up in peace for the day ahead before the gaffer gets in."

"No chance, sergeant," smiled Copper in reply. "I was also looking forward to a couple of minutes of quiet contemplation before duty kicked in, but it seems that the gods of crime have willed it otherwise. That was Control on the phone. They obviously thought we ought to start the week as they would like us to go on. They have a suspicious death for us."

"I don't remember being wicked over the weekend," muttered Radley rebelliously. "So, what's it all about?" he added aloud, taking a surreptitious sip of his coffee.

"There's a dead body aboard a boat at Sea Village Marina in Porthampton, and it seems that the local Uniform who were first on the scene think that it may well be one for C.I.D. So put down that drink and pick up your notebook, because we're off to visit the boating fraternity."

"Can't I bring my coffee with me, boss?" pleaded Radley. "You know I'm useless without my morning caffeine hit."

"Oh, all right," sighed Copper, "as long as you promise not to spill it on my new upholstery. I've seen

36

the state of your car."

"Promise, boss. And how about ...?"

"No." The inspector cut his colleague off before he even had the chance to voice his request.

"You can leave those on your desk, and hope that they're still there when you get back."

"Fat chance," murmured Radley, attempting to slide the plate of doughnuts into an already over-full drawer. "If those vultures in the other offices get a whiff of doughnut, I can kiss these goodbye."

"Then it'll be another chance for you to exercise your detectional skills in attempting to discover the thief or thieves," said Copper. "But in the meantime, we have bigger challenges on our plate." He made his way out of the door and headed along the corridor in the direction of the car park.

*

A uniformed P.C., forbidding hand raised, stepped in front of the car, as Dave Copper drove into the entrance of the car park in the shadow of Porthampton marina's Grand Village Hotel.

Porthampton's Sea Village was an impressive re-purposing of what had once been part of a large docks complex from which, in the 1950s, stubby steamers had plied their trade across the English Channel, carrying passengers and freight between the U.K., the Channel Islands, and France. The area was completely unrecognisable from its former incarnation. Where once a mixture of brick-built and corrugated-iron-roofed warehouses and passenger sheds had surrounded the dock basin, there now rose glittering blocks of smart apartments, their ground floors given over to a selection of restaurants ranging from the informal to the chic, offering cuisine from every corner of the world. Elsewhere, groups of town-houses clustered around immaculately-maintained shrub-filled gardens and courtyards. A modern hotel, its architecture reminiscent of the silhouette of an ocean liner, hugged the waterfront, while the pontoons of a busy marina, host to boats of every description from the humblest motorsailer to the swankiest gin palace, almost filled the basin.

"This area's closed to the public," declared the uniformed officer, as the inspector wound down his window and looked up enquiringly. "You can't park here."

Copper delved into a jacket pocket and produced his warrant card. "I think you'll find I can, constable. Likewise Sergeant Radley here."

The officer stepped back. "Sorry, sir. I didn't realise who you were."

"No reason why you should," smiled the inspector. "I prefer not to announce my arrival with a flourish of blues and twos if I can avoid it. So, what's what? Where's our body?"

"It's on a boat down in the marina, sir. If you park over there and go round the corner of the hotel, you'll see a little metal gate. Go through that and down the ramp to the pontoon, and that's where the boat's moored. My oppo's down there, so he can tell you all about it."

"Thank you, constable. We'll do just that."

Following instructions, the two detectives climbed out of the car and rounded the end of the hotel building.

"Bloody hell, boss!" was Pete Radley's instinctive reaction to the sight before him. "That's not a yacht. That's a cruise ship."

"What were you expecting, sergeant?" smiled Copper. "A twelve-foot dinghy? A place like this isn't just where money talks. It stands on a box and bellows at the top of its voice." He led the way through the propped-open metal gate which gave on to the pontoon. "Hmmm," he remarked. "Keypad-controlled I see. But not much point in that if it's going to be left open like this. So, let's see what we're dealing with." He descended the slope to where another uniformed officer stood at the foot of the small gangway leading on to the deck of *Red Buccaneer*.

"Good morning, sir," the officer greeted him. "My mate just radioed to say that you were heading this way."

"Good. This is D.S. Radley, and I'm D.I. Copper. And you are ...?"

"P.C. Kapoor, sir."

"Right. Well, first things first. Where's this body?"

"It's up here on the main deck, sir. If you want to follow me." The officer led the way round to the stern and up a short set of stairs to a partially-open deck set with a dining table and chairs under the covered portion, while at the extreme rear, open to the sky, sat a large hot tub, faint wisps of steam still wreathing from its surface. And below the rippling surface, completely submerged, could be discerned the body of an elderly man wearing nothing but a pair of red speedos, a dressing gown cast casually on a nearby chair.

"Well, that's not a sight you see every day," remarked Radley. "Who is he?"

"The boat's owner, sarge. A gentleman by the name of ..." The young constable fumbled in a tunic pocket for his notebook. "... Sir Lionel Butler."

"No doubt one of the great and the good," murmured Copper in an aside to his junior colleague. "This will have complications, or I'm a Dutchman. And who found him?" he continued aloud.

"One of the boat's crew, sir. A kid by the name of Rayle. He discovered the body, and the chap in charge of the boat phoned 999. And when we got here, I reckoned there was something odd about the situation ..."

"You could say that," put in Radley in his own aside to the inspector.

"... so I got on to Control and suggested we needed C.I.D."

"Good instinct, Kapoor," approved Copper. "It's not exactly run-of-the-mill, finding a corpse in a hot tub. We'll certainly be wondering how that came about. So where is this young man you spoke of?"

"One deck up in the wheelhouse, sir, together with the rest of the crew."

"Oh? How many are there?"

"Four of them, all told, sir. Of course, that's not counting the family."

"They've got their families on board?" queried Radley. "What was this, an outing for the nearest and dearest?"

"Not theirs, sarge. Sir Lionel's family. But I've kept them separate. I've kettled them up through there, in the main saloon." He pointed towards a floor-to-ceiling set of folding glass doors, through which could dimly be seen the silhouettes of a group of people seated and standing about. "They told me they're the dead man's three sons and their wives. I didn't bother to get any more details, sir," said the P.C. apologetically, "because I knew someone would be on their way as soon as we'd called it in. But they've been in there quite a while, and I've got a feeling they're getting a bit restive."

"Don't worry about that, constable," Copper reassured him. "We'll take it from here. But there is one more thing you can do. Get on to County at Westchester and tell them I need them to send somebody from Forensics over. We'd better find out what we're dealing with. In the meantime, I ought to speak a few soothing words to the family, and then have a chat with the first person to find the body. And if you'd stand guard where we first found you, I'd be grateful."

"Will do, sir." The constable drew himself up and gave a salute, bringing a quiet smile to the inspector's lips.

"Now, sergeant, we'll make a start." Copper led the

way through the folding doors and into the saloon, where he was met by Robin Butler, bristling with indignation.

"Look, this isn't good enough," barked Robin. "My father's dead, and I want to know what's going on. For a start, by what right are we being kept here?" He looked the detectives up and down. "And who are you?"

"My name is Detective Inspector Copper, sir, and this is my colleague, Detective Sergeant Radley." The two displayed their warrant cards. "And I have to offer my apologies for any inconvenience," replied Copper in his most emollient tone. "I'm afraid that these things are bound to happen in the event of an unexpected death." He surveyed the group of people scattered around the saloon. "And may I first of all express our sincere condolences for your loss. I understand that you are all members of the late gentleman's family."

"Yes, that right," said Robin, calmed slightly by the inspector's words. "I'm Robin Butler, Sir Lionel's eldest son, so I imagine that makes me the senior member of the family, and I'm ..."

Copper held up a hand in interruption. "All in good time, sir. I shall be wanting to have a word with each of you in turn. But before that, I need to learn more about the exact circumstances of your father's death. I understand that it was a member of the boat's crew who was first on the scene, so I think I'd better start with him. I'm told he's in the wheelhouse, so if you'd be so kind as to tell me how I get there ...?"

"Oh." Robin seemed rather taken aback at his dismissal, gently couched as it was. "It's up those stairs and turn left." He pointed to a staircase at the side of the bar.

"Thank you, sir. And if the rest of you would remain here for the time being, I shall try not to keep you too long. Sergeant, you're with me." Accompanied by Radley, the inspector climbed the stairs to the upper

41

deck, to find three members of *Red Buccaneer*'s crew perched around the wheelhouse. "Good morning, everyone," he began, before introducing himself and his companion. He paused, frowning. "I understood there were four people in the crew."

"That's right, inspector." An older man stepped forward. "I'm Bob de Waters, sir. Sir Lionel's skipper. It's just our engineer who's not here. She's gone down to her engine room to check up on a few things. I can call her back up if you want."

"Not just at the moment," said Copper. "But I shall be needing to interview each of you in due course, and I'd like to start with the person who discovered the body." His eye fell upon the youngest person present, standing hunched in one corner of the wheelhouse, his every fibre radiating nervousness. "And I'm thinking that must be you, Mr. ... Rayle, didn't my colleague down below say?"

"That's right, sir," quavered Taff.

"Now, I wonder where we might have a quiet chat on our own, just to put me in the picture," said Copper. It was plain that the witness would need to be handled with care.

Bob spoke up again. "Can I suggest you might like to go through to the owner's suite, inspector. It's private there, and you won't be interrupted."

"That sounds very suitable, Mr. de Waters." Copper smiled his thanks.

"Well then, you show the officers the way through, Taff," said Bob. "And if it's all right by you, inspector, can Trey here go down to make some coffee and breakfast for the family?" He indicated the steward. "Only they won't have had anything since we came back on board ..."

"... and hunger and thirst are not likely to make them feel any happier about the situation." Copper completed the thought. "Very well. But please don't discuss matters with them until I've had a chance to speak to them," he instructed.

"As you wish, sir," said Trey, and started down the stairs to the saloon.

"Now, perhaps you'd like to lead the way, Mr. Rayle," suggested the inspector, and with Radley in tow, he followed in the young deckhand's footsteps across the small landing towards the owner's suite.

*

Copper seated himself in one of the chairs on the suite's small private outer deck, indicating to Taff that he should take the other, while Radley positioned himself discreetly behind the young man, out of his eyeline, notebook at the ready.

"So, it's Taff, isn't it?" began the inspector comfortably.

"That's right, sir," replied the other in a broad Welsh accent.

"But I'm guessing that 'Taff' isn't what it says on your birth certificate," smiled Copper. "I'd better have your real name, just to make sure Sergeant Radley here has all the details right."

"It's actually Albert, sir," said Taff. "Albert Rayle. After my Da's grandad. He was a miner, but then he died in the war. But after my parents moved to England, everyone at school started calling me Taff, because, well, you know ..."

"I think I can work that one out for myself," said the inspector. "So, how long have you been working as boat crew?"

"Ever since I left college, sir. I got offered a holiday job one summer, and I sort of stuck. Don't know why. There's no sailors in my family."

"And you've been working for the Butler family for how long?"

"Just over a year, sir. The guy before me had left, and Captain Bob was a friend of a friend of the people I

43

was with at the time, freelance-like, and he offered me the job on *Buck*."

"Buck?" queried Copper.

"Sorry, sir. *Red Buccaneer*, I mean. We all just call her *Buck* for short."

"I see. So, coming on to this morning. How did that come about?"

"Well, we'd all been ashore overnight, sir," began Taff. "Us crew, that is. Because we got back in yesterday, and we'd been given the night off because the family were having dinner ashore. And we were coming back on board this morning, and I was first on ..."

"What sort of time was this?" interrupted Radley, pencil poised.

Taff twisted round. "About half-past seven, I guess. Anyway," he continued, "I was coming round the stern when I thought I could hear the rumble of the hot tub bubbling. And I thought to myself, somebody's up early. I hope the noise isn't waking everyone else up. So I peeped up to see who was in it, and I couldn't see anyone, so I thought I'd better switch it off. And I came up, and looked in, and I could see ..." He gulped.

After a pause, Copper helped the young man out. "You saw Sir Lionel. And did you try to help him?"

"I ... I couldn't touch him, sir. And I knew he must be dead, because his eyes were wide open under the water. Staring at me, they were." Taff shuddered at the memory.

"Is it the first time you've seen a dead body?"

Taff nodded. "And I didn't know what to do. I called Captain Bob, and he and the others came up, and they could see ... what I'd found, so then he said we had to call the police, so he did, but then Trey said 'What about the family?', because there wasn't any sign of the others, and the skipper said they must not be up yet, thank goodness, but they ought to be told, so Trey said he'd do that once

44

the police got here, and then Flix – she's our engineer, sir," he put in, in response to Copper's enquiring look - "she wondered if we ought to switch off the tub, and the skip said no, he'd been told we mustn't touch anything. So we just sat down there waiting until the police car arrived. And then you and the sergeant got here and ... and then it was now." Taff gave a sigh at the end of this breathless narrative.

"I see." The inspector paused for a few moments in thought. "Well, I think that gives us a fairly clear picture, so far as it goes, so thank you for that, Taff. If you'd like to rejoin the rest of the crew for the time being ..." As the young man disappeared towards the wheelhouse, Copper stood, and as he did so he caught sight of a familiar figure approaching the gate at the top of the pontoon. He turned to Radley. "I see the cavalry's arriving. That didn't take long. We'd better head straight down and let her know what we know. And in the meantime, I shall have to put the family on hold again."

"That's not going to go down too well with that bloke with the red face, is it, boss?" remarked Radley.

"I can't help that," returned his superior. "I shall just have to devise the soothing answer that turneth away wrath." He led the way down the stairs, to be met with six pairs of eyes swivelling immediately in his direction, as Trey hovered in the background, coffee pot in hand. "I'm so very grateful for your patience, ladies and gentlemen," he said, before any of those present could utter a word. "And I assure you that I shan't keep you waiting a moment longer than necessary. But the fact is that a colleague of mine has just arrived, and I'm sure her input is going to be crucial in reaching a swift conclusion to this unfortunate matter. So if I can ask you to bear with me for just a few minutes longer, I shall be back as quickly as I can." Without giving anyone a chance to react, Copper strode out on to the deck and down to the pontoon, where the newcomer was just approaching the officer on guard, who seemed disposed to halt her progress.

"Sergeant Singleton!" the inspector hailed the white-overall-clad individual with a broad grin, while giving the constable a nod to indicate that all was well. "What a pleasure. Quick off the mark as ever. So once again we have the dream team on the case."

"Hi, Una," said Radley, somewhat more muted in his greeting.

"Of course I was quick off the mark," smiled Una in response. "When C.I.D. calls, what can we minions in the Forensics Department do but obey? Although," she added in lowered tones, "you might at least give me a chance to get my feet under the desk in the morning before hauling me out to one of your dead bodies."

"What is it they say, love?" replied Copper. "'No man knoweth the hour of his death', or something like that. And I have a feeling that, in this case, our victim wasn't exactly prepared for his. There are factors. Want to come and take a look?"

"That's why I'm here." Una followed the detectives up to the hot tub.

"Sergeant Radley, while we're taking a look here, would you like to go through to the saloon and keep a friendly eye on the family gathering," suggested the inspector. "And if there are curtains, maybe they ought to be pulled across those doors. I don't think we particularly want an audience for our activities."

"Will do, boss." Radley made his way through into the saloon, and moments later could be seen to be drawing the curtains across the glazed partition.

"That," remarked Una, putting down her equipment case and gazing down at the body in the tub, "is going to be a very unhelpful corpse."

Chapter 5

"How so?" enquired Dave Copper.

"Do we know how long he's been in there?" asked Una.

"Not at this point," replied her husband. "I hope I'll know more, once I've had a chance to carry out some interviews. All we know at the moment is that he was discovered at around half-past seven this morning."

"Because," explained Una, "we probably don't stand a chance, unless there's some corroborative evidence, of establishing a time of death. If he's been in there in the hot water for at least that length of time, I shan't be able to tell you anything, either from the temperature of the body, because it won't have cooled down in textbook fashion, or from any state of rigor mortis. And there's a very good chance that the constantly moving hot water will have effectively washed away any forensic traces." She sighed. "And why do we think that there's anything suspicious about this death anyway? Why do we think he didn't have a heart attack, or just slip and drown?" She regarded her husband with a searching gaze.

"It's the eyes," said Copper. "The first officer on the scene said he had an instinct that there was something off about the situation, but he didn't say why. And I had the same feeling when I first saw the body, but again, I couldn't put my finger on it. But then the kid who first found him said something. He said he knew the chap was dead because he was staring up at him from underwater. Now, correct me if I'm wrong, but I don't think drowning victims usually die with their eyes open."

"Good point," conceded Una. "Okay. Well, there's little we can do here. You'd better get somebody to drain this tub, and I'll call for the van to come and have the dead man taken away. Further and better particulars when we've got him back at the lab."

"I will leave you with it," replied Copper. "I'd better get interviewing." He passed into the saloon, where Radley stood amidst an uneasy silence. "Pop up and have a word with the captain, sergeant," the inspector murmured into his ear. "Tell him we need the hot tub emptied so that we can remove the body. Una's sorting things out from there."

"Will do, boss." Radley disappeared up the stairs towards the wheelhouse, and Copper focussed his attention on the six people before him.

"Once again, apologies for the delay, ladies and gentlemen," said Copper. "But I'd now like a few words with each of you in turn." He addressed Robin. "Perhaps I should start with you, sir, as I think you said you are the late gentleman's eldest son."

"That is correct, inspector," began Robin, "and this is my wife Dee. We are ..."

He was interrupted in mid-flow by Leo. "Just a second, inspector. Is this going to take long?"

"That I can't say at the moment, sir. It will take as long as necessary. Why do you ask?"

"Because I have to be in London on a very important matter this afternoon, so I can't sit around here all day."

"I'm afraid that the necessities of the law will have to take priority over whatever you have planned, Mr. ...?

"Leo Butler, inspector. Queen's Counsel, for your information. So when you talk about the necessities of the law, I rather think that the fact that, as a Q.C., I need to be present for an extremely important court case at the Old Bailey this afternoon rather trumps your little chats with us."

Dee Butler spoke up. "Oh, for goodness sake, Leo, don't be so pompous. The inspector has his job to do. Just get on to the court and ask for a delay."

"It's not that easy, Dee," said Leo, "as you well know."

Dee sighed. "It's not rocket science, Leo. If you're leading counsel, you've got a junior, haven't you? You just need to instruct your junior to get up on his hind legs and ask the judge for an adjournment until tomorrow. Who's your junior?"

"Young Gavin. But it's his first case at the Bailey."

"Oh, you can easily make up some plausible reason. Say that there's some query about disclosures. Who's the judge?"

"Sir Philip Eade."

Dee laughed. "Well then, problem solved. Old Eade's a sucker for a pretty face. I bet Gavin'll be able to twist him round his little finger."

"Well, if you think so ...," demurred Leo.

"Get on the phone to chambers," insisted Dee. She looked over at Copper. "That's if it's all right with you, inspector."

"Perfectly fine, madam," replied Copper. "Although perhaps you should be a little vague about the circumstances, Mr. Butler," he suggested. He turned to Robin. "In the meantime, Mr. Butler ..." He sighed. "I'm afraid that this may all get very confusing."

"Oh, just call me Robin," was the exasperated response.

"I think I'd rather keep things a little more formal, sir. But I suppose calling you Mr. Robin will be quite acceptable. So unless you've any objection, I think we'd probably be more comfortable in the suite where I had a chat with your young crew member."

"Fine," said Robin shortly. "Let's just get on with it." But as he started to climb the stairs to the upper deck, he was forestalled by the appearance of Pete Radley at the after end of the saloon.

"Can I have a word, sir?" said the sergeant.

"Now?"

"It's quite urgent, sir. Una ... I mean, Sergeant Singleton needs to show you something."

"Excuse me one second , Mr. B... Mr. Robin." With a slight roll of his eyes, Copper followed Radley out on to the open deck, where Una stood waiting alongside the emptying hot tub. "So, what's up?"

"Take a look at this," said Una. She indicated the head and shoulders of Sir Lionel Butler as the body slowly emerged from the water. "See the forehead?" She pointed to an area which seemed somehow out of alignment with the rest. "That's the result of a considerable blow to the skull. If I'm not much mistaken, that's actually produced a depressed fracture, which would be quite enough to bring about more or less instantaneous death."

Copper peered more closely. "I see what you mean. So could he have slipped in the water and banged himself on the head?"

"Not in that position," replied Una. "If he'd fallen forward and hit himself, he wouldn't have ended up lying backwards as he is. I think there's only one likely explanation. He was hit. And I suspect I know what he was hit with."

"And what's that?"

"Look at the bottom of the water. There's a bottle down there. We couldn't see it before because it was concealed by the legs, but the body's shifted position as the water's started to drain. And unless my eyes deceive me, that looks to me like a champagne bottle. Which accords with the champagne glass sitting in that holder there."

"But if he'd had a whack that bad with a bottle," wondered Radley, "wouldn't it have broken?"

"Not necessarily," responded the inspector. "We've seen plenty of news footage of ship launches where they've had to have several goes at breaking the bottle. Champagne bottles are pretty sturdy."

"So, bludgeoned by Bolly, eh, boss?" grinned Radley. "That's a new one on me. We've never come across that before, have we?"

"I'll go over the bottle for prints once we've fished it out," said Una, "but I'm not terribly hopeful, if it's been in moving warm water for any length of time. And I'll also go over the controls of the tub, just for the sake of form, although I suspect that in this scenario I'm likely to get either everybody's prints or nobody's. I'll scan everyone's prints before I go, just in case. But I'm pretty definite about one thing. This isn't just a suspicious death – this is murder."

*

The inspector was solemn-faced as he and the sergeant returned to the saloon and addressed Robin. "Perhaps we can continue, sir. If you'd like to lead the way."

"About time too," muttered Robin as he climbed the stairs, settling into the chair previously occupied by Taff. "Now, inspector, can we get on? It's obvious that there's been a terrible accident, but I don't see why there should be all this cloak-and-dagger kerfuffle. It's a tragedy, but that's surely something for the family to sort out and recover from."

Copper sighed. "I wish I could agree with you, sir. But I'm afraid that we have a pretty clear indication that Sir Lionel's death was not accidental. In fact, it was brought about deliberately."

"But he would never ..." Robin broke off as he studied Copper's grim expression. "You don't mean that someone else ...?"

"I'm afraid it looks that way, sir."

"Murder?" Robin looked aghast. "But how? I mean who ...?"

"And that is something I hope you will be able to help me answer, sir. In order to do that, I need to be able to form a picture of who was where, and when. So for a start, can you tell me, when did you last see your father?"

Robin still seemed stupefied by the inspector's words. "It ... it was last night. We'd all been ashore to have dinner in the restaurant at PORC."

"Sorry, sir? Pork?"

"Porthampton Ocean Racing Club, inspector. It's the yacht club here in the marina. My father is ... was ... a member. And they have a rather good restaurant in the clubhouse."

"And you say 'all'. Does that include the crew as well?" asked Copper.

"Well, yes and no, inspector. We – the family – we were in one of the private dining rooms. But my father arranged for the crew to have a table in the restaurant – a sort of thank-you for their hard work over the last week."

"The last week, sir?"

"Yes. It was one of the things my father liked to do every year. He would invite the family on board for a week's cruise together. Not usually anywhere special – just some ports in northern France or around the Channel Isles. We flew down to meet him in the Canaries once, but that wasn't the norm."

"I see. And you got back here to Porthampton last night?"

"Yes. Around six, I think. And then we had drinks, and went over to the clubhouse, and then the six of us came back on board after dinner."

"Six? Sorry, sir, but I make it seven, if you include Sir Lionel. Was he not with you at the time?"

"Actually, no. When we left the clubhouse, he was talking to Piers Moore - that's the club commodore - so we came on ahead." A reflective pause. "And I didn't see him after that."

"And your crew?"

"I've no idea, inspector. There was no sign of them when we came out through the dining room, and they weren't on board when we got here. Goodness knows what they were doing."

"So the six of you came back here. What sort of time would that be?"

Robin reflected. "About ten or so, I suppose. Not late. And then I think we all dispersed down to our cabins."

"Nobody went into the saloon for a chat or a nightcap?" Copper sounded faintly surprised.

"I think we'd probably all had quite enough socialising for one evening," was Robin's rather dry reply.

The inspector filed away the tone of the response in the back of his mind, but decided to move on. "Tell me a little about Sir Lionel. I'm afraid I hadn't heard of him before this morning. I take it he was a wealthy man?"

Robin snorted. "Look around you, inspector. Boats like this don't come cheap. Draw your own conclusions." He reined in the sharpness in his tone. "Yes, he was. He was a very successful businessman."

"In what area, sir, may I ask?"

"These days he mostly sticks to being Chairman of the Pirate Group. Properties mostly – commercial, industrial, some residential development. But he still keeps his finger in various other pies. Mine, among them."

"Yours, sir?"

"Yes. Butler Steels. It was what the group originally built from. Then Dad passed it on to me. I'm the CEO, but he's still Honorary President." Robin passed a hand over his face. "I mean, was. I'm having trouble getting used to the idea. So I suppose now it's just me in charge."

"And your brothers? Are they also involved in the family's business activities?"

"Not so's you'd notice." Again, the tone of voice was dry. "Leo managed to cut and run years ago. As you are aware, he's a barrister. And Tyrone was always the tearaway, with a taste for fast cars and fast women, so Dad tried to keep some measure of control over him by setting him up with his own motor racing team. Barbarossa. I dare say you've heard of them."

Copper snapped his fingers. "Of course! I thought I half-recognised his face, but I couldn't think from where. So, is that the extent of the family? Other than wives, of course. I'm assuming Sir Lionel was married."

"Divorced," replied Robin, with a look that discouraged further enquiry.

The inspector raised a slight eyebrow, but elected not to pursue the point. "So, to recap, your father was a wealthy and, I'm presuming, powerful businessman. I'd be surprised if a man like that hadn't made some enemies along the way. So can you think of anyone who might have wished him ill?"

"What kind of question is that, inspector?" retorted Robin. "Of course there were people who would have been only too happy to see him lying in a gutter. But where are they supposed to be? How could anyone have got to him? There's nobody on the boat except us." The import of his words struck him, and he stopped short. "Oh."

"'Oh' indeed, sir," said Copper. "If there was nobody else present on the boat, then I'm afraid that I have a very limited field in which to pursue my enquiries into your father's death. So let me ask you again. Who might have wished him ill? Can you think of any reason why one of the family might have wanted to harm Sir Lionel?"

"I've no idea why you would think so," replied Robin.

The slight evasion did not escape the inspector. "Or you yourself?" he pursued. "Might you have had anything against him?"

"Don't be ridiculous, man!" snarled Robin. "Of course not. He was my father, dammit!"

*

"That went well, boss," remarked Pete Radley, as the sound of Robin Butler's footsteps faded as he stamped his way back down the stairs to the saloon. "Not absolutely forthcoming in all departments, was he?"

"Not so's you'd notice," agreed Dave Copper. "I have a feeling that there's quite a lot going on under the surface. Maybe we'll be able to glean rather more from brother number two."

"Assuming that number one did actually pass on the message that you wanted to speak to him, boss. He didn't strike me as the sort of chap who much enjoys doing what he's told."

"Which could easily have led to resentment if Robin's trying to run a company, and his father was determined to keep sticking his fingers into the pie, as he so graphically put it," observed the inspector. "So we'll bear that thought in mind. I think there's probably a lot of background to be looked into here. And you'll notice that Robin talked about Leo having 'cut and run'. One wonders what he might have been escaping from."

"You're going to get the chance to ask him any second," murmured Radley, as the sound of someone climbing the stairs could be heard, and Leo Butler appeared in the doorway of the suite.

Chapter 6

"My brother sent me up, inspector," said Leo, as Dave Copper beckoned him in. "No, actually, that's wrong," he said, with a mirthless laugh, taking the seat facing the inspector. "For him to send me up, that would have required a sense of humour, and that's something Rob has never been accused of having. Anyway, I gather you wanted a word."

"I do, sir. But first, I hope you've managed to sort out your difficulties over your court case."

"What?" Leo looked nonplussed for a moment. "Oh. This afternoon, you mean. I hope so. In fact, I've delegated it to Rob's wife Dee. She's very good at manipulating people into doing what she wants, and she did used to work at our Chambers, so she was going to call our senior partner and organise things. I'm sure she'll have managed it. I expect she'll tell you all about it if you ask her."

"I dare say I shall do so, sir," smiled Copper in beguilingly friendly fashion. Pete Radley, standing alongside, was not fooled by his superior's apparently relaxed manner. "Perhaps you'll ask her if she'd pop up and have a word when we're done here. But first, as I say, I think you and I ought to have a chat."

"Although I'm a little puzzled as to why," frowned Leo. "I don't know what I can tell you about this morning that Rob wouldn't already have mentioned. Trey came and knocked on our cabin door this morning and told us that, sadly, Dad had been found dead. That's about it. The patrol car crew who were already on the scene said we weren't to go out on deck until someone more senior arrived to take charge, which I assume was you, and we've been hanging about in the saloon ever since."

"And your brother didn't say anything else?"

Leo looked quizzical. "No. What was there to say?"

Copper took a deep breath. "I'm afraid I have some distressing news for you, sir. My forensic colleague has taken a preliminary look at Sir Lionel's body, and I'm afraid that she is of the opinion that his death wasn't natural."

"Oh, good lord! I just thought it might have been a heart attack. But ..." An expression of shock swept across Leo's face. "Just a minute, inspector. Are you trying to tell me that Dad was killed?"

'Not telling you very successfully, apparently,' thought Copper to himself. "I'm sorry to say so, sir," he confirmed. "There is evidence of an attack which led to his death."

Leo still appeared stunned. "But who on earth ...?"

"That is what I have to establish, Mr. Butler." The inspector changed tack. "Suppose we go back a little, sir. What can you tell me about the events of last night?"

"Hasn't Rob already told you?" asked Leo.

"I'd rather hear it from your own lips, sir," insisted Copper. "Let's take it from the time the boat arrived back here in the marina."

Leo paused for thought. "Well, Dad had arranged for everyone to go ashore to have dinner in the yacht club. I suppose he thought of it as a sort of signing-off from the trip. We'd all been away together for the week on the annual cruise, you see."

"So I gather, sir. A jolly family get-together, in fact."

"I suppose you could put it like that." Leo sounded doubtful as to the accuracy of the description. "Anyway, we had cocktails on board first – Trey makes a wicked Buck's Fizz, and it's not the usual recipe – and then we headed for the restaurant. Well, the crew were in the restaurant. Dad had arranged a private room for the rest of us."

"For any particular reason, do you know, sir?" enquired Copper.

Leo shrugged. "Not really. I just suppose to stop people staring or eavesdropping."

'At what?' wondered the inspector. "And after the meal, sir?"

"We sauntered back here – well, most of us did. Dad hung about chatting."

"Just one thought occurs to me, sir. I noticed when I arrived this morning that there is a barrier with a sort of metal security gate at the access to this pontoon, but it was propped open. Is that normally how it stands?"

Leo laughed. "Lord, no, inspector. This is a private pontoon. It's leased from the club for Dad's exclusive use. You couldn't have just anybody wandering along and coming aboard."

"Well, that's what I was thinking, sir. And there seems to be a keypad controlling it, so I'm assuming there's a security code. My question is, who has that code?"

"We all do," replied Leo. "The family, the crew, everyone. We'd never be able to get back on board if we'd popped ashore otherwise, would we?"

"So anybody with knowledge of that code would be able to gain access to this vessel?"

"They would," agreed Leo, "but they'd have to be pretty quick off the mark, because it gets changed to a new number every Sunday at noon. The security system in the club's computer does it automatically. So we were given the new number, which I expect we all promptly forgot, when we got in last evening. Fortunately Dee remembered it when we came back to *Buck*, otherwise we'd have been cooling our heels up on the quayside for ages waiting for Dad to reappear. Which, it turned out, he never did before we went to bed."

"So the last time you saw your father was when you left the yacht club's premises last night?" Copper sought to confirm.

"Correct, inspector."

Copper reflected for a moment. "Tell me, sir. During the past week, have you become aware of any tensions emerging among the family?"

Leo suddenly became wary. "I don't quite see what you mean."

"Oh, I'm sure you can see what I'm driving at, Mr. Butler," responded the inspector. "I'm sure that, as a barrister, you're well used to weighing up evidence. You see, as you yourself have clearly explained to me, nobody outside the family circle, other than this boat's crew, could have gained access to the vessel between your return last night and the discovery of Sir Lionel's body this morning. The crew, it appears, were not on board overnight, although I'm uncertain as yet as to why. But the fact remains that the only people who would have had the opportunity to kill your father were the members of his own immediate family. So I ask again, have there been any quarrels, or even anything less obvious, which might have led one of the people aboard this boat to wish Sir Lionel ill?"

"My father," said Leo, his look and his voice unexpectedly haughty, "was the rock on which this family was built. To suggest that any of us would want to harm him is very dangerous thinking, inspector. I would advise against it."

*

"That's us put in our place, boss," remarked Pete Radley, after Leo had stalked out of the suite. "Did that sound ever so slightly like a threat to you?"

"If it was, I wish him the best of luck," responded Dave Copper. "Our barrister ought to know better than to mess with a police investigation."

"One barrister down, one to go," observed Radley. "And speak of the devil," he added in a whisper, as Dee Butler appeared in the doorway.

"Mr. Copper," she said. "Here as requested."

"Mrs. Butler, do come in and take a seat," Copper welcomed her. "Your brother-in-law evidently mentioned that we wished to speak to you."

"He did growl something of the sort, inspector," said Dee. "I don't know what you've done to put him in an even grumpier mood than the one he was already in."

"Nothing, I hope, Mrs. Butler," smiled Copper blandly. "I assume that he was still unhappy about the disruption to his schedules for today. Which I hope you've been able to resolve for him, being a fellow-barrister."

"I have. A little persuasion goes a long way. Oh, and it's 'ex-barrister', inspector," Dee corrected him. "Leo and I used to work in the same chambers in the Temple, but no longer."

"That must have been potentially confusing, having two Q.C.s called Butler in the practice," remarked Copper.

"Not at all," replied Dee. "At that time, I was still using my maiden name"

"Which was?"

"Fender, inspector. Plain Miss Desdemona Fender. But anyway, Leo was the only Q.C. in the family. I never got around to applying for silk, and I left shortly after Robin and I were married, so the confusion never arose."

"Ah. Well, thank you for clearing that up." Copper turned to Radley. "I take it you have that noted, sergeant." A silent nod from his junior colleague. "Sergeant Radley is taking notes for me," he explained to Dee. "May I take it you have no objection?"

"Of course not, inspector. Why should I?"

"I cannot imagine, ma'am. So we'll move on. I'd like you to tell me what you can about the events of yesterday, that being the last day that your father-in-law was seen alive. Unless you can tell me otherwise, of course?"

"I can't. And as to the events of yesterday, that would make a very short list."

"Really, ma'am? I understood that there was something of a celebratory dinner last night."

"I'm not certain you could call it that," replied Dee wryly. "Perhaps we were all celebrating our release from a week's dutiful attendance on Lionel. But I thought you were speaking of the whole day, which was singularly uneventful. We sailed from Guernsey shortly after breakfast, and after that it was simply a question of sitting there watching the English Channel roll by, with the occasional wild excitement when we spotted a container ship on the horizon. But then, as I gather you know, we got into port yesterday evening and went across to the yacht club for dinner, after which we returned on board."

"You didn't linger to socialise after that, I gather."

"We didn't. I for one had packing to do, because we had planned to get away early this morning. My husband has a slew of meetings this week. But that plan seems to have gone out of the window."

"I fear so, Mrs. Butler," sympathised Copper. "But I'm afraid that, as you doubtless realise, with your experience in the law, murder does tend to disrupt everyone's plans."

"You're wrong, Mr. Copper," retorted Dee, slightly to the inspector's surprise at the sharpness of her tone. "I have no experience whatsoever of murder, or indeed any other criminal activity of the kind. My area of expertise was in commercial law. I leave the grubbier aspects of the law to my brother-in-law."

Copper flicked a glance at his colleague, one eyebrow fractionally raised. "And now, from what you say, I understand that you've left the law altogether. Since your marriage, did you say?"

"I had no need to stay," said Dee, her manner

verging on smug. "Forgive the cliché, but the law is a jungle. Yes, even in the apparently dry field of business law, although that may surprise you. Some of the conflicts can be brutal. And my marriage to my husband meant that I was very well provided for, with no need to fight my colleagues for a living. Robin's position leaves us extremely comfortably off, so I am now in the situation of being able to indulge myself." Her hands played unconsciously with the ring she wore, a significant emerald surrounded by diamonds. "Which I do."

"Forgive me if I point out a slight contradiction, Mrs. Butler," said Copper mildly, "but you spoke just now of your 'dutiful attendance' on Sir Lionel for the past week. That sounds very much as if you weren't exactly pleasing yourself."

"Oh that," scoffed Dee. "A small enough price to pay. Lionel had some fanciful image of what the ideal family ought to consist of, and part of that was coming together in unity and following some sort of norms of behaviour. And since he holds the whip hand as the nominal head of Robin's company ..." She broke off. "Although, of course, not any longer," she mused, half to herself.

Copper reacted swiftly to the comment. "And does 'holding the whip hand' imply any kind of conflict between your husband and your father-in-law?" he enquired. "Because, of course, if it did, we would have to look carefully as to whether that might provide a reason for you or your husband to wish Sir Lionel ill."

"The idea's absurd," said Dee dismissively. "Why on earth would either of us do anything to jeopardise a perfectly satisfactory situation?"

*

"We seem to have a talent, sergeant," observed Dave Copper mildly, after Dee's tense departure, "for rubbing up the members of the Butler family the wrong way."

"Seems like it, boss," agreed Pete Radley cheerfully. "But if you think about it, might that not be a good thing? Potentially, I mean. You've talked about the 'trapping more flies with honey than with vinegar' thing, but if people are a bit off balance or on edge, couldn't that mean that something might slip? Because I for one don't buy this 'happy family all on a jolly holiday together' story for one moment."

"I'm not at all sure that I do," said Copper. "There seem to be cracks. The question is, which one of them is wide enough to let a motive for murder slip through?"

"You're pretty confident that one of this lot is responsible?"

"It certainly seems that way. Obviously we have to confirm the whereabouts of everyone else, by which I mean the crew, but it's hard to think outside the family. Unless, of course, we have a completely unknown interloper from outside, about whom we know nothing. Plenty of questions still to be asked."

The detectives' musings were cut short by a female voice asking tentatively, "Is it in here, inspector?", as Cordelia Butler stepped hesitantly into the suite.

Copper stood. "Come in, Mrs. Butler. I'm assuming it is 'Mrs. Butler'?" he asked with a smile. "My only question would be, which one?"

"I'm Cordelia, inspector. Leo's wife. Cordy for short, if you wish."

"I think I'll probably stick to Mrs. Butler, or perhaps Mrs. Leo, if that's all right by you." Cordelia shrugged assent. "And am I right in detecting a slight Southern Hemisphere accent? Australia?"

"New Zealand, actually," said Cordelia. "Born in Christchurch."

"Christchurch?" queried Radley, pen hovering. "That's in Dorset, isn't it?"

"Christchurch, South Island," explained Cordelia with a smile. "But I've lived in the U.K. for quite a few years now."

"And are you also involved in any of the family's business activities?"

"Oh, no. I plough my own furrow, inspector." Cordelia laughed. "Actually, that's very appropriate, if you think about it."

"Oh? How so?"

"I have a garden design practice." She produced a card from a slim wallet drawn from the pocket of her designer jeans. "As you can see, I work under my maiden name of Cordelia Lyne. I prefer not to carry the baggage of the Butler name in my work."

"You think it might be some sort of a handicap?" queried Copper, intrigued.

"Oh no, nothing like that," said Cordelia. "But sometimes people with money, who are the sort of people who might want my services, hear the name 'Butler', and they might think they can go through me to get some kind of advantage. Ridiculous, of course, but there it is. So I avoid the situation."

"So I wonder how your different worlds managed to collide, Mrs. Butler."

"Oh, that's easy. I designed a garden at Chelsea sponsored by Leo's law practice. He and I met at the Flower Show and ... well, we went on from there."

"And now you take part in the family's activities," said Copper, sliding seamlessly into the situation in hand. "Such as this last week aboard Sir Lionel's boat."

"It's quite a useful opportunity," said Cordelia. "Sometimes it gives me a chance to visit gardens which wouldn't be on my normal beat. I'm always on the lookout for fresh inspiration."

"And was this trip suitably inspiring? Did it produce the results you were hoping for?"

Cordelia gave the inspector a look, as if suspecting that there was a hidden meaning behind his words. "I think I managed to enjoy myself, if that's what you mean, inspector," she replied guardedly. "Until ..." She stopped short.

"Until the unhappy events of this morning, I assume," said Copper.

"Of course. The others say that you have some idea that Lionel was killed. Murdered. Is that really true?"

"I'm afraid it looks that way, Mrs. Butler. Now, I have a fairly clear picture of the events of yesterday, up to the point where everyone left the yacht club premises. Beyond that, the situation is unclear. So, of course, I find myself in the position of having to ask everyone if they can think of anyone who might have a motive to kill your father-in-law."

Cordelia shook her head. "It's a mystery, inspector. Unless it was some kind of business rival. But surely that's too melodramatic."

"Perhaps so, madam. But in the absence of any motives within the family, we may have to investigate that possibility. And if you can think of none ...?" The inspector let the question hang in the air.

"None at all, Mr. Copper. Surely we aren't that kind of family."

Chapter 7

Dave Copper took a deep breath. "Well, sergeant, I don't know about you, but it's all sounding rather samey to me. Unless your notes are packed with earth-shattering insights which have somehow escaped me."

"No such luck, boss," grinned Pete Radley in response. "Except that everybody has dropped just the tiniest hint of cracks in the united family façade. One of those is bound to open up sooner or later."

"Thank you for the optimism," said Copper with an answering smile. "You sound like the old me, with the power of positive thinking that I used to drive Mr. Constable mad with."

"I've just learned from the best, boss."

"Anyway, we'd better get on. Four down, two to go."

"Right. Just the two young celebs left."

"Sorry?" Copper sounded puzzled. "I know it's Tyrone Butler and his wife, and I'm quite prepared to count him as a celebrity, if that's how we're defining things these days. But I've no idea who she is."

"Ah. That's because you don't read the same sort of magazines as my missus, boss," smiled Radley. "Sharon's never happier than when she's leafing though the pages of 'Hi!' or one of those other mags that send the paparazzi out to stalk footballers' wives or Eurotrash royals."

"True. Una's more a National Trust magazine woman, leavened with the occasional true crime periodical for a little light relief."

"But if you had been looking over my Sharon's shoulder," continued Radley, "you would have known that Mrs. Tyrone is one of those models who seem to get paid loony amounts of money to stand there looking half-starved. Jessica Bell, if I'm not much mistaken."

"Which I'm sure you're not. So, one of those golden couples the social media are apparently so fond of. That'll make a change from the rather dour fare we've been offered so far. Well, let's have one or other of them up here."

As if in response to the inspector's wish, Tyrone Butler swung breezily through the door of the suite. "Guys! I figured you must be in need of someone else to grill by now. Cordy didn't say anything much when she came down, and it seemed to have all gone quiet up here, so I thought I'd volunteer myself as your next victim. Do you want me to sit here?"

"That would be good, Mr. Butler," replied Copper after a moment's pause, slightly taken aback by the other's exuberance. "Do indeed take a seat."

Tyrone threw himself into the suggested chair. "So, inspector, what can I tell you that you don't already know? I suppose the others have probably already given you chapter and verse about the past week?"

"Not comprehensively, sir," said Copper, charmed almost against his will by the other's friendly openness. "But we'll start, if I may, just for my sergeant's notes, with what I think I already know about you. You're lead driver for the Barbarossa F1 team, which I have been given to understand was initially financed by Sir Lionel …"

"Lead driver, maybe," interrupted Ty with a laugh. "I wish I could say 'leading driver', but if you've been following the season, you'll know that that's not exactly a claim I can make. Next to bottom in the rankings at the moment, I'm afraid. Still, there's always another race, isn't there?"

"I'm faintly surprised you can find time to take a holiday at this time of year," remarked Copper.

"Squeezed it into the schedule, inspector," said Ty. "And after all, when the team's owner requests your presence, you can't very well make an excuse that you're too tied up preparing for the next race. I just leave the mechanics to tweak the car while I'm away and then jump into it when I get back."

"And Sir Lionel was content with this approach to your racing career?" wondered Copper.

"Oh, Dad was never happy unless you were top of the heap," laughed Ty. "But that's just the way he was. Why?"

"Because," said the inspector, "as I'm sure you are aware by now, all the evidence so far is pointing to the conclusion that your father has been unlawfully killed. This means that I am searching for reasons. Now I don't know a great deal about the motor-racing world, but one thing I'm fairly certain of is that it's not for those without deep pockets. Not, I gather, that this would be a problem for Sir Lionel Butler. But I imagine that to pour a great deal of money into a venture which produces unimpressive results might lead to a certain amount of dissatisfaction on the part of the sponsor. There might well be questions asked. Conflicts could arise. I'm sure you can see where I'm going with this, sir."

"Do you mean to say that Dad might have had a downer on me because I wasn't producing enough wins for him, and so you've got me in your sights because we might have argued about it?" demanded Ty, his former easy manner transformed into belligerence. "You think I killed him?" He half-rose out of his chair.

"I haven't said so, Mr. Butler," replied Copper evenly, "and I'm sure we shall get on a great deal better if you remain calm." Ty slowly subsided back into his seat. "But you must understand that I am seeking possible motives for the murder of your father. And the scenario I offer is not really so far-fetched, is it?"

Ty managed a rueful laugh. "I suppose not, inspector. Sorry. And in a way, you're right. Dad did have a bit of a go at me over dinner because he reckoned that Barbarossa wasn't really pulling its weight in the grand scheme of things to boost the image of his Pirate empire, but I wasn't the only one to get on the wrong side of him. But to murder him over that? No, inspector. You've got that all wrong."

"I'm glad to hear you say so, sir. So let's carry on from the end of the dinner last night. You all came back to the boat together."

"Except Dad."

"Yes, sir. That we know. And did you see him after that? At any point between your return and this morning? Because so far, I've heard from no-one who did."

"And I can't help you there either, inspector. Jezza – that's my wife - and I went back to our cabin pretty much straight away."

"And you were together there all the time after that?"

"Not exactly. I was, but Jezza did go out for a while."

Copper's attention was alerted. "Indeed, sir? How so?"

"She's got a guilty secret, inspector." Ty laughed. "Oh no, nothing illegal. But she smokes." He held up a hand. "I know – it's not the worst thing in the world, but you don't expect it these days. It wouldn't do her image any good if anyone found out. And Dad wouldn't have the smell of cigarettes anywhere within a mile of him. So it's not been easy for her this week. She's had to sneak off ashore whenever she could. And last night, after we got back, she crept ashore when she thought everyone else was out of the way so that she could have a sly ciggy round the back of the bike sheds, or whatever it is they have at the hotel. But then she came back, and we were together until Trey came knocking this morning."

"That's our first absence of alibi, isn't it, boss?" Pete Radley sounded quite excited, after the two detectives had waited for the sounds of Tyrone's departure to fade away.

"It is," agreed Dave Copper. "And as soon as the young lady gets here, which I imagine is only going to be a few moments away, we'll see what more we can find out about her little trip ashore. If that's indeed what she did. For a start, the timing may be crucial."

"Not that we know what time Sir Lionel came back on to the boat, boss," demurred Radley. "So far, nobody's clapped eyes on him after they left the yacht club."

"True. But we'll see if we can elicit more details from the people there in due course." Copper lowered his voice, as the sound of someone approaching could be heard. "In the meantime, we have the third Mrs. Butler on our plate, I think. Do come in, Mrs. Butler," he said at normal volume, as Jessica appeared hesitantly in the doorway. "We've just been waiting for you. I hoped your husband would have mentioned that we wanted a quick word."

"Yes, Ty told me to come up," faltered Jessica.

"Well, take a seat, Mrs. Butler," smiled Copper in his friendliest voice, thinking as he did so, 'Seems as if the kid gloves are going to be needed for this one'. "That's if you don't mind me calling you 'Mrs. Butler'. Because according to my sergeant here, who apparently knows much more about these things than I do, I gather you're quite the celebrity in your own right. A model, he tells me."

"That's right." Jessica seemed to gain in confidence, and she preened slightly. "I've done a few covers," she murmured, gazing up through her eyelashes in what was evidently one of her signature looks.

"So shall I call you 'Miss Bell'? I think that's the

name, isn't it? Unless you only use that when you're working, of course."

Jessica gave the inspector a nervous look. "But I don't ... I mean ..." She seemed oddly unsettled.

"I'll tell you what. We'll stick to 'Mrs. Tyrone', shall we?" suggested Copper. "Then I won't get confused."

Radley flicked a sideways glance at his superior. 'Confused?' he thought. 'That'll be the day.'

"Now," resumed the inspector, "I'm hoping you can give me a little more information about what happened yesterday."

Jessica brightened. "Oh, I had fun," she announced with sudden childish glee. "I drove the boat."

Copper was slightly taken aback by the abrupt change of mood. "Sorry?"

"On the way back," explained Jessica. "Bob let me steer the boat for a while. I'd never done it before. It was exciting."

"This would have been on your way back from Guernsey, I assume. But unfortunately I am more concerned with the events which occurred later on, once you'd arrived back in Porthampton. I've been told that the family all went for a meal together ashore, and that you all came back together. But when you returned to the boat, Sir Lionel wasn't with you."

"No. He stayed behind."

"I wondered if you might have any idea why he might have done so?"

"No." Jessica shrugged prettily. "He was just talking to some old man when I last saw him."

"Ah, so you didn't see him after that?" asked Copper. "Not after you'd arrived back on board?"

"No."

"Not even when you left your cabin and came ashore again?"

"How ... how did you know about that?" Jessica's

nervousness returned.

"Your husband mentioned it," said Copper mildly. "He revealed your guilty secret to us." And as Jessica merely gaped at him, he smiled. "The smoking."

"You won't tell anyone, will you?" pleaded Jessica. "Only the people I model for, all the fashion companies, they're all so anti-smoking. None of the magazines will run cigarette adverts. And Lionel, he absolutely hates ..." She broke off, and her hand went to her mouth. "Oh."

"So I imagine you need to indulge in a certain amount of subterfuge," suggested Copper after a moment's pause. "So tell me, how did you manage to avoid detection last night?"

"I just crept out and went round to the smoking area at the back of the hotel. And when I'd finished, I popped a mint and came back."

"Did you see anyone else during the course of this? Anyone who might verify your movements?"

"No, nobody," replied Jessica. "I was lucky."

"And it was also lucky that you remembered the security code for the pontoon gate," said the inspector.

"Oh, you don't need it to get out. It just opens from the inside."

"But surely you do need it to come back in," pointed out Copper. "Otherwise you could have been stranded out there. Your brother-in-law Leo has already told us that he'd forgotten the number when you all returned to the boat."

"So had I," confessed Jessica with a guilty smile. "But I propped the gate open when I went out so that I could get back. But I closed it again afterwards."

"And there was nobody to be seen? Not Sir Lionel? Not any other members of the family? No crew members? No strangers?"

Jessica shook her head. "No, no-one at all. Everything was very quiet."

"So you didn't, by any chance, hear any noise from the hot tub? Because I should think the sound would be quite audible in the silence."

"It does get quite loud," nodded Jessica. "I said that to Lionel when we were in it earlier on, and he said 'What?'" She giggled. "He was funny."

"And now," said Copper, with harsh solemnity, "he is unfortunately dead. Someone has killed him. Which means I need to ask you, Mrs. Butler, if you can think of anyone among your family who might have any reason to wish your father-in-law harm?"

Jessica turned a wide-eyed gaze on the inspector. "Oh no. Surely none of us would want to hurt Lionel. He was always so good to me. And to Ty," she added quickly. "And the others too, I suppose." She sounded less positive. "But why the family?" she challenged. "Why couldn't it be somebody else? What about the crew?"

"They were all apparently elsewhere," returned Copper.

"Well, someone else," insisted Jessica with increasing desperation. "Somebody could have come on board, couldn't they?"

"They could," agreed the inspector heavily. "But only if they were able to take advantage of the fact that you had left the pontoon gate open and unattended."

*

"Drat!" burst out Dave Copper, after Jessica had been dismissed.

"Watch it, boss," chuckled Pete Radley. "You're going to lead me astray if you start using such words in front of me."

Copper joined in the chuckle ruefully. "Sorry about the intemperate language, sergeant. But that was just what we didn't need. Here was I, thinking we had this reasonably closely sewn up, with a conveniently short list of half a dozen suspects among the late lamented's

73

nearest and dearest, and the nautical equivalent of a nice locked room mystery, so beloved of detective fiction authors. Then the lovely Jessica throws a spanner in the works by confessing that she left the door open for some person or persons unknown to pop in and cause our dead man to pop off."

"With a bottle of pop," added Radley, "if Una's right."

"Well, let's not strain the imagery too far," said Copper, growing solemn-faced.

"What next then, boss?"

The inspector reflected for a moment. "First thing, clarify this business about the crew's absence. Why on earth were they away from the boat overnight? And then we'll see if we can get any more information about what Sir Lionel did after he'd let the rest of the family go on ahead at the end of the meal last night. Where did he disappear to, I wonder?"

"Don't forget the crew still hanging about in the wheelhouse, boss," Radley reminded his superior.

"Precisely. First item on my list. So nip through and ask Mr. de Waters if he'd care to join us," instructed Copper. "And we'll see if we can gather some more data for your little notebook."

*

Bob de Waters settled into the seat opposite the inspector and looked enquiringly at him. "Are you getting anywhere, Mr. Copper?" he asked.

"Early days still, Mr. de Waters," replied the inspector. "Or is it 'Captain'?"

"Oh please, it's 'Bob'. Nobody calls me 'Mr'." Bob chuckled. "Or you can be like Taff and call me 'Captain Bob'. Or 'Skipper'. Please, anything but 'Mr'."

"I think, under the circumstances, we'll stick to the formalities, sir," said Copper drily. "Let's try 'Captain'."

"That sounds very ominous, inspector," said Bob. "I

hope that doesn't mean that you think I had something to do with Sir Lionel dying."

"Not so far as we can tell at this stage, Captain. But there is one thing that is puzzling me, which I hope you can resolve. How did it come about that none of the crew were on board this boat last night? I should have thought that at the end of a week's voyage, which I gather this has been, you would all have had your various duties here."

"And so we have, inspector. Which is what we came back early this morning to see to. And that's when Taff found Sir Lionel."

"So explain to me, please, the sequence of events. As I've been told, the crew all went ashore for dinner yesterday evening at the same time as the family left the boat. Is that correct?"

"More or less, inspector. Sir Lionel had very kindly said that we should all have a meal at the yacht club last night as a sort of reward for looking after everybody during the trip. His treat. He was a very generous employer. So we had the meal, wine and all." A rueful smile. "Maybe a drop too much wine all round, if the truth were told."

Copper smiled. "So you might have been a touch noisy, coming back on to the boat last night? Is that the reason? But I still don't see ..."

Bob shook his head with a laugh. "Oh no, inspector. It's much worse than that. You see, Flix – that's Felicity Witcher, our engineer – had this mad idea of going clubbing afterwards. There's a place up in town she knows. I told her not to be so daft – me going clubbing at my age? But she insisted, and the boys were up for it, so against my better judgement, I let myself be persuaded." An embarrassed grin. "Actually, it was great. I hadn't been to a club since God was a lad, and I think I'd forgotten how to have fun. Anyway, several hours and a few drinks later – okay, quite a few – we rolled out of the place at something past two o'clock, with Trey and me practically carrying Taff. And to crash back on board in that state would not have been popular. Sir Lionel might have been a generous gentleman, but I couldn't always say the same for some of his family."

"So what did you do?" wondered the inspector.

"I've got a house," explained Bob. "Just a little terraced place, a couple of streets back from the marina. I bought it so's I'd have somewhere to live between trips on *Buck*. If you saw my shoebox down below, you'd see why. So anyway, we rolled back there and got our heads down for a few hours. I figured we wouldn't be missed after everyone had gone to bed, and if we came back on board early enough, nobody would be any the wiser. But then ... well, you know what happened then."

"We do, Captain," said Copper. "So you're telling me that all four of the crew were together for the whole of the time between your leaving the boat yesterday evening and your return this morning. There are no unaccounted-for absences?"

"No chance, inspector," stated Bob. "And before you ask, nobody could have sneaked past me in the dead of night to get out of the house. I let Flix have my bedroom, and the chaps squeezed into the spare room while I kipped on the sofa downstairs, right close to the front door. And I'm a light sleeper. No, if you're looking in that direction, you're going to have to look elsewhere."

Copper nodded slowly. "Thank you for that, Captain. I think that's all very clear. Now, I wonder ..."

"Did you want to speak to the others?" asked Bob, standing. "Because I'm sure they'll all tell you the same."

The inspector reflected for a moment. "Not at this point, I think. Because I still have unanswered questions about the movements of Sir Lionel himself. I don't suppose you can help me with that?"

"Sorry, no, inspector. The last I saw him was when

76

he and the family were heading over to the clubhouse for dinner. After that, nothing."

"Then I think, Captain, you and your colleagues can stand down for the time being, although I shall certainly want a word with each of them later. But first, I'd better break the news to Sir Lionel's family that I shall need them to stay put on board for the time being. Perhaps we can soften the blow by arranging some further refreshments for them," suggested Copper.

Bob looked at his watch. "I'll get Trey to do them some cocktails, and then start on lunch, if that's okay by you, Mr. Copper."

"Good idea, Captain. And then I think the sergeant and I will follow in your footsteps of last night, and ask some questions at the yacht club."

Chapter 8

The Porthampton Ocean Racing Club building was a short walk around the edge of the marina basin from the top of the pontoon. A flagpole in the forecourt flew a briskly-snapping Union Flag, accompanied by a burgee bearing the club's logo, a crowned wreath encircling a stylised breaking wave, with alongside the flagpole a marble stela with a bronze plate commemorating the opening of the building by a minor member of the royal family. A double-horseshoe flight of steps led up to the pillared portico of a classical building in the style of a Greek temple, gleaming in white Portland stone, with a gilded statue of Poseidon adorning the pediment.

"I think we can safely say," observed Dave Copper, "that there is evidence of quite a lot of money floating around in this establishment."

"Do you reckon they'll let me in, boss?" enquired Pete Radley. "I mean, I did put a tie on this morning, and I remembered to check that I'm wearing matching socks, but are we sure that's posh enough?"

Copper chuckled. "I shouldn't worry too much, sergeant. Despite appearances, I'm hoping that the place isn't quite as snooty as one of those London gentlemen's clubs that I'm guessing it was designed to look like. As long as you remember not to wipe your nose on your sleeve, I think we'll be all right." He led the way up the steps and in through the heavy brass-mounted doors.

"Can I help you, gentlemen?" A middle-aged man in dark trousers and a striped waistcoat appeared in a doorway and advanced into the foyer, a look of slightly aloof enquiry on his face.

"You were saying?" muttered Radley in an undertone to his superior.

"I'm sure you can," responded Copper to the man, unintimidated. "We'd like to speak to someone in authority, please."

The man looked the detectives up and down. "With regard to what, may I ask ... sir?"

"With regard to the sudden violent death of a member of this establishment," said Copper firmly. He produced his warrant card. "My name is Detective Inspector Copper, and this is my colleague Detective Sergeant Radley." He surveyed the other man in his turn. "And unless you are the person in charge, I should like to speak to your most senior official." A pause. "Please."

"Of course, inspector." An ingratiating smile was suddenly produced. "If you'd just like to wait for one moment ..." The man crossed the foyer and tapped on a door, entering in response to a gruffly-barked 'Come!'. A murmured conversation could be heard, before an older man sporting immaculate white naval whiskers in the style of King George the Fifth, resplendent in a blue blazer with dazzling brass buttons and a crested top pocket, teamed with white trousers with knife-edged creases, advanced into the foyer.

"A detective inspector, I gather?" The man advanced, holding out a hand in greeting, and then shaking Radley's hand in turn. "And a detective sergeant to boot. The forces of law and order turning up mob-handed, eh? Well, I can guess what this is about. My name's Piers Moore. I'm the Commodore of the club. You'd better come through to my office, gentlemen." He turned to the other man. "And that will be all for now, Harvey. I think you can safely return to your duties in the bar."

Piers led the way into a large office, comfortably furnished in the style of an Edwardian study with deep leather armchairs and walls studded with paintings and prints of nautical scenes, and waved his visitors to a chesterfield sofa as he took his place behind an imposing mahogany desk. "Do excuse Harvey's rather frosty reception, inspector. I'm afraid he's the most dreadful snob, and is firmly of the opinion that it was a sad day when the club began admitting members without titles during the 1930s, but as our sommelier, he does keep a remarkably good cellar. Not that you're here to talk about our wine stocks, of course. This will be about Lionel Butler, no doubt."

"It is, sir," smiled Copper. "I see news travels fast."

"Not that it had far to travel," responded Piers. "But yes, the sight of a police car appearing amidst unusual activity aboard the vessel of one of our more prominent members was bound to get people wondering what was afoot. But I'm asking myself, what exactly is it that is afoot? Lionel has died, that much we know. But what is it that brings a pair of detectives to our door?"

"The nature of the death, sir. I'm afraid that our forensic colleague has drawn a preliminary conclusion that Sir Lionel did not die a natural death. So we must ask certain questions."

"Are you telling me that he's been murdered?" Piers sounded horrified. "But that's ghastly. Do you have any idea who was responsible?"

"That's what I'm in the midst of trying to find out, sir," said Copper. "And since I understand that he spent some of his last hours on these premises, I'm hoping that you can provide some helpful information."

"Of course, inspector," replied Piers readily. "Anything I can do to help. Ask your questions." He sat back and waited.

Copper took a second to gather his thoughts. "Sir Lionel dined here last night with his family, I'm told."

"That's correct, inspector. Not that that was anything unusual. He used the club frequently whenever he was down on *Red Buccaneer*. And I had a call from him yesterday to ask if we could reserve one of our private dining rooms for him and the other members of his family, which we were happy to arrange. Several of our members like to do that from time to time, if it's in the nature of a celebration or perhaps a confidential meeting. Not that we encourage the discussion of business on the club's premises, of course. It isn't thought to be quite the thing, if you understand me. But naturally, in a private setting, we don't trouble ourselves too deeply about the convention."

"And it wasn't only the Butler family who were here in the club, I believe."

"Also correct. When Lionel arrived, he asked if we could provide a table in the restaurant for the four members of *Red Buccaneer*'s crew, as his guests, to be charged to his club account. Of course, that was not a problem, and in fact they arrived a few moments after Lionel and his party had gone through to their dining room."

"So the two groups were entirely separate?"

"So far as I can tell, inspector," said Piers. "I myself was in the restaurant with a couple of friends a little later, and I certainly didn't see any to-ing and fro-ing. Why should there be?"

"No reason, Mr. Moore," responded Copper. "I'm simply trying to form a clear picture. But the thought occurs to me, that with everybody from Sir Lionel's boat present in the club, that might have given an opportunity for some other person to gain access to *Red Buccaneer*."

"Aha!" chuckled Piers. "I'm afraid Lionel was ahead of you there. Because he asked me to get our security chap to keep a particular eye on the boat while she was unoccupied, and to make sure that nobody unauthorised gained access to the pontoon. Not that they'd find it easy to do so without being detected, of course."

"How so, sir?" wondered Copper. "Surely if someone had knowledge of the code to the gate, there would be nothing to prevent them?"

"They could get in," agreed Piers, "but not without our knowing about it. Here, let me show you." He rose from behind the desk and moved to a wall of bookshelves, where he slid aside a section, to reveal that some of the shelves formed a dummy façade concealing a keyboard and a bank of monitors. "We may look old-fashioned here," he remarked, smiling at the detective's evident surprise, "but we aren't totally averse to the benefits of the twenty-first century. We have all our pontoons covered by CCTV, and all the gates have individual access codes linked to a central monitoring system. We can tell whenever someone punches in the number for a particular gate, and at what time."

Copper's eyebrows rose. "I'm impressed, Mr. Moore."

Piers moved a wheeled leather chair to the unit and took a seat at the keyboard, as the detectives rose to stand at his shoulder. "I'll give you a demonstration." He gave a few clicks at the keyboard, and an image of one of the marina's pontoons appeared on a screen. "Here's Sir Lionel's private pontoon at present, with *Red Buccaneer* alongside. So let me scroll back to yesterday ..." More clicks. "... and there she is moving into position on arrival. Now we can roll forward ..." The picture moved forward like a jerky silent movie. "Ah look, there's Lionel's skipper coming ashore to check in at the clubhouse. And a little while later, he heads back on board, and if we look at this other screen here ..." Further clicks. "... we can see the time at which he keyed in the code to go through the gate to get back on board."

"That is some system, sir," marvelled the inspector.

"It's necessary," replied Piers simply. "There are some very expensive craft here, and the members of the club have every right to expect us to exercise all possible measures to take care of them."

"It's just a shame the coverage doesn't extend to

the whole boat, boss," put in Radley. "You've only got just the edge of it, plus that gangplank thing, or whatever you call it."

"On-board security is the owners' responsibility," said Piers. "We can't cover everything, so we just monitor the pontoons."

"So can we follow the events of later yesterday evening?" requested Copper.

"Very easily." Piers turned back to the keyboard. "If I speed things up a little more ... there, Lionel and his family are going ashore ... and a few minutes later, there go his crew. And if I roll on a couple of hours ... there are his family heading back on board, and if you check the other screen, you can see the time recorded for when the gate code was entered. And not a single soul in between," he finished triumphantly.

"I'm grateful, sir. That clarifies things considerably," said the inspector. "Just one or two things more, if I can trespass on your kindness a little further. Could you run the recording on a little more. I'd like to verify something I've been told about an individual who may have gone ashore after the family's return to the boat."

"Of course," said Piers, sounding faintly puzzled. The recording advanced, until a figure could be seen making its way up the pontoon and out of shot, propping open the security gate as it went.

"There she is, boss!" exclaimed Radley. "That's Jessica, nipping ashore as she said. So that proves that what she told us was true."

"Agreed," nodded Copper. "Oh. Just a minute." His attention was caught by further movement. "Well, well. There's one question answered. If I'm not much mistaken, that is Sir Lionel returning to the boat. In Jessica's absence, which may or may not be interesting. And ..." He frowned. "Here's an odd thing. He doesn't close the gate. If he's so bothered about security, why not?"

"Maybe he saw Jessica coming, boss," suggested Radley.

"Maybe you're right," nodded the inspector. "In fact, look. There, after a moment, back she comes, and the gate is closed behind her."

"So the family's all back on board. But how about the crew?" queried the sergeant.

"That was my second question. Mr. Moore, could you take the recording forward to early this morning – say from around sixish?" And in response to Piers' further clicking, "Nobody on the pontoon in the interim. And then there they are. All four of them, coming back through the gate ..." A check on the other screen. "... at the time they said they did. Any doubt helpfully removed. So I think that's probably all your system can tell us, sir. Thank you."

"My pleasure. So, unless there's anything else ...?"

"There is, sir."

With an interrogatively raised eyebrow, Piers sat behind his desk once more as the detectives resumed their seats on the sofa. "Ask away, inspector."

"I'd be grateful if you could tell me a little more about Sir Lionel himself, Mr. Moore."

"What's this then?" asked Piers with a smile. "Know the man and you know his murderer? That's the saying, I believe, isn't it?"

Copper echoed the smile. "Something like that, sir. So, can you help us in that respect? Were you and Sir Lionel friends?"

"Friendly would be a better description," replied Piers after a moment's reflection. "I mean, we never spent a great deal of time in one another's company, but he always seemed a thoroughly pleasant chap. Self-made, of course, but I've never been one to hold that against a man, unlike some of our crustier members. But one of the best things about him was that he seemed to wear his money lightly. You probably know what I mean. Some people like to flaunt their wealth in a brash way, which doesn't always make them popular."

"Trash with cash, do you mean, sir?" put in Radley.

"Not sure I'd express it exactly like that, sergeant," replied Piers, amused, "but I suppose that's the general gist. Whereas Lionel seemed quite content to spend his money without making too much of a song and dance about it. All right, I imagine *Red Buccaneer* will have set him back a pretty penny, and I'm told he is somehow involved in motor racing with one of his sons, which I'm sure doesn't come cheap. But for all I know, it was a case of quiet enjoyment on his part. At least in public." A chuckle. "Of course, you never know what goes on behind the scenes."

"So you wouldn't have any knowledge of anyone who might wish him harm, Mr. Moore?" enquired Copper.

"Enough to murder him? Not the slightest clue, inspector. As I said, we don't encourage business talk within the club. But I imagine that, as a prominent businessman, he would have had his share of enemies. Just don't ask me who they were."

"Then I shall have to go looking for that information elsewhere, sir," said Copper, getting to his feet. "And I shall also have to try to find out where Sir Lionel went after he left your premises last night."

"Oh, I know that," said Piers. "And in fact, you may well be able to kill two birds with one stone." He cleared his throat in slight embarrassment. "If that isn't too distasteful a way of putting it."

"Sir?" Copper regarded the commodore enquiringly.

"Yes. He went across to see Lady Butler."

85

"His wife?"

"Ex-wife, I think, boss," Radley quietly reminded him. "Didn't Robin say that they were divorced."

"So he did," said Copper. "And are you saying she lives nearby, Mr. Moore?"

"You could say that," laughed Piers. He gestured out of the window. "She lives there." The detectives turned, to glimpse the edge of a block of apartments rising over the marina. "Sea Village House. In the penthouse. I suppose you'd like a word with her?"

"We shall certainly wish to do so, sir."

"Two ticks." Piers picked up the phone on his desk, consulted a flip-up address file, and dialled. "Hello, Sylvia ... yes, it's Piers at the yacht club ... yes, we heard. Isn't it appalling? ... Now the thing is, I've got a couple of police chappies here, and they wonder if you could spare a couple of minutes for a chat ... That would be excellent. I shall send them straight over ... yes, we must ... I shall speak to you soon." He replaced the receiver. "All sorted, inspector. Lady Butler is expecting you. When you get to the foyer, just press the lift button marked 'P' for the penthouse and it'll take you straight up."

*

As the detectives descended the steps of the yacht club building, their eyes rose to survey the apartment block which towered in front of them.

"That's got to be the tallest building for miles, boss," remarked Pete Radley. "How many floors do you reckon that is?"

"Looks to be about twenty to me," answered Dave Copper, "although I don't propose to get a crick in my neck trying to count them. If you're that bothered, just look at the floor numbers in the lift."

Radley sighed. "And that's why you're an inspector and I'm just a humble sergeant," he grinned. "D'oh!"

The pair made their way between two extremely

smart-looking restaurants and into the block's foyer, clad in marble and rising through several storeys, with an impressive chandelier in multi-coloured glass cascading down in the centre.

"I'm sensing more money than you can shake a stick at, boss," said Radley. "Probably not going to be putting an offer in for one of these flats any time soon."

"Let alone the penthouse," replied the inspector. "I suspect that Lady Butler lives in some style. Well, we shall soon find out." He pressed the button marked 'P' next to the lift doors.

"*Yes?*" crackled an unexpected voice from the small speaker grille alongside the button.

"Detective Inspector Copper and Detective Sergeant Radley to see Lady Butler," responded Copper into the grille.

"*Very well. I'll authorise the lift for you. Press 24 when you get in.*"

"Thank you." But the owner of the disembodied voice had already gone, and Copper stepped into the lift as the doors opened, Radley at his side.

Chapter 9

As the detectives emerged from the lift, Dave Copper couldn't help but be taken aback as he absorbed the vista spread before him.

Pete Radley was more vocal. "Bloody hell, boss! That's a view and a half!"

He was not wrong. The outlook from the twenty-fourth floor of Sea Village House was breathtaking. Directly below lay Sea Village itself, a toytown cluster of wriggling streets lined with a variety of houses and small blocks of apartments with roofs of slate and tile in a multitude of colours, while alongside the pontoons of the Porthampton Ocean Racing Club could be seen yachts of all sizes, sail and motor, with *Red Buccaneer* notable as the largest vessel in the pack. Beyond the marina stretched the approach to the harbour, with the commercial port to one side, a car transporter taking on its cargo as an ant-like procession of vehicles progressed up its loading ramps into the cavernous interior, while behind the slab-sided leviathan rose the more graceful outline of a cruise ship gleaming white in the sunshine, a wisp of smoke emerging from its twin funnels. Further away, the colour of the waters of the port approaches changed gradually from a murky grey to a more ethereal blue, the margins dotted with clusters of housing interspersed with patches of woodland, and as the horizon faded into a milky haze, there could just be discerned the ghostly shape of an island standing guard at the mouth of the estuary.

As the officers marvelled at the sight, a man in his forties, dressed in white shirt and black trousers, emerged from a room at the far end of the corridor. "Please come through to the drawing room." He remained in the doorway and announced "The gentlemen from the police, madam," before turning to

Copper, stepping back, and saying "Lady Butler will see you now, sir."

"Oh, for goodness sake, Alan, don't be so grand," came a voice from within the room. "Do come in, officers."

The woman who advanced to meet the detectives was not at all what Copper had anticipated. In her late sixties, with a frizz of curly pale blonde hair, she was short in stature, with a shape which could best be described as grandmotherly. She wore a bright purple dress teamed with slightly incongruous leopardskin high heels, and her fingers sparkled with a profusion of rings. She bustled over to a pair of oversized brocade sofas flanking a marble fireplace, beckoning to her visitors to follow as she seated herself and indicating that they should do the same. "Now, what can I do for you boys?" she enquired in an unreformed East End accent.

The detectives exchanged amused glances at the unexpected form of address. "I'm Detective Inspector Copper, and this is Detective Sergeant Radley," began Copper, as the two produced their warrant cards. "We've been speaking to the commodore of the yacht club …"

"Oh, Piers," interrupted Lady Butler. "Lovely man. The most beautiful old-fashioned manners, and no side to him at all, for all that he's a viscount. Anyway, do go on."

'Oh good grief,' thought Copper to himself. 'Should I have addressed him as 'my lord'? Oh well, it's a bit late for that now.' "And he told us," he continued valiantly, " that you may be able to give us some helpful information regarding your late husband … I mean, your former husband … I mean …"

Lady Butler let out a peal of merry laughter. "Or as I called him, dear, 'the old goat'." Her face grew solemn. "No, I shouldn't laugh. Not today. I mean, we obviously had our ups and downs, or else we'd still have been married, but for all that, we had some very good times, and we managed to stay friends, even after the divorce. So I'm sad that he's dead. And especially because he's been murdered, or so Alan told me they're saying. So, how can I help?" She regarded Copper expectantly.

"Well, firstly, your ladyship ..."

"Now that's enough of that," she broke in. "You call me Sylvia. And your names are ...?"

Copper frowned in slight puzzlement. "As I said, I'm Detective Inspector ..."

"No, no, no. I mean your first names. We shall get on so much better if we don't have to fiddle about with titles. My cousin Rachel has been married to a bobby in Golders Green for over thirty years, so I've heard enough talk of police ranks to last me a lifetime."

"Oh. Well, in that case ..." A slightly reluctant pause. "I'm David."

"Peter, ma'am," said Radley, desperately trying to conceal a grin. "I mean, Sylvia."

"There. And now we're all friends. Now, just one second." She raised her voice. "Alan!"

The man appeared almost immediately. "Madam?"

"A fresh pot, please." Sylvia indicated the silver coffee-pot on the table beside her. "And two more cups for the officers."

"Of course, madam." Alan hesitated. "And what would you like me to do about luncheon?"

Sylvia glanced at the elaborate cherub-festooned porcelain timepiece on the mantelshelf. "We'll have that in twenty minutes." She turned to Copper. "You'll stay, of course?"

The inspector blinked in surprise. "No, really, Lady Butler ... Sylvia ... we really mustn't take up your time."

"Nonsense!" she retorted. "We're going to be having a nice long chat, and I shall need my lunch, so you may as well stay and share it with me. It'll be a treat for me to have guests. And don't worry, it isn't anything elaborate. Just quiche and cold meats and some salad. So please stay. Because if I know anything about police work, I'm sure you won't have had anything to eat this morning."

"Not since breakfast," admitted Copper.

"I almost had a doughnut," murmured Radley wistfully.

"Then that's settled. Alan, can you please set up for three in the dining room?"

"Of course, madam." Alan disappeared as noiselessly as he had arrived.

"If you're absolutely sure," said Copper. "Because we really wouldn't want to cause any extra work for your ..." An uncertain expression came over his face. "Would he be your butler?"

Sylvia's merry laugh returned. "What? Lady Butler's butler? Wouldn't that be just too much?

No, Alan is my steward. I inherited him at the time of my divorce, together with this flat. He used to be Lionel's steward on the first *Red Buccaneer*. Ah, here's the coffee. Thank you, Alan. I'll pour. Now, David," she said, as she busied herself with the coffee-pot and cups, "what would you like me to tell you?"

"Two things," replied the inspector. "I gather from Mr. Moore ... sorry, should that be Viscount Moore?"

"Just Piers, dear," replied Sylvia comfortably. "Anyway, go on."

"He mentioned that Sir Lionel came over to visit you after the family dinner in the yacht club last night. I'd be interested to know if he may have said anything which would be helpful to our enquiry. And also, I think it might be useful if we knew a little more about Sir Lionel's background, and I can't think of anyone who would be better placed than yourself to provide that."

"You want the ancient history, David?" Sylvia

smiled. "Well, there's plenty of that. So shall we start there?"

"If you like," said Copper. "And I hope you won't mind if Sergeant Radley makes a few notes."

"You go ahead ... Peter," said Sylvia pointedly. "Now ... where to begin?" she mused. "Well, I suppose, at the beginning. We were at school together. Childhood sweethearts."

"So you've known Lionel Butler a good long time?" The inspector sipped his coffee.

"Oh, he wasn't 'Butler' then, dear," chuckled Sylvia. "That came later. In those days he was Lionel Rotlieb. But his father decided to change the family name to 'Butler' when he started to expand his business. It's almost 'Rotlieb' back-to-front, and he thought a more English-sounding name might open up a few more opportunities."

"Oh, so Sir Lionel comes from a family of businessmen?"

Sylvia laughed. "You could put it that way, David. But maybe not in the way it sounds. His grandfather Isaiah was a scrap metal dealer in the East End after the First World War, and his father Isaac turned that into a small metal-working firm when he took over. Screws and brackets – hardly the big time, dear. But he made sure that Lionel started at the bottom and learned the whole of the business. That's what made him such a successful entrepreneur later on – he knew how things worked. So when he took over after his father died, he was already on his way. But of course, we were married by then."

"I wonder how many childhood sweethearts end up married," commented Copper. "Not many, I'd imagine."

"Oh, we were always suited," said Sylvia. "And to be honest, when he proposed, I couldn't wait to say yes so's I could change my name. I'd been saddled with being

'Sylvia Silver' for quite long enough. Funny the way some parents don't give a thought to how their children's names are going to work out, isn't it?"

"I've come across a few odd cases," nodded Copper. "So tell me a little more about how Sir Lionel came to achieve the great success which he obviously did."

"Flair, dear. And an eye for the main chance and the worthwhile opportunity. He looked around, and whenever he saw a small firm that might be struggling, he jumped in and took control. And it wasn't too long before he started to attract attention, and there were articles in the business papers about this rising star." A laugh. "One of them even called him the East End Pirate because of the way he'd suddenly appear and seize these little companies and turn them into treasure. And then the headlines started talking about the 'Buccaneering Businessman'. He loved it."

"Ah, so that would be where the name of the yacht came from," deduced the inspector. "But why 'Red', I wonder."

Sylvia chuckled. "Oh, Lionel could always turn anything to his advantage. There was a time, when he was still young and working for his father on the shop floor, that the workers decided they had some sort of grievance, so they wanted to strike. It was just one or two troublemakers at the heart of it – communists, apparently. But Lionel took the lead, put himself at their head, even joined the Communist Party for about five minutes, and then managed to defuse the whole thing. But the story came out later, and one of the papers ran a headline about him being the Red Buccaneer, and that was it. Ridiculous, of course," she scoffed. "He was no more a communist than my Auntie Miriam, and she used to think that even Churchill was a bit of a pinko. But you know what journalists are like. They'll make up anything to sell papers. Anyway, after that, Lionel renamed the

93

group of companies 'Pirate Industries', and then when he bought his first boat, what else could he call it but '*Red Buccaneer*'?"

"Perfectly logical," smiled Copper. "And from what you're saying, it seems the business empire grew and grew."

"So it did. As did the family. Three sons. What mother could ask for more? My son the businessman, my son the lawyer, and ... well, then there's Tyrone, and what mother can't help loving her youngest just that little bit more? All successes in their own ways." A slight shadow crossed Sylvia's features. "Well, more or less."

A soft throat-clearing was heard from the doorway. "Excuse me, madam, but luncheon is on the table."

"Thank you, Alan. We'll serve ourselves, so if you have things to do ...," responded Sylvia meaningfully. As the steward disappeared, she stood. "I swear that man thinks he's Jeeves," she murmured to the detectives. "He has a habit of materialising when you least expect it, and I don't think he needs to know everything, does he?"

"That depends on what the 'everything' consists of," replied Copper, intrigued, as he and Radley followed Sylvia through to a dining room with a view just as stunning as that from the drawing room.

"Help yourselves, boys," said Sylvia, indicating a buffet of cold items laid out on a side table. "And because I know you're on duty, Peter, I'll leave it to you to pick out a bottle of sparking water from the wine fridge there."

Once again, Copper smiled quietly to himself at the older woman's assumption of command as the sergeant carried out her request.

"Now, where was I?" wondered Sylvia, after the three had seated themselves around the end of a large glass table laid with elegant white china and crystal glasses, with an enormous floral arrangement as the

94

centrepiece.

"You were speaking of the successes of your three sons," Copper reminded her.

"Ah yes," Again, there was a hint of reserve in Sylvia's response. "Of course, it was always going to be obvious that Robin would follow in his father's footsteps as head of the business. That's why Lionel made him chief executive of Butler Steels, which is what the old metal-working firm grew into. But then Leo took a slightly different path, because he was always that bit cleverer, so he decided to study law at university. He's a barrister now, and quite well thought of, I believe."

"So I gather."

"He has ambitions, I think. Not like his younger brother." A fond smile. "No, I don't think Tyrone ever had an ambitious bone in his body. Not for business, anyway. He just wanted to have fun. And it turned out that he had quite a talent for it, especially driving too fast. That's what made Lionel decide to create a race team for him, after Tyrone had got one speeding conviction too many and only just managed to avoid getting sent to prison, thanks to Leo. So in his usual fashion, Lionel bought up a race team that was on the brink of going bust and renamed it 'Barbarossa', and gave it to Tyrone as his grown-up toy. He's done fairly well, and it keeps him out of mischief. Or so I hope."

"Why Barbarossa, I wonder?" enquired Copper.

"Oh, it's after somebody called the Red Pirate, apparently. Something to do with the Ottoman Empire. Another one of Lionel's little conceits. I don't really know the history. Anyway," said Sylvia, putting down her knife and fork and taking a sip of water, "I don't think that's the sort of history you wanted, was it, David? You're more interested in Lionel's."

"That's true, Lady Bu … Sylvia," said the inspector. "And what I was wondering is, would you be aware of anyone among all these various business deals you've spoken of who might have held a grudge against your husband?"

"Nobody I can offhand think of, dear," responded Sylvia after a moment's reflection. "But you must remember, I'm five years out of date. Since we got divorced, I've been well away from all of Lionel's business doings."

"But yet you remained friends?" ventured Copper.

"Oh, we were always that," said Sylvia. "But there came a time when ... well, how shall I explain it? Lionel always had an appetite for excess. Not flash, but he liked the best. He was very talented with money, for a start, both making it and spending it. But it meant that he ... strayed, shall we say? Very often, actually. As I said, I used to call him 'the old goat'. It was never serious, you understand. But there was very often a close female friend, usually rather younger, alongside him whenever his picture appeared in the papers. One of the perks of his position, you might say, and he always assured me that these ... friends ... meant nothing, and I believed him. But in the end, the cumulative effect just became too much, so we decided that a divorce was the most sensible thing to do." She broke off and took a look at Radley's plate. "Now you just get up and have some more, Peter. You look as if you could manage a second helping."

"Well, I am still a bit peckish, ma'am," confessed Radley.

"You go ahead," insisted Sylvia. "I always used to tell my boys, eat! You might be hungry one day." And as the sergeant got up to refill his plate, she turned back to Copper to continue. "Now, what was I saying? Oh yes, the divorce. Actually, it was all thoroughly civilised. Lionel was very generous. I didn't want the house in Surrey – it's far too big anyway, and too far away from anything. But I have the flat here, and the little house in Mayfair, and a very large portfolio of shares in the Pirate Group which mean that I am extremely comfortable, and I can please myself. And the upshot is that we have always been on good terms with one another. And he always felt that he could come and talk to me."

'And now we come to it,' thought Copper. "And that is what happened last night," he stated.

"It is," confirmed Sylvia. "He was … troubled."

"About what, may I ask?"

Sylvia sighed. "It was several things, really. Not that he was too specific about anything, but he'd found himself in a position where he wasn't sure what the future of the family was going to be."

"How so?"

"He said that all sorts of whispers had come his way, and once he had hard facts, he would know how to act. But that was always Lionel's way." Sylvia smiled at the memory. "Knowledge, he said. That was the key to success in anything. He always insisted that, without his sources, he'd never have been half the man he was."

"What kind of sources?" enquired Copper.

"The usual commercial ones. Lionel kept his ear very close to the ground when it came to rumours running around the business world. Hints in the press, gossip he might have overheard in a lift or when he was out to lunch – it all came in useful. And then, of course, there were his tame investigators."

"You mean private detectives?" The inspector sounded surprised.

"Oh yes, dear," nodded Sylvia. "Lionel employed all sorts of people. Probably not always completely ethical, but he did say that all was fair in love, war, and business. But I'm sure he'd never break the law. I think it was more a question of getting hold of some confidential details about a company's affairs that might make it vulnerable, or else finding out some personal information about a rival which could mean that they could be influenced to act in a certain way. As I say, we never talked business in too much detail. But this time, I think he'd put his people on to looking into some of the family's activities, and he wasn't too happy with what he thought they might have come up with. So he said he'd put them all on notice."

"And do you know what he meant by that?"

"He'd warned them. He said that he told them all last night that he was expecting to have reports in front of him when he was back at his desk, and that he'd know what action to take, once he'd digested them."

Copper thought for a moment. "And I'm assuming that he would have planned to return to his office today. In London, would that be?"

"Yes. The Pirate Group headquarters is in the City. He'd usually get Giles to bring the car down from town, and then drive him back to be at his office after lunch." Sylvia caught her breath. "In fact, about now. Oh my goodness. I wonder if they know up there. Will somebody have told them?"

"I imagine that one of your sons will have been in touch," the inspector reassured her. "But, just so that I understand clearly, you said that Sir Lionel wasn't too specific in what he said to you? No particular names were mentioned? Nobody was singled out?"

"I'm sorry, David." Sylvia shook her head. "I don't think he wanted to say more before his suspicions were proved to be correct. So there wasn't a lot more said. He murmured something to himself about history, but I didn't catch what. We reminisced a little over a couple of drinks – I always kept a bottle of his favourite champagne chilled and ready whenever I knew he was around – and then he went back to the yacht." She pulled a scrap of handkerchief from her sleeve and wiped away the start of a tear. "That was the last time I saw him."

Copper took the cue to push back his chair. "Lady

Butler … Sylvia … thank you for your kindness. And please accept our condolences. But I think we must get on and see if we can get to the bottom of the situation. Perhaps, in the light of what you've told us, your family may be a little more forthcoming. So if you will excuse us …"

"Of course, dear." Sylvia stood. "If you won't stay for a coffee? No? Well, in that case, I wish you well. Let me see you to the lift." She led the way out into the hall and pressed the button, and as the lift arrived, she placed her hand on the inspector's arm. "You just find out who killed my Lionel. Because for all our troubles, he was the father of my children, and in my way I still loved him."

The detectives stepped into the lift. "Rest assured, ma'am, we'll do our best," declared Copper. The lift doors closed.

Chapter 10

"That was instructive, if not particularly illuminating," remarked Dave Copper, as the two detectives made their way across the precincts of Sea Village towards *Red Buccaneer*'s mooring.

"You mean it tells us everything and nothing, boss?" said Pete Radley.

"That's exactly what I mean," replied Copper. "At least we know quite a lot more about the kind of man Lionel Butler was, and there are pretty strong indications that he wasn't the sort who enjoyed being taken advantage of. It seems that there have been some goings-on among the family members. All we need to do is find out what they are."

"Sounds simple enough," grinned Radley. "So you're happy to rule out the members of the crew?"

"I think so. With the evidence from the marina's security system, and the apparent fact that they were all together from the time they left the yacht on Sunday evening to the time they returned early this morning, I can't see any opportunity for any of them to have been on board at the requisite time, whatever that may have been. Maybe Una's forensics will be able to tell us something about timing, although from what she said, it doesn't seem very likely. And we'll be interviewing the crew anyway, so if there are any cracks in the account of their activities, they're bound to show up fairly quickly."

"So back on board and carry on quizzing people, boss?"

"Exactly so." A thought struck the inspector. "That's if we can get back on board, of course. Do you happen to know the security code for the gate?"

Radley shook his head. "Sorry, boss. That's one of the things my notes do not cover."

"Then we'd better get hold of the number, in case

there's nobody around to let us through."

"Leave it to me, boss." The sergeant trotted off in the direction of the PORC clubhouse, returning a few minutes later, puffing slightly, to find his superior gazing out across the marina, wrapped in thought. "Got it," he said, waving his notebook in triumph.

"You know, I've been thinking, sergeant," began Copper.

"Me too, boss," said Radley. He was obviously attempting, not particularly successfully, to rein in something which was causing him considerable amusement. "You see, if you're counting out the crew, that only leaves one possibility."

Copper raised a suspicious eyebrow. "That possibility being ...?"

"Well, clearly the only candidates left as murderer are the members of Sir Lionel's family. So, although at this stage we can't tell which one it is ..." The laughter threatened to escape.

The inspector sighed in resignation. "I have a horrible feeling I know where this is going. Carry on, sergeant. Get it off your chest."

"It's just got to be said, boss," gurgled Radley. "Obviously, a Butler did it!"

*

Having negotiated the security gate successfully, the detectives descended the pontoon's ramp to find P.C. Kapoor still standing guard at the yacht's gangway.

"Anything interesting to report, Kapoor?" enquired Dave Copper.

"Not really, sir," replied the young officer with a rueful grin. "Other than the fact that they seem to be getting rather restive. One of the men keeps coming out on deck, scanning the marina as if he's looking for something, and then sounding off with something between a sigh and a snarl, before he goes back inside

101

again."

"I bet I can guess who that is," commented Pete Radley.

As if on cue, the door from the saloon to the afterdeck opened, and Robin Butler appeared, glaring down at the quayside. "Oh, there you are, inspector," he growled. "And about time too. I don't suppose you're actually managing to make any progress, are you?"

"In some ways, yes, Mr. Butler," replied Copper mildly. "And I'll be up to join you, if you'd just like to wait one second. I'd hate for you to have to keep shouting down to us and strain your voice." He and Radley stepped aboard and made their way up to the open deck, to find that Leo Butler had joined his older brother in the saloon's doorway.

"Is there any prospect of letting us get on with our lives any time soon, inspector?" demanded Leo. "As I told you, I have very important matters awaiting my attention in London."

"And I have a company to run," added Robin. "More than one now, it seems. And the sooner I can get back to take the reins, the better. I hate to think what the effect will be in the City, once the news of my father's death gets out."

"Perhaps we'd better all go inside," suggested Copper. "I think it's easier if I can speak to everyone together."

With a testy 'harrumph', Robin pushed his way back into the saloon, leaving his brother and the detectives to follow. "So what are you intending to do next, inspector?" he asked, seating himself next to his wife. "Surely you don't expect us to sit around here eternally while you poke about into goodness knows what."

"Unfortunately, Mr. Butler," replied Copper, "poking about, as you so graphically put it, is exactly what I have to do. You see, I have received indications that there may be factors in this case which require further looking into, chiefly the relationship between each of you and Sir Lionel."

"Indications? What indications? Who's been talking about us? And what nonsense have they been saying?"

"As to whether it's nonsense, that's what I need to discover, sir," said Copper. "And as for who, I don't think it should come as a great surprise that my source is another member of your family."

"What? But why ...?"

Leo interrupted, emitting an exasperated sigh. "Oh, you idiot, Robin. Who do you think he's talking about? He's been speaking to Mother."

"Is that where you've been all this time?" asked Robin. "Well, no wonder you took so long. I dare say she's been rattling on, the way she usually does."

"Lady Butler was kind enough to give us some very helpful background information about your late father," responded Copper. "And yes, as a result, there are some very pertinent questions which have to be asked."

"Then hadn't you better get on and ask them, Mr. Copper?" suggested Dee Butler silkily.

"All in good time, Mrs. Butler."

"I fail to see what's holding you up," she remarked, lifting a supercilious eyebrow. "You've interviewed each of us. Surely we've already told you all we know?"

"You may have, Mrs. Butler," conceded the inspector. 'Or you may not,' he thought privately. "But I still need to speak to the members of the yacht's crew. And while Lady Butler may well have provided a certain amount of long-term history, what she hasn't been in a position to do is tell us about the events which have led up to this morning's situation. For that, I need the input of Mr. de Waters and his colleagues."

"Oh, for heaven's sake!" exploded Robin, his face

suffused with an angry flush. "Now we're expected to wait around at their beck and call? And how long is this going to take?"

"As long as it takes, Mr. Butler," replied Copper, refusing to be ruffled. "It's possible that I may need the rest of the afternoon. So I cannot promise that I will be able to continue my conversation with you and your family before tomorrow."

"That's ridiculous," joined in Leo. "You want us to stay cooped up on this boat until tomorrow? I for one won't stand for it!"

"And," added Dee, "I may be a little out of practice since leaving the legal profession, but is there not the small question of unwarranted detention? You can't hold us here against our will."

Copper smiled, a wolfish expression which he had learned over the years from his former superior Andy Constable. "I haven't the slightest intention of doing anything of the kind, Mrs. Butler. You are all of course free to leave at any time." The smile faded. "But I do hope you'll all see the sense in remaining voluntarily and assisting us in whatever way you can. I'd hate to misunderstand anyone's reasons for failing to co-operate."

"Of course we'll all co-operate," said Tyrone languidly, rousing himself slightly from his position lounging on one of the saloon's sofas. "Don't be such a pain, you lot. Let the inspector do his job, and we can all get out of here."

"Which I can't wait to do," said Cordelia. "A week on this boat is quite enough for me. I don't relish the thought of another night in this atmosphere." A pause ensued, as all the family members regarded one another with varying degrees of unease.

Eventually, Jessica spoke up. "Um ... couldn't we get rooms in the Grand Village hotel?" she suggested timidly.

"We'd have heaps more room, and they've got a lovely pool with a bar."

"At last," sneered Robin. "Some sense from someone, even if it is Jessica. Dee, get on to them. Book some rooms – a suite for us, if they have one." He turned to Copper. "There, inspector. Will that satisfy your strictures about not leaving the scene of the crime?"

"Admirably, sir," replied Copper calmly. "I'll leave you to arrange it."

*

As the members of the Butler family disappeared towards their various cabins, Robin and Dee through to their suite at the forward end of the main deck, while Tyrone and Jessica followed Leo and Cordelia down the spiral stairs to the deck below, Pete Radley directed a quizzical look at his superior.

"Some of them seem fairly anxious to put some distance between themselves and 'the scene of the crime', boss," remarked the sergeant. "Especially the red red Robin. Do we reckon there's anything in that?"

"Hard to say offhand," mused Copper. "Some people just don't particularly like being told what to do. Whatever the reasons may be, we may discover more about them, once we've had a chance to chat to the other occupants of the boat. The only question being, who to start with?"

A soft throat-clearing from the far end of the saloon caused the inspector to whirl round in surprise. "Good grief! Where did you spring from?"

Trey stepped forward from a corner of the galley area. "I been here all the time, sir."

"And I completely failed to notice you," smiled Copper. "Trey, isn't it? You certainly have a talent for fading into the background."

"It's one of the things you learn to do pretty quick when you do my job, sir," grinned Trey. "Comes from the time when I was working as a waiter. You try to be invisible. You don't want to interrupt people when they're in the middle of a conversation, specially if it's something like a proposal. Or an argument."

"Which," observed the inspector, "could be exactly the talent we need at this moment. You'll have heard me saying that we need to know as much as possible of what's gone on during the past week. I think you may be just the man to help us. So come and sit down, and we'll see if I'm right." He lowered himself into one of the armchairs and gestured to Trey to seat himself alongside him. "And Sergeant Radley will make a few notes, I have no doubt."

"Notebook at the ready as always, boss," responded Radley, pulling out a chair from the dining table. "So hadn't we better start with the full name? I've only got you down as 'Trey'."

"That's what they all call me," said Trey in his lilting accent. "But in full, it's Treymain Loader. And I reckon I'd better spell that first name out for you, because nobody ever gets it right." He did so.

"Thank you, sir," said Radley, a quizzical eyebrow raised. "I'd never have got that first time. Or even second or third," he added under his breath.

"So, Mr. Loader, ..." began Copper.

"Oh, please, inspector," interrupted Trey, "you better call me Trey, just like everyone else. If you start calling me 'Mr. Loader', I'm gonna think my father's turned up behind me. And that would be a worry, seeing as he's been dead for ten year." A cheerful guffaw.

Copper smiled. "Very well. 'Trey' it is. So tell me, how long is it that you've been working for Sir Lionel?"

"That'll be about five year now, sir. He took me on back in Barbados, about the time he bought *Buck*. I was working in a hotel, and he needed somebody to be steward on his new yacht, and we just sort of fell

106

together."

"Good employer?"

"One of the best, sir. Always generous with his money too. He paid me well – and not just me, but the whole crew, I reckon. And he always wanted the best of everything, like champagne and so on, and I never had to stint on the food. He was never a man to put up with second best. And I tell you, sir, it's a real big shock that someone's killed him. And for why, I want to know."

"That's what we're all trying to find out, Trey," replied the inspector. "And the unfortunate fact appears to be that it was somebody within the family circle that was responsible."

"This is what I don't get, sir. Because, alright, Sir Lionel, he was a big businessman, and you hear of all sorts of rivalries in that world, so I guess he must have had some enemies. But the family?" Trey shook his head in bewilderment. "You got to stick together in the family."

"So you're aware of no tensions within the Butler family that might have caused a clash between members?"

"Ah, no, sir. I didn't say that. Because what I meant to say was, family got to stick together, no matter what."

Copper's attention was alerted. "It sounds as if you're telling me that there were times when all was not, as you might say, sweetness and light. Would you like to expand on that? What reasons might there have been?"

Trey hesitated. "The thing is, sir, I might have seen or heard things which might not have gone down too well with Sir Lionel if he'd known about them. But I couldn't say if he did."

"I think we're coming back to your talent for being unobtrusive, Trey, aren't we?" remarked the inspector. "I'm willing to bet that you've had the opportunity to see or hear plenty of things that weren't intended to become generally known."

"I never mean to eavesdrop, sir," protested Trey.

"But you have information," insisted Copper. "So I need you to share it."

"Well, some of it, I couldn't say exactly what it means," began Trey. "Like, for instance, on Saturday when we were in Guernsey. I had some time free, so I thought I'd take a trip. When I got ashore, there was a lady from the tourist office on the quay, and she told me there's a bus which goes all round the island, and it's not dear, so I thought, why not? But the next bus didn't go for half an hour, so I just had time to go into the town church there. I hadn't been for a week, you see, so it was about time."

"You're a churchgoer?" enquired Copper.

Trey chuckled. "You might say that, inspector," he said. "Mother brought all us kids up to go to church regular, every Sunday, no excuses, and in the week too, if she could manage to get us all together. So I was missing it."

"Surely you could have visited a church in France?" suggested Copper.

"A Catholic church? Oh no, sir. I don't think Mother would approve. Strict Anglican, she is. She wouldn't hold with that. So it was good to find the old church in St. Peter Port while I was hanging around for the bus. I just had time to go in to say a few prayers."

"I'm not sure where this is leading, Trey," remarked Radley. "Am I supposed to be writing all this down, boss?"

"Hold your horses, sergeant," responded the steward. "I'm coming to that. Because when I was coming out of the church, I saw Mrs. Butler ... that's Mrs. Dee, Mr. Robin's wife ... and she was coming out of a jeweller's shop across the road. And I waved, but she didn't notice me, and she went off down a little side lane straight away. But then a few seconds later, a young chap in a suit came jumping out of the shop doorway. Seemed like he was in a panic, and he looked all up and down the road, but then it was obvious he couldn't see whatever he was looking for, and he sort of slumped and went back into the shop. So I thought, maybe Mrs. Dee had forgotten something like a purse or a credit card and left it behind, so I went over and asked if I could help. I mean, I explained about Mrs. Dee and who I was, because the shop assistant looked at me a bit funny, but he said no, it was nothing, and I wasn't to worry. And then I noticed a clock in the shop window and saw it was time for the bus, so I ran, and I just caught it."

Copper mused for a moment. "And the shop assistant maintained that there was no problem?"

"That's what he said, sir," replied Trey. "But it didn't quite ring true. And I don't like to say what I was thinking. So I went on my way."

"Exciting times in Guernsey, boss," said Radley, giving his superior a sideways look. "And that's it, is it, Trey?"

"Oh no, sergeant. I got more."

"Indeed? I'd be glad to know what," said Copper. "Provided it's relevant to the question of Sir Lionel's death, that is."

"Well, you'd be the best judge of that, inspector. But since Sir Lionel got mentioned, maybe it is."

"Then please go ahead." Copper leaned forward, intrigued. "Let's have the details. Stand by, sergeant." He directed a faint amused smile towards his junior colleague.

"Good job I've got plenty of lead in this pencil, boss," murmured Radley in response.

"It was like this, you see," began Trey. "I got on my bus, and off we went. And it goes in and out, round all the lanes and pretty villages. They got some very nice scenery round that island." Radley emitted a soft sigh of despair, which Trey ignored. "And about halfway round, up the top of the island, the bus makes a stop for a while. And on the top of the cliff, just close by, there's a big concrete building, like a fort. The tourist lady on the quay had told me that there were lots of them on the island, because they were built by the Germans when they were occupying Guernsey during the war." Trey broke off to laugh. "Actually, it was quite funny, because as she was saying it, we were surrounded by a load of people off the German cruise ship that was visiting the same day, and she got quite embarrassed in case they'd heard. She probably thought they wouldn't want to be reminded of that. But as it turned out, looks like she was wrong."

"Really? In what way?"

"Well, inspector, I thought I might as well go up and take a look at this fort. There was just time. And when I was looking around, what did I hear, just round the corner from me, but the voice of Mr. Tyrone."

Copper's eyebrows rose in surprise. "Tyrone Butler?"

"That's right, sir. And I was surprised too, you can bet. I thought, what's he doing up here? And I was just going to say hello, but then I could hear he was talking to someone. And the thing is, the other man sounded German."

"What, another tourist?"

"Maybe, inspector, but it didn't sound like tourist talk. Because Mr. Tyrone, he was saying 'You can't expect me to do that, not after what happened in Portugal', and the German guy, he said 'I don't care about that. But you'd better take Garcia out in Monza, or else we're going to have to talk about money'."

"Sounds a funny time to be organising somebody's social life," quipped Radley.

"Was there anything else?" enquired Copper, ignoring the sergeant's intervention.

"Yes, sir. Mr. Tyrone said 'Now look here, Von Staffen, just because your grandson is your blue-eyed boy ...', but then the other man cut him off and said 'My grandson is good enough to take care of himself. But how long will you be your father's blue-eyed boy if he hears what you've been doing?" And then the German came round the corner – old guy, he was, with white hair and a stick – and he almost knocked into me and went off down the hill. And I heard the bus toot its horn and I realised I only had a minute or two to catch it, so I run back down, hell for leather, just in time to see the German get into a big car with a chauffeur. Off he went, and I got back on the bus. And that was it."

"So you didn't actually see Tyrone Butler at all? You just heard his voice?"

"That's right, inspector. But I know it was him, no mistake."

"Hmmm." Copper reflected for a moment, before turning to Radley. "Any of that make any sense to you, sergeant?"

"Maybe, boss. I'm not sure. But I've got all the names noted down, and I bet I know one person who can unpick it for us."

"That person being ..."

"Anna in Intelligence. She's the best researcher I've ever met. Well, that's why you helped get her the job, wasn't it, after the business at Witch's Holt? I'll have a word."

"Do that, sergeant. In the meantime, Trey, is there anything else you can think of that might shed any light on the past week's events?"

Trey considered. "Well, maybe one thing, inspector," he replied doubtfully. "But I don't really know what it was about, so I can't tell you if it's relevant."

"Why don't you let us be the judge of that," replied Copper. "Just tell us what you know."

111

"It was sometime at the start of the week, sir," said Trey. "I can't remember which day exactly. But anyway, I'd just made Miss Jessica a drink, because she'd come into the saloon and she wanted one of my special cocktails. She's got a bit of a taste for them, to tell the truth. But anyway, I'd mixed it for her, and I'd used up the last bit in the bottle of Curaçao I had behind the bar, so I was crouched down to get a fresh bottle out of the cupboard down at the bottom, when in comes Mr. Robin. I think he must have been through in his suite. But when he saw Miss Jessica, he said 'I see you haven't lost your taste for the high life', and she said she didn't know what he meant, and he said that from what he'd heard on the grapevine, his father wasn't the first man to keep her in luxury. And he said it in that sneering voice he has sometimes, and I thought 'Well, I'm not going to get caught in the middle of this', so I kept my head well down and hoped he wouldn't notice me."

"Which presumably he didn't?"

"Oh no, inspector. I made sure of that. I like my job. I didn't want Mr. Robin causing trouble for me. But it sounded like that's what he might be planning to do for Miss Jessica. He said that what she was doing now was a bit of a step up from her old job, and Miss Jessica, she said she didn't know what he was talking about, because she'd always been a model, and Mr. Robin said 'That's one way of putting it'. 'I suppose a girl has to work', he said, with a bit of a sneer, like he does sometimes. And he said he wondered who'd be most interested if he passed on what he'd heard. Would it be Mr. Tyrone, or would it be Sir Lionel? And she said to him that he ought to watch out, because she had better friends than he knew. And he sort of laughed, as if he didn't think much of that, and then he went out on to the deck, and I think I heard Miss Jessica going down the stairs to her cabin. And I said to myself, 'What was that all about?'."

Chapter 11

"Thank you, Trey. I think that'll probably do for now," said Dave Copper. "Although ... one last point. There was a champagne bottle found at the scene."

"Oh, no surprise there, inspector. Sir was fond of his champagne, all right. And only out of the best glasses too. Nothing other than Baccarat Crystal would do."

"Really?"

"That's right, inspector. Here, let me show you." Trey moved to a display cabinet and opened it to show a rack of exquisite champagne flutes. "Hey, there's one missing."

"That would have been the glass Sir Lionel had been using at the time of ..." Copper left the rest of the explanation unsaid.

"But hold on," said Trey. "What's this? There's one that looks as if it's been put away dirty. Who would do that?" He reached for the glass.

"Please don't touch that glass!" ordered Copper swiftly. He gave a meaningful look to Radley. "Sergeant, would you carefully take possession of that glass. Have you by any remote chance got any plastic evidence bags concealed about your person?"

Radley laughed. "You know me so well, boss," he said, producing one from his jacket pocket. "Always prepared."

"Good," nodded Copper. "Then bag it up. Who knows, Forensics may be interested to examine it."

"Do you want me to scoot it over to them, boss?" asked Radley, having carried out his superior's instructions.

"No need. Set it to one side, and I'll give it to Una this evening. So now, Trey, I think we can leave you to your duties." And as Trey returned to the kitchen, the inspector directed a tilt of the head to his junior colleague, before leading the way from the saloon out on to the open deck. "Better if we stay out of range of any potential prying ears," he continued. "So, our steward friend raises a very pertinent question when he talks about Jessica. What indeed was that all about?"

"The young lady obviously has some kind of a past, boss," replied Pete Radley. "And if there's one thing you love, it's secrets in people's pasts, isn't it?"

"How would we ever manage to track down a murderer without them?" smiled Copper in response.

"So I bet you know what I'm going to suggest, boss. I'm already down to have a word with Anna Logue to see if she can decode that conversation between Tyrone and this mysterious German guy. Why don't we broaden that out and have her see what she can dig up about the entire Butler clan? They're all public figures in one way or another, so there's bound to be something on the net."

"That, sergeant, is an excellent proposal. I can't imagine why we didn't think of it before. Give her a call. And while you're doing that, I'll see if I can track down someone else from the crew."

"Start at the top and work down, boss?" offered Radley. "Maybe the captain's lurking up in his cockpit or whatever it is? It's worth a punt."

"I shall punt accordingly," smiled Copper. "Come up and find me when you're off the phone."

Bob de Waters looked up from his perch at the chart table as the inspector entered his domain. "Something I can do for you, inspector?"

"Actually, I'm hoping there is, sir," replied Copper. "Although I wouldn't want to interrupt you if you're in the middle of something complicated."

"Nothing of the kind," replied Bob. "I'm just glancing through the log of the past week's trip to make sure I haven't failed to note anything significant."

"Funnily enough, captain," smiled Copper, "I was

hoping to do very much the same thing."

Bob looked puzzled. "Don't follow you, inspector."

"The thing is, captain, as you can imagine, we're on the hunt for reasons why an assailant, as yet unidentified, should wish to attack Sir Lionel. And it may well be that events of the past week would have a bearing on this. So I'm hoping that you and your colleagues on the crew will be able to cast your minds back for any helpful information."

Bob scratched his head. "Now you're asking." He pulled out the companion high stool to his own from under the desk and gave a nod towards it. "You'd better take the weight off, inspector. It's been a long week."

"Oh?" Copper was intrigued. "What makes you say that, sir?"

"Hard to put a finger on exactly. I suppose I should say it's not been sunshine and roses all the way. There seem to have been tensions. Not that I've wanted to tune in on anything in particular. After all, Sir Lionel just employed me to drive the boat. So anything else isn't really my business."

"But it's very much my business, Mr. de Waters," responded Copper. "So I hope you'll put aside any thoughts of being discreet out of loyalty to your employer. Surely that loyalty would mean that you'll want me to find out who killed him as swiftly as possible."

Bob nodded slowly. "Well, of course, when you put it like that, inspector ..." He paused for a few moments as if in reflection. "I suppose there was one thing that involved Sir, because there were a couple of the others tied in, but I haven't any idea what it was all about."

"Suppose you just let me have the bare facts, captain," said Copper, "and leave me to draw any conclusions."

"We were in Guernsey," began Bob, when he was

interrupted by the arrival of Pete Radley.

"Sorry to have taken so long, boss," apologised the sergeant, puffing slightly. "I got caught up on the phone."

"With Anna?" queried Copper.

"Oh, not just her," replied Radley. "I mean, yes, I did speak to her first. Told her about the chat that ..." He broke off to give a sideways glance at Bob. "... that our witness told us about in Guernsey."

"Excellent," said the inspector. "Mr. de Waters here was about to do something similar. So we can look forward to her coming back to us with whatever she can make of that."

"Not just that, boss. I mentioned the context and suggested that she might trawl through the whole ... er ... group of people, if you catch my drift, and she said she'd pull up whatever she could and compile us a dossier. She sounded quite excited at the prospect."

"I swear we'll have that girl working in C.I.D. before we're all much older," smiled Copper. "Right. On we go then, captain."

"Hang on, boss," said Radley. "There's more. Because just as I was finishing with Anna, the phone rang again. This time it was Una."

"Oh yes? Do you mean to say she's got her forensic results for us already?"

"Not quite, boss. There's been a hold-up. She and Suzanne got diverted. There's been a nasty RTA near Camford. Dead driver at the end of a car chase, and naughty substances suspected. Drugs Squad are all over it, but they needed to bring in Forensics for an initial assessment of man and vehicle. So our chap is on the back burner until tomorrow morning."

Copper shrugged. "Well, it can't be helped. We shall get the information in due course. And it's not as if we haven't got plenty to occupy our time with. Like, for instance, Mr. de Waters' input. Which makes your arrival very opportune. You can make some notes." He turned back to the yacht's skipper. "So, captain, you were saying. Guernsey?"

"Right. Yes. Do you know Guernsey at all, inspector?"

"I don't, sir."

"Fascinating place," said Bob reminiscently. "Great waters for a seaman. D'you know, they've got one of the biggest tidal ranges in the whole British Isles? And some of the rocks round there! You have to watch your step if you're trying to navigate your way through them. Bit of a challenge, but if you're an old sea-dog like me, that's all part of the fun." He gave a chuckle.

"This is all very well, captain," said Copper, "but I don't quite see where this is taking us."

"Sorry, inspector," apologised Bob. "Didn't mean to veer off course like that. But it's all relevant to how come I heard what I did. You see, I managed to get ashore for a bit while we were there, even though we were anchored off. I didn't think I would, what with the family going to and fro in the tender, but then Flix – that's Felicity, our engineer – came back earlier than I expected, so I thought I'd take advantage because I wanted to go to the castle. That's Castle Cornet, you know, just on the edge of the harbour. I've always had a bit of an interest in history, and because of the dangers of the seas round there, like I was saying, they've had a lot of shipwrecks, and they've got some good stuff in the castle museum. And I'd been having a look round inside, and then I came out to take a look out over the ramparts towards Sark, when I heard Sir's voice just down below me on the lower level. I had no idea he was even ashore."

"And did you speak to him?" asked Copper.

"I was about to go and say hello," replied Bob, "when I realised who he was talking to. It was Mr. Leo."

"Indeed? And what was the nature of this

conversation? I imagine they weren't simply talking about the view or the weather, or it wouldn't have sparked your attention."

"I don't rightly know what it was about," frowned Bob, "except that Mr. Leo obviously had some sort of problem, which Sir seemed to think was quite serious. And I guessed it must have been something to do with his job. You know he's a barrister, inspector?"

"We were aware of that, captain. But why would you suppose that the problem related to his law work?" wondered Copper.

"Because of what Sir said to him. He said, if I remember right, 'You'll need more than Dee's defence skills to extricate you from that'. And he said something about a career ending, so I thought maybe Mr. Leo's got some big case on, trying to put some criminal away, and it's not going his way. And of course, Mrs. Dee used to be a lawyer, but she packed that in, so whether it was her career they were on about, I don't know." Bob shook his head. "I couldn't really fathom why Sir sounded more angry than anything, but I didn't want them to catch me eavesdropping, so I moved on. But then, a bit later, something else clicked."

"And what was that?"

Bob scratched his head. "Well, it might have been the same thing, or it might not. But it was certainly the same person."

"What ... Sir Lionel?"

"No, inspector. It was Mr. Leo again. But not in Guernsey this time. It was earlier on in the week, and I can't remember where it was exactly. Maybe when we were under way, or it might have been in one of the French ports. Granville, maybe. Actually, I think it must have been, because of where I was. Couple of days before St. Peter Port, that would have been. But Guernsey got mentioned, you see, so maybe it was all tied up together.

I couldn't say."

"Well, please just say what it was," said Copper with gentle insistence, trying not to show his growing perplexity at the skipper's haphazard narrative, "and we'll see if we can help you make sense of it."

"Oh. Right. Well, I was down at the stern on the landing platform – that's how I know it must have been in port, because you wouldn't go down there when we're under way. Anyway, I could hear Mr. Leo on his phone on the deck above me. He must have been sitting in one of the chairs by the hot tub. You know, that's where ..." Bob tailed off.

"I think we have the picture, captain. So, you overheard a telephone conversation?"

"Part of one," said Bob. "And it was Mr. Leo saying that the only thing would be to meet in Guernsey, although he wasn't too keen on the idea. And he said something like 'What time does the ferry from Jersey get in?' and then whoever it was must have said, because Mr. Leo said he'd meet him just after that, and he said that there would have to be a great deal involved, because evidence doesn't just lose itself. You see, inspector, that's why I thought it might be tied up with his work."

Copper nodded slowly. "Yes. I can see that, captain. But you didn't pick up any indication as to who Mr. Leo was speaking to? Or what it related to?"

Bob shrugged. "Not a clue."

The inspector looked over his shoulder towards his colleague. "Got all that, sergeant?"

Radley pulled a face. "Done my best, boss. But it's not exactly crystal clear what it's all about, is it?"

"Then it seems we shall have to have further conversations with Mr. Leo Butler in order to clarify matters," remarked Copper.

"You might as well have a word with his brother while you're about it," commented Bob unexpectedly.

"With Tyrone Butler, do you mean?" enquired Radley. "Yes, we're already planning to have a chat with him about his time on Guernsey."

"No, not him, sergeant. The other one. Mr. Robin."

"Oh yes?" Copper's interest was piqued. "You seem to have had a very lively end to the cruise."

"Oh no, this wasn't at the end," said Bob. "This was right at the start."

The inspector gave a faint sigh. "I wonder if it might be useful if we had an itinerary of your trip, captain. Since you have your log handy. Sometimes a timeline can be helpful in deciding what event relates to which. Isn't that right, sergeant?"

"Oh yes, boss," replied Radley heavily, turning over to a fresh page in his notebook. "I'm always up for a good timeline. Go ahead, Mr. de Waters."

Bob reached for the logbook and scanned it. "We started off from here almost a week ago," he said. "That's last Tuesday." He broke off. "Lord, is it only a week? Seems like forever, what with everything that's gone on. Anyway, first day, we went over to Deauville – that's up to the east. And we stayed there berthed overnight, because some people wanted to go off on trips, like to Rouen and some garden place that Mrs. Cordelia was interested in. That was Wednesday. Then on Thursday we were round in Granville ... that's on the west coast of the Cherbourg peninsula, sort of opposite Jersey," he added in response to Radley's enquiring look. "... and Friday we nipped across to St. Malo. Then on Saturday morning we headed back to Guernsey and spent the day there, before we started back across the Channel on Sunday. Yesterday, in fact. And we got in here around six." Bob consulted the log once more. "Six minutes past, if you want to be exact," he concluded.

"And I think we're fairly clear on the sequence of events after that," said Copper. "So let's return to the start of the trip. You said something about Deauville, I think."

"I did, inspector."

"A very smart resort, from what I've heard," observed the inspector. "With quite a celebrated casino, if I'm not much mistaken."

"Funny you should say that, inspector," responded Bob, "because there was mention of that at the time."

"This was in the conversation involving Robin Butler?" Copper sought to clarify.

"That's right," nodded Bob. "It was the night we docked. Some of the family had gone ashore for an evening out, and I was up here when they came back. I just happened to hear voices, so I looked out to check who it was, just in case, but it was only Sir Lionel and Miss Jessica with Mr. Robin and his wife, and then I saw Mr. Tyrone coming along a little way behind. So I couldn't help overhearing what they were saying as they came aboard."

"And what was that, exactly?"

"Well, it started out with Miss Jessica. She seemed all bubbly and excited, and she said she didn't know yet what she was going to buy with her winnings, and she said thank you to Sir for giving her the chips to start with. And then Mr. Tyrone came up and said they ought to go in and have another drink to celebrate, so those two disappeared into the saloon, and that just left Sir and Mr. and Mrs. Robin still at the top of the gangway. And then Sir said, a bit dry like, that he supposed that the other two wouldn't have much to celebrate, and that if Mr. Robin kept on racking up losses like that, he'd have had his chips good and proper, or something like that. He said something about it 'taxing his finances', and Mr. Robin got a bit flustered and said 'What did he mean by that?', and then Mrs. Dee jumped in and said that everything was under control, and that Sir ought to concentrate on

121

his own business instead of fussing about matters he'd already passed on to others. And Sir said 'Everything's my business, and don't you forget it', and then he started up in this direction to go back to his suite, I suppose, so I just popped my head back in and made as if I wasn't there. And that was it."

*

"Interesting little snippets there, boss," commented Pete Radley in a low voice, as the two detectives seated themselves at the far end of the saloon from the kitchen, where Trey could be heard moving about.

"Quite," agreed Dave Copper. "Wrangles over money are always fertile ground when we're on the lookout for motives for anything, let alone murder, and I'm inclined to guess that money wrangles among the rich may quite possibly be even more intense, far beyond the comprehension of the rest of us mortals."

"The only time Sharon ever has a bit of a go at me is when I can't believe the amount she's spent on clothes for Tommy," chuckled Radley. "You just wait till you and Una have to start forking out for kids' stuff. Any plans?"

"So far as I'm aware, sergeant," responded Copper drily, "we haven't quite got to that stage yet, nor are we planning to. And at the moment, Una and I have more urgent matters on our plate. Like identifying the murderer of a prominent businessman, for instance."

'Oops,' thought Radley. 'Better get back to safer ground'. "So what next, boss?" he asked. "Carry on talking to the crew?"

"I think so," said Copper. "Which means that we'll be wanting to track down the engineer." He stood. "Trey!" he called.

The steward appeared in the galley entrance. "Sir?"

"Can you suggest where we might find your engineer lady?"

"Flix? Oh, I expect she'll be down in the engine

122

compartment, inspector. That's where she spends most of her time. Hold on a second." Trey lifted the telephone receiver on the adjacent wall and pressed a button. "Oh, hi Flix. I thought you'd be there. Only the police guys want a word. Shall I send them down? ... Okay. They'll be right there." A laugh. "She loves that engine, sir. Calls it her baby. So if you want to find her, just you go down these stairs here, and at the bottom there's another little door that will take you down below. And mind your head," he warned. "It's a bit cosy down there."

"We'll manage," said the inspector, and started down the steps, with Radley close behind.

Chapter 12

"Brace yourself to tackle some old boiler, boss," quipped Pete Radley as the inspector reached for the handle and pushed the door open, squeezing into the rather confined space inside.

Since Dave Copper's maritime experience to date had consisted solely of taking an unscheduled cruise which had turned into a murder investigation, along with viewing footage of stokers mired in coal-dust, toiling in a cacophonous hell, in clips from the film 'Titanic', the engine compartment of *Red Buccaneer* came as a considerable surprise. Everywhere was the gleam of spotless metal and flawless paintwork, relieved by reflections from shiny plastic and glass surfaces, with in the background the muted hum of machinery going about its discreet business. The custodian of the compartment was equally unexpected, both in terms of her youth and her glamorous appearance. 'So much for Peter's old boiler,' Copper reflected wryly to himself, as Felicity Witcher, clad in an immaculate set of white overalls, turned from polishing the faces of a bank of gauges to welcome her visitors.

"Good afternoon, Miss ... Witcher, isn't it?" began the inspector.

The young woman laughed. "Oh please, call me Flix. Everyone does. And you, I assume, are the police."

"That's right, miss ... er ... Flix. My name is Detective Inspector Copper, and this is my colleague Detective Sergeant Radley." The pair produced their warrant cards.

"Bob said you were on your way down. And you've got questions about Sir, of course." Flix shook her head disbelievingly. "I still can't quite realise that he's dead."

"Not just dead, miss, but murdered," responded Copper bluntly. "Which is why we need to gather as much information as to who might have had a reason to do such a thing."

"And you think I may know something? I can't imagine what. I don't think I've ever heard a bad word said against him. But then, down here, I suppose I wouldn't. And as for Sir's business world away from *Buck*, I'm afraid I haven't a clue."

"Perhaps your recollections of the events of the past week may trigger something useful," suggested Copper. "Even if no further back than that. Tell me, how long have you been working for Sir Lionel?"

"Almost two years now."

"And have you found him a good employer?"

"I don't think I could have asked for a better one," smiled Flix. "I mean, this has really been my dream job. Just look around." She gestured to the equipment crowding the compartment. "Everything is the best there is, and if anything ever needs attention or repair, I can have whatever I want, no questions asked."

"Mr. de Waters did mention that you enjoyed your work," said Copper, echoing the smile. "So Sir Lionel was as generous to you as he seems to have been to the other crew members?"

"Oh yes. Not that I ever had that much to do with him personally," replied Flix. "I mean, Trey and Bob were in contact with him all day every day. But I've always been quite happy making sure that everything on *Buck* was running smoothly. And of course, there have been the perks. I've had the chance to visit some lovely places when we've been in port."

"Which brings us neatly round to the question of this past week's trip," said the inspector. He shifted, trying to find a more convenient position as he leaned against a rather lumpy piece of metalwork.

"I'm so sorry, inspector," said Flix. "You can't be comfortable. I suppose it's pretty cramped in here if you're not used to it. Would you both like to sit down?"

"I'm sure we'd love to," responded Copper gratefully, looking around, "but ..."

Flix laughed. "But not in here. True. We are a bit short of space. Come through here." She made her way past the main bulk of the engine and through a narrow doorway, the police officers following in her wake, to climb a very steep set of metal steps and open a further tiny door which brought them, to Copper's surprise, out on to the rear deck just above water level. "There," she announced, pulling a pair of benches out from their recesses in the wall. "Welcome to the landing platform. This should be a bit more like it. Take a seat."

"That's a bit of a turn-up, miss. You don't expect to find a secret passage on a boat," observed Radley, as he subsided with a sigh on to the bench.

"Emergency exit, sergeant" explained Flix. "In case the other door is blocked. There's another from the passenger cabins up to the bow. We have to have them for health and safety." She turned back to Copper, and her face grew solemn. "Not that you're really interested in the finer points of yacht design, are you, inspector? You have other worries."

"I do, miss. So if, as you say, you're aware of no reasons outside the context of this yacht why anyone should wish Sir Lionel harm, that would then bring us to more recent events. Have you been aware of any conflicts between members of the family during this trip? Because although you say that you spend the majority of your time in your own little engineering kingdom, you also mentioned that you've had the chance to visit some interesting places when the boat has been in port. I'm guessing that this trip would have been no different. So perhaps you might have had the chance to see or hear something which might be helpful to us. Anything. However small." Copper regarded the young woman encouragingly.

Flix sat for a moment in thought. "I suppose there may have been a couple of things," she said eventually. "Not that I'm one for eavesdropping. And I couldn't say if they meant anything at all."

"So what sort of thing would we be talking about?" coaxed Copper. "Let's start with your most recent port of call. That was Guernsey, wasn't it? I gather from the captain that you were anchored in the harbour there, so did you manage to get ashore at all?"

"Actually, yes," replied Flix. "And I remember now, because it was in the harbour. Taff had run me ashore at the same time as Leo and Cordelia, and I was up on the quayside when one of the tenders from the German cruise ship came alongside, and a whole lot of passengers got off, including a group who sounded as if they were from Australia or New Zealand. Actually, I'm sure they were Kiwis, because I heard someone mention Christchurch, and that's New Zealand, isn't it? I think a lot of people from down there like to take cruises in Europe during the summer because it takes them away from their winter."

"I don't quite see what this has to do with Sir Lionel," remarked Copper.

"Well no, it doesn't," admitted Flix. "It actually sounded as if it had something to do with Lady Butler, but it just seemed a bit odd at the time. You see, everyone on the quayside was all mixed up together, and one of the women in the crowd suddenly grabbed Cordelia by the arm and said 'It's you, isn't it? Fancy that! Long time no see'. And Cordelia said sorry, she didn't know what the other woman meant, and the other woman said she was desperately trying to remember Cordelia's name, and it was on the tip of her tongue, and Cordelia insisted that she must have made a mistake, and that she was sure they'd never met. But then the New Zealand woman suddenly said of course they had. 'I'm Nyree', she said, 'and you're Cordy, aren't you? I'm a great friend of your mother-in-law back home'. And Cordelia almost tore herself away, and said the woman must be thinking of somebody else, and she practically ran to get back to Leo, who was some way away, and the woman's husband asked what all that was about, and the woman was quite put out. 'How rude,' she said. 'Wait till we get home'. But then everyone went off in different directions, so I didn't hear any more."

"You remember Cordelia told us she came from New Zealand, boss," remarked Radley.

"That doesn't necessarily mean that she knows everyone there," countered the inspector. "Tell me, miss, has *Red Buccaneer* been down to New Zealand while you've been working on board?"

Flix laughed. "I wish. I've always wanted to go. But I think that might be a trip too far for *Buck*. We've got the range to get across the Atlantic, but I think a round-the-world would be a bit ambitious."

"So Lady Butler wouldn't have visited there on this yacht," reflected Copper. "Although, of course, there's nothing to have stopped her going there at any other time."

"I couldn't say," shrugged Flix. "Actually, I did ask Sir if *Buck* had ever been Down Under, and he said 'Why?', so I told him about what I'd heard, and he said it sounded all very odd. But as far as he knew, Lady Butler had never been there."

"And you've met Sir Lionel's former wife?" queried Radley. "You know who she is?"

"Of course," answered Flix. "She's visited us a couple of times when we've been here in port, but she's never sailed with us while I've been here. She and Sir Lionel were divorced before I came to work for him, but they've always seemed quite comfortable together

128

whenever I've seen her." She gave a small smile. "Sir always seemed to get on well with women. I think he had quite a taste for female company."

Copper's eyebrows rose. "Do you have any special reason for saying that, miss? Any particular recent occasion you can think of?"

Flix frowned. "I don't know what relevance it would have to your enquiries, inspector," she said, "but again, I overheard something which just seemed a bit odd."

"And when and where was this?" asked Copper.

"We were in Granville," replied Flix. "I don't know if you know where that is, inspector. It's a little town on the western side of the Cherbourg peninsula. Pretty little place, with an old port – quite touristy, so I took a break ashore to do some sightseeing. And I couldn't believe it, but they've got a museum there all to do with Christian Dior. Apparently he was born there, and the house was his childhood home. Who knew?"

"Who indeed?" smiled Copper. "The sergeant and I are not exactly well-informed about the world of *haute couture*."

"While I," laughed Flix, "am a total slave to fashion, as you can tell." She indicated her utilitarian overalls. "Although actually, there was a time when my mother was rather worried by my liking for what she thought of as unsuitable male pursuits like engineering, and would have loved me to be more of a girly girl, so she used to ply me with fashion magazines in the hope of diverting my career plans. It never worked, of course, but I've always liked the look of designer clothes, even if I can't afford them. So anyway, when I saw that there was a museum here, I thought I'd pay a visit." A slightly misty look came into her eyes. "And some of the dresses on display ..." A sigh. "Oh well. Not for me. But I did treat myself to a bottle of perfume from the shop. That's a week's wages gone!"

"So, you visited the museum," prompted Copper. "And something happened?"

"I was just coming out of one of the rooms," explained Flix, "when I heard Sir's voice up on the landing above me. And I was surprised for a moment, but then I realised that he was talking to Jessica – you know, Tyrone's wife – and I thought to myself, 'Well, obviously', because she's a model, so she'd be interested in fashion. But the thing was, it's the first time I'd ever heard him speaking in that tone of voice."

"How do you mean?" enquired the inspector.

"Well, you know I said just now that Sir always seemed to get on with the ladies. He was quite a smoothie, for an older man. But it didn't sound much like that this time."

"Because ...?"

"Because he said something about her hiding something from him, and she said that she didn't want to talk about the past, and why couldn't they think about the future, and he asked how much Tyrone knew, and she said 'Nothing, but he's bound to know sooner or later', and that some things can't be kept secret for ever. And he hissed something to her which I couldn't quite catch, except for the word 'betrayal', and then she started to cry, and I could hear them starting down the stairs, so I just ducked back into the room and stepped behind one of the displays, but fortunately they carried on down the stairs, so they can't have known I was there. And when I came out of the museum, they must have left, and when I came back on board *Buck* there was no sign of them."

"Intriguing," mused Copper. "And evidently out of character for Sir Lionel, from what you've told us. But perhaps Jessica will be able to enlighten us further."

"Oh!" said Flix suddenly.

"You've thought of something else, miss?" asked

Copper.

"Yes. I've just remembered. You know I said that the time in the museum was the first time I'd heard Sir speak like that to one of the wives. But it wasn't the last time."

"Really? So when was this, and who was he speaking to?"

Flix reflected. "Gosh. It must have been only yesterday, because it was when we were on our way back from Guernsey."

"So what are we talking about here?" persisted the inspector.

"You see, we were in mid-Channel, and everything down in my engine-room was going smoothly, so I thought I'd pop up to the wheelhouse for a moment, just to have a chat with Bob and to get a breath of fresh air. Which I did, and then I came back out on to the landing, and just as I was about to come back down, I could hear Sir speaking to someone in his suite. It was Robin's wife Dee."

"And can you remember what was said?"

"Not a lot, actually. And it sounded as if it was all about business, which doesn't really interest me that much. But it seemed to be about the company that Robin runs. I think that was the original family firm that Sir's empire started with. You know, the steel company." Flix giggled. "It's quite funny. Bob told me that the whole business started when Sir's grandfather was a rag-and-bone man, or something like that, in London back in the old days. And the way he tells it, it sounds like those old repeats of 'Steptoe and Son' I've seen on the television. You can't believe something like that could turn into something like this." She gestured to her surroundings.

"But clearly is has," said Copper drily. "Evidently proof of the old saying that where there's muck, there's brass. So go on, miss. You say Sir Lionel mentioned his

131

original company. Butler Steels, isn't it, sergeant?"

"That's right, boss," confirmed Radley.

"Yes, that's what he was saying," continued Flix. "He said, 'Butler Steels. That's not the sort of headline you want to see in your daily paper, is it?' and Dee said something about not being responsible for what had happened, and he said she'd better make sure that he never heard of anything of the sort again. He said that Robin's neck could easily be on the block as well if the story got out." A shrug. "I didn't think Dee was involved with Robin's company, but as I said, I don't pay that much attention to these things. Anyway, I didn't want to hang about in case they came out, so I just carried on back down below."

"So there wasn't any sort of explanation as to what this 'story' related to?" queried the inspector.

Flix shook her head. "Sorry, Mr. Copper. The only thing I know is that whenever Trey brings the papers on board, which he always does – every time we call into a port, Sir makes Trey go ashore and get copies of the business papers – if ever there's a story about one of Sir's companies in the Pirate group, or if there's a report on one of Tyrone's races, Sir always gobbles them up. At least, that's what Trey jokes when he shows them to me afterwards. Don't they say there's no such thing as bad publicity? You'd have thought Sir would be pleased if he's in the papers again."

"That would all depend," mused Copper to himself. He rubbed his hands together. "Well, Miss Witcher, I dare say you have things to do, and we must get on as well. I'd like another word with your young colleague Taff, if you can suggest where he might be."

"Well, he can't have gone far, can he, inspector?" smiled Flix. "*Red Buccaneer* isn't that big. You could try up on the foredeck."

"We'll do that," said Copper, rising. "Round the side

132

here, presumably."

"Or," interposed Radley, "couldn't we go straight up the middle, miss? Didn't you say there was another one of your secret passages going up to the front of the boat?"

Copper sighed. "Humour him, miss. He's a child at heart. It's all these mentions of pirates. He's probably hoping Captain Jack Sparrow will jump out of the scuppers, whatever they may be."

"No problem," laughed Flix. "Follow me, and mind your head on the way in." She retraced the route down and through the engine compartment, holding back the door through which the detectives had entered. "Go up one deck to the guest cabins, and then there's another little door which just looks like wood panelling, and that will take you through the passage and up into the rope locker and out on to the foredeck. But it's all a bit of a squeeze," she warned.

"Anything to keep my sergeant happy," replied Copper. "It's a small enough reward for all the cups of tea he brings me." He started up the stairs.

Chapter 13

"Whoa!" Pete Radley leapt back as a jet of water splashed perilously close to his feet, as the detectives emerged on to the foredeck.

"Oh, sorry, sergeant." Taff appeared round the corner of the yacht's superstructure, hose in hand. "It got away from me for a second," he apologised. "I didn't mean to splash you. Are your shoes okay?" he fretted.

"No harm done," Radley reassured him. "It takes more than a drop of water to damage a pair of police-issue footwear. They're as tough as old ..." He laughed. "Well, you get the idea."

"And now that we've dealt with that little burst of excitement, Taff," intervened Dave Copper, "we're hoping you can spare us a moment for another little chat."

The young man looked nervously over his shoulder in the direction of the hotel building rising alongside the quay. "Well, I suppose so," he faltered. "Although I'd better not be too long, or Mr. Robin will have my hide."

"Oh yes?"

"Yes. He's made it quite clear that he's the boss now. He got me to help carry all the cases over to the hotel because he said the family are all staying there for tonight, and then he told me to get on with all the jobs I usually do when we get back from a trip. You know, cleaning the boat down and everything. There's always a lot of salt spray when we're going fast like we were yesterday, so I have to make sure all the windows are cleaned, and wipe off all the metal fixtures, and hose down all the decks. I like to make a good job of it. And Sir was always saying that he appreciated my efforts in keeping *Buck* looking at her best."

"And obviously Robin wants to follow in Sir Lionel's footsteps," said Copper.

"Well, maybe." Taff sounded dubious, and sneaked

another nervous glance up towards the hotel.

"But perhaps a rather sterner taskmaster than his father?" deduced Copper.

"That's not really up to me to say, inspector," replied Taff uneasily.

"Then let me reassure you on one point," said the inspector robustly. "At the moment, you are assisting the police with their enquiries into Sir Lionel's death. So if your newly-instated employer has any queries about the use of your time, you just direct him to me. Is that all right?"

Taff gave a faint grateful smile. "If you say so, sir."

"I do. So, turn off that hose, because we need to have a talk."

"Oh. Right. Yes." The young man dropped the hose end to the deck and disappeared for a moment, reappearing as the flow of water eased to a trickle, before ceasing altogether. He cast another nervous look towards the balconies on the top floor of the hotel.

"I'll tell you what, Taff," suggested Copper. "Why don't we find somewhere comfortable to sit, away from any possibility of being overlooked? Somewhere like ... how about the covered deck outside the saloon? I expect it's easiest to go along here, isn't it?" Without waiting for a reply, he moved past Taff and made his way along the side deck towards the stern, leaving Radley to shepherd the deckhand in his wake. On arrival, the inspector took one of the chairs flanking the dining table, while gesturing to Taff to seat himself opposite, as Radley placed himself discreetly behind the young man, out of his line of sight, notebook at the ready.

As the three sat, Copper observed Taff giving a sideways look in the direction of the after-deck's hot tub. "Is it really true what they're saying, inspector?" queried the deckhand. "Sir Lionel's death wasn't an accident? I mean, it wasn't because I'd done something wrong with the tub's settings or anything like that?"

"I'm afraid not, Taff," replied Copper. "That's to say, I'm afraid it wasn't an accident, so I'm glad to be able to say that there's no way you can be blamed. No, it seems very likely that the gentleman was killed."

"Murdered, you mean?" Taff gave a shudder. "That's horrible."

"Indeed," agreed Copper. "Which is why I need all the help you can give me in trying to find out what has led to the present situation. So, Taff, tell me a little about Sir Lionel," he continued. "Was he an easy man to work for?"

"Oh, he was great," enthused Taff. "I mean, he always knew what he wanted but he was, you know, nice with it. He never spoke a cross word – well, not to me, anyway, even if I didn't get something quite right the first time."

The inspector was swift to seize on the implication. "But not so forgiving with others, perhaps? The other members of his family sometimes got on the wrong side of him?"

Taff wriggled uncomfortably. "Well, I don't like to say, inspector ..."

"I need to know everything," stated Copper firmly. "If there have been any tensions within the Butler family, particularly during the past week, that information could be vital. Do you understand that, Taff?"

The deckhand nodded.

"So," pursued the inspector, "let's take our thoughts back to Sir Lionel's oldest son Robin. You implied that he was not so easy-going in his attitude to you as his father was. And we've had a couple of conversations with Robin Butler, so I think we already have an impression of the occasional shortness of his fuse. My question is, did you ever see this manifested in the context of the father-son relationship. In either

136

direction?"

"I don't think Mr. Robin would have dared to speak to Sir the way he spoke to other people," responded Taff. "But maybe Mr. Robin got on the wrong side of Sir sometimes. I mean, I did hear one time ..." He hesitated.

"This was a conversation that took place during the past week?" encouraged Copper. "Tell me about it."

Taff took a deep breath and seemed to gather his courage together. "I can't remember which day it was," he said. "But I was out here by the hot tub, giving it a wipe round where the water had splashed over, and I could hear voices coming from the balcony of Sir's suite on the deck above. Not that I heard much, because there were other people about here, and I didn't want to look as if I was listening in."

"Obviously not. But you did hear something? Words passed between Sir Lionel and Robin?"

"That's right. Oh ... I've just remembered when it was. It was the morning after the night we spent in Deauville, because Mrs. Dee had asked Trey if he'd managed to get any newspapers, and Trey said yes, but Sir had first dibs on them like always, but he'd let her have them later. And it was talk about the papers that made me prick up my ears, because that's what I heard Sir saying. He said to Mr. Robin, 'Have you seen this? You're going to have to provide me with some answers when we get home, my boy, and pretty damn quick!' He sounded quite hot under the collar. But then Mr Robin said something about there being nothing to worry about, and everything was under control, but then Sir said 'So why is my company being trashed in these rumours that seem to be going about?', and Mr. Robin said that his company was perfectly sound, and Sir got even crosser and said '*My* company, boy, and don't you ever forget it!'. But then I realised that Mrs. Dee was looking at me a bit funny, as if she knew I was listening in

137

to something, so I finished up quick and nipped off before she could say anything."

Copper reflected for a moment. "Interesting exchange, sergeant," he remarked to Radley. "And if I remember correctly, you'll have some notes on a similar conversation at another time."

Radley nodded. "It's all in here, boss," he confirmed, tapping his notebook.

"I look forward to doing a 'compare and contrast'," said the inspector. He turned back to the young deckhand. "So far, so good, Taff," he smiled, "so let's see if there's anything else helpful you can recall. Because as your colleague Trey told us, one of the useful things about being a member of the crew who's always around is that, very often, your presence isn't actually noticed. Which probably gives plenty of opportunities to hear conversations which weren't necessarily meant for your ears. So having heard about Robin, let's carry on down the Butler family. What about his younger brother Leo? Any thoughts?"

"Not really," replied Taff. "I can't remember Sir having a go at him like with Mr. Robin, if that's what you mean." He gave a sudden laugh. "But there was one time when Sir was talking about Mr. Leo, but it was with Mrs. Cordelia."

"Relevant to what we're investigating? Because what I'm looking for, Taff, is some sort of motive for somebody to kill Sir Lionel," Copper reminded the other. "Murder doesn't always just happen. Sometimes it's planned, and for a reason."

"You couldn't say that good planning was what Sir were talking about," responded Taff with a continuing smile. "It sounded more like the opposite to me."

"In what way?"

"'Damned incompetent!' Sorry, inspector, but that's what he said. And he said something like, if he'd been any

138

judge, there'd be questions asked."

"Judge?" queried Copper. "Are you absolute sure that that was what he said? The exact words? It could be important." He regarded the young man intently.

Taff wrinkled his brow in thought. "It might have been 'If he'd been the judge'. I was down on the platform aft, and they were up here, so I might have got it wrong."

"Was there more?"

"Sir said that from what he'd read, it took a particular kind of fool to lose under those circumstances. Unless there was something odd going on. And Mrs. Cordelia just said that nobody could win every time, and Sir would be better off forgetting about her husband and talking to Mr. Tyrone about things like that. But that was all I heard, because Captain Bob called me to do something."

"But you had the distinct impression that Sir Lionel regarded some action of Leo Butler's as incompetent?"

Unexpectedly, Taff laughed. "Well, he wouldn't have been the first, inspector."

"Really?" Copper was surprised at the young man's statement. "Why, who else has said so?"

"Oh, it's nothing to do with your case, inspector," said Taff hastily. "No, I was just remembering what one of the guys who crews on one of the ocean racers at the yacht club told me one time. I crewed the foredeck for them once or twice. And he told me this funny story."

"About Leo Butler?"

"That's right. You see, the man who owns the big racer, he's one of Sir's friends, and I think he's also quite high up in the law. Lord Somebody-or-other – I can't remember exactly. Anyway, Mr. Leo apparently thought he could get in with him, so he got Sir to ask if he could wangle him on to the crew for one of the races at Cowes Week. Not that he'd ever done any real sailing before." Taff started to chuckle. "So anyway, it got arranged, and they were out in the middle of the race, and the chap I know was helming, and they were about to tack." Taff broke off, as his rising level of mirth threatened to overwhelm his narrative.

"Yeah, that can be a bit of a dodgy moment," intervened Radley. "I've been caught out at moments like that," he added, to Copper's astonishment.

"Sergeant?" The inspector looked at his junior colleague in puzzlement. "I never had you down as the nautical type."

"Not really, boss," admitted Radley. "But when I was at school, we had a sailing club that had a few pram dinghies we used to take out on the local reservoir. Nothing serious."

"You evidently have hidden depths, sergeant," smiled Copper.

"Good job the reservoir didn't, boss," said Radley. "The number of times people fell in. Anyway, sorry to interrupt. Carry on, Taff."

"So they were about to tack," resumed Taff, "and the helmsman gave the usual stand-by call of 'Ready about!'. And then ..." The chuckling grew in volume.

Suddenly Radley burst out laughing. "Oh no! He didn't?"

"Yes, he did," responded Taff, almost helpless with mirth.

"Would somebody please explain what is going on," demanded the inspector, baffled and frustrated.

Radley took a deep breath. "It's like this, boss. When you're sailing, sometimes you have to change course, so that the wind is coming at you from a different direction. It's called tacking. That is, unless the wind's going across your stern, and then it's gybing, which can be a bit trickier, because ..."

"Is this master-class in sailing techniques taking us anywhere soon?" demanded a slightly irritated Copper.

"Sorry, boss. Anyway, the point is, when you're about to tack, the man on the wheel or the rudder shouts 'Ready about' to warn everyone to watch out for the boom on the mainsail, which is going to swing from one side of the boat to the other. Okay?"

"I think I follow," said the inspector cautiously.

"And then after you give the warning, you put the helm over and shout 'Lee oh!'" Radley began to laugh afresh.

"And that's what my mate at the helm did," continued Taff, trying to keep a straight face. "He shouted 'Lee oh!', and Mr. Leo was in the yacht's cockpit, and he stood up and said 'Yes?', and the boom caught him smack on the back of the head and knocked him flat. He was out cold, so they had to abandon the race and call an ambulance. He was okay, just shaken up a bit, but the owner said he'd never have that idiot on board ever again."

"Hmmm," said Copper, attempting not to join in the laughter but failing. "I take his point. But it rather takes us away from the matter in hand, although perhaps it does at least give us an insight into the way things may have stood between Sir Lionel and his second son. Which reminds me ... I'm intrigued by Cordelia's reaction to Sir Lionel's remark about Leo, when she seemed to want to divert her father-in-law's criticism away and towards the youngest brother. I wonder what that was about."

"Well, I'm not exactly sure ..." said Taff. "But maybe ..."

"You've remembered something else?"

"Only because you reminded me, inspector," replied the crewman. "And that was something Sir said about not coming up to expectations, or something like that."

"And this was when he was speaking to Tyrone Butler?"

"That's right, inspector," confirmed Taff. "You must think I'm an awful snooper, going around listening to people's conversations."

"I'm perfectly content to take my information from wherever it comes," declared Copper. "And in any case, as your colleague Miss Witcher pointed out, *Red Buccaneer* isn't that large. You are all to an extent on top of one another. You're bound to overhear things. So tell me, what in particular are we talking about?"

"We were in port," said Taff. "I can't remember which one, except that it can't have been Guernsey, because we were alongside. And I was down in the rope locker sorting some things out, and the hatch was open, and I could hear Sir speaking to Mr. Tyrone. They must have been on the quayside."

"And the nature of the exchange?"

"It was about money."

"Money?" The inspector sounded surprised. "I would have thought that was the last thing for the members of this family to be worried about. There doesn't seem to be any lack of it on show here. So, was Tyrone complaining of a shortage in his pocket-money allowance? Or was Sir Lionel displeased because of some kind of extravagance on the part of his son?"

"No, it wasn't like that, inspector. Although Sir did sound a bit annoyed. And it was to do with Tyrone's racing. He wanted to know how come Mr. Tyrone wasn't getting the results he ought to, and he said 'Are you trying to tell me that my money's not good enough?'. He said that he expected better, and he was beginning to wonder if there was some factor he wasn't aware of, and Mr. Tyrone said that nobody could magic up a win every time, and Sir said that the only thing his sons seemed to be able to magic up was losses. And then it went quiet, and I popped my head out of the hatch just in time to see Sir storming off, and Mr. Tyrone sort of slunk back on board."

"It seems Sir Lionel was a man with high expectations," reflected Copper, turning to Radley. "And it sounds as if the failure to meet them wasn't contributing to the game of Happy Families which you'd think this cruise was intended to foster. Many thoughts to ponder." He turned back to Taff. "Is there anything else you can remember that might help us?"

Taff scrunched up his face in thought. "Not that I can think of, inspector," he replied. He shifted uneasily. "And if it's all right by you, I ought to be getting on with my work. On account of, you know, Mr. Robin and all ..."

"Yes, I understand. And it's probably a good thing if you can carry on working as normally as possible. It'll help settle your mind after the shock of finding your employer the way you did. You must have had a great surprise this morning, discovering Sir Lionel in the hot tub like that."

"No, not really, inspector," came the unexpected reply. "No, I mean it was an awful shock finding Sir dead like that, but it wasn't surprising that he was in the tub early on. He very often used to do that. Sometimes he'd be in there before any of us crew were up and about. Or even last thing at night, I'd hear the tub going and think 'Oh, Sir's having one of his late night wallows'." Taff glanced up furtively at the clock on the bulkhead. "So, is that all? Only I ..."

"Yes, go," said Copper. "The last thing we want to do is get you in trouble." And as he regarded the young man's retreating back, he remarked to his junior colleague, "Well, that's a fistful of information to plough through." He also took a look at the clock above him. "And I think we'd probably best do our ploughing with fresh brains in the morning. I'm not at all sure that there's anything left to do here today."

"We'd better scoot off then, boss," said Radley, a

hint of relief in his voice. "And it's not as if we won't have plenty to get on with tomorrow anyway. There's the forensic results, and I wouldn't mind betting Anna will have turned up something from her web-surfing activities."

"True. A policeman's lot, eh?" smiled Copper. "So, let's find Captain Bob and tell him we're signing off and that the ship is his for the night, and then I think we can safely let the Uniform chaps go on their way for this evening. Nothing for them to keep watch over at present, although we'll get them to come back and hover in the morning, just to maintain the presence. And then we can look in to the hotel and let the family know that we'll be back tomorrow at some time and that we'll without doubt want further words with them, so they will need to stay put ..."

"That'll go down well, boss," grinned Radley. "I'll leave that bit to you."

"And after that, it's 'England, Home, and Beauty'."

"And a beer!"

"No arguments from me, sergeant," smiled Copper. "So let's be on our way."

Chapter 14
Tuesday

"Good morning, inspector! Hello, sergeant!" The sunny greeting, accompanied by a bright smile, came from the young woman seated at a group of computer screens and keyboards in a cubicle in the Intelligence department on the upper floor of the police station, the room's slightly grimy windows overlooking the station's car park with its high wire fences, and an uninspiring view of a jumble of buildings beyond. Anna Logue provided a complete contrast to her less than glamorous surroundings. In her early twenties, petite, and with pert and lively features topped by short dark hair cut in an elfin style, she had originally come to Inspector Copper's notice when he and Sergeant Radley had been called to investigate a somewhat bizarre death at an institute at a country house, where her job as resident I.T. specialist had proved invaluable in helping to discover the solution to the crime. But that solution had also brought about an end to Anna's employment at the institute, at a time when a stroke of luck meant that someone of her talents was needed by the Intelligence team at the detectives' base. A discreet word or two in the right place had helped to secure the position for Anna, and her internet research skills, together with her bubbly and unquenchable enthusiasm, had since proved an invaluable asset to the force.

"Sergeant Copper tells me you have some information for us, Anna," smiled Copper in response. "That was quick off the mark. He says you'd phoned down first thing this morning, before I'd even arrived, let alone had a chance to get behind my desk."

"I know you don't like to hang about, inspector," replied Anna in her cheerful Scots accent. "And once the sergeant here had put me on to finding out about the people in your latest case, I got quite caught up in it. And the more I looked, the more I found. They're an interesting bunch, to say the least."

"I look forward to hearing what you've unearthed."

"Well, sit yourselves down a wee while, and I'll take you through it." Anna looked about her. "Inspector, you'd better have this other chair. And I'm sure Sergeant Radley can scrounge another one from around the office somewhere."

"Leave it to me, boss," said Radley, before popping to the adjacent booth and, after a murmured exchange, returning with another chair which he squeezed into the somewhat crowded space, as Anna turned back to her computer screens and began clicking at a keyboard.

"So, inspector, where would you like to start?" enquired the young woman.

"I suppose we may as well begin with our dead man," suggested Copper. "I imagine the more we can find out about him, the more likely we are to be able to identify any motives for anyone wishing him dead."

"Oh, I know this one," chuckled Anna. "What's the formula? 'Know the man and you know his murderer'." She laughed at Copper's reaction, his eyebrows raised in surprise. "Oh, don't look so astonished, inspector. I got that one from Sergeant Peter here. Isn't it one of your favourite sayings?"

"And my former guvnor's before me," admitted the inspector with an answering smile. "And now everyone seems to be quoting it back at me. Not that there's anything wrong with some of the old truths. And I dare say it's good to know that they're trickling down the generations to some of the children in the organisation. No offence, Anna."

"None taken, inspector," she responded chirpily. "We kids are happy to learn from the experience of some of the old fogeys in the force. No offence, sir."

146

"Cheek!" muttered Copper, and the three shared a laugh, before the inspector sobered. "So come on, Anna, let's hear what you've got on Sir Lionel Butler."

"Here we go, then." A burst of clicks, and Anna's screen was filled with dense script. "There's quite a lot to tell. How far back do you want me to go?"

"We've already had something of a potted family history from the victim's divorced wife," pointed out Copper. "So I'm not sure we need to go too far back. And in case you start wondering, as far as we can ascertain, the divorce was perfectly amicable, and the lady can be exonerated because of an absence of opportunity. Not that the same can be said for the other members of the close family, but we'll come on to them later. For the moment, let's stick to Sir Lionel."

"Okay." Anna scanned the information in front of her. "Well, if you just want a précis, let's just say that he was an extremely wealthy man – and I do mean 'extremely', inspector. I did a quick tot-up of his declared assets, and I nearly ran out of zeros. Which for the grandson of a boy from a family from the East End of London, born without any kind of spoon, never mind a silver one, has got to be pretty impressive. If you really want me to, I can bring up a list of his companies."

"I think we'll settle for 'extremely wealthy' for now, Anna," said Copper. "But I'm guessing that it would be safe to assume that he didn't get to where he was without a few struggles along the way. Challenges, conflicts, and probably quite a few toes trodden on. But for now, we'll take that as read. Because what I'm most interested in is more recent history. Did anything pop up by way of a particular current enemy, for instance?"

"How would that work out, boss?" queried Radley. "If we're confident that our suspect list is restricted to the members of the family who were on the boat on Sunday night, why should anyone else be in the frame?"

"Because," explained Copper, "it's not beyond the realms of possibility that a third party could have influence over some member of the Butler family, and that family member might have been compelled or pressured or influenced to carry out the crime. We can't rule that thought out."

"Oh, right. Hadn't crossed my mind," admitted Radley. "So, Anna, have you found anyone who would fit the bill?"

"Sorry to disappoint, sergeant," replied Anna, "but Sir Lionel doesn't seem to have been involved in any what you might call boardroom scraps in the last few months. His latest big takeover was at the end of last year, and that one seems to have been smiles all round, according to the press photos. And the other party walked away with very full pockets. The whole business was a very open book. So I've got nobody for you there."

"That's unfortunate. So Sir Lionel himself is a bit of a dead end then, boss." Radley sounded crestfallen. "To coin a phrase."

"Not so," contradicted Anna. "I've got a couple of things for you that aren't quite as open-book. And they relate to the past week or so."

"Really? I'm intrigued," said Copper. "Do tell."

"I took a look at Sir Lionel's phone records. Yes, I know," said Anna, in reaction to the inspector looking askance at her. "Probably highly unorthodox without a search warrant, but I won't tell if you won't. And it's not as if I was listening to voice-mails or anything like that. I just had an idea that it might tell us something if we could identify who he'd been talking to. Business contacts and the like. Which actually it turned out to be, for the most part. The numbers pretty much all belonged to other companies in his Pirate group, or friendly competitors, or personal things like restaurant bookings. Nothing sinister." A pause. "Except ..."

"Except ...?"

"Except for two numbers," explained Anna. "Both untraceable mobile numbers. Burner phones, if you like. And incoming calls only. Sir Lionel never called them."

"And what can you tell us about these burner phones?" wondered Copper. "Are they related?"

"Not by the look of it. They have completely different patterns of use. One of them I can trace to having been used around central London over quite a long period of time. Usually calls several minutes long. If I had to guess, I'd say that somebody has been providing information to Sir Lionel on a fairly regular basis, but that's just supposition. The calls never went to voice-mail. They were either answered, or the caller rang off. But one of the calls came during the past week. In fact it was ..." Anna checked her screen. "Wednesday."

An interrogative glance towards Radley. "And the yacht would have been where at that point?"

A riffle as the sergeant looked back through his notes. "Deauville, boss."

"Interesting," said the inspector. "And how about the other phone?"

"Maybe even more interesting," smiled Anna. "Because Sir Lionel only received one call from that one. And this time the caller wasn't in London."

"No? So where were they?"

"Jersey!" declared Anna triumphantly. "But there's more. I've got no track of that number being used at any other time, except for once."

"A genuine burner," mused Copper. "Use and throw away. Except for this one other call, you say. Which was when?"

Anna took another look at the computer screen. "That was on Thursday."

"At which point, sergeant, the yacht was in ...?"

Another riffle. "Granville, boss. That's where Sir

Lionel was looking around that Dior museum."

"And have we any idea who the recipient of this second call was?"

"We have," said Anna. "It's a mobile number registered to another member of the Butler family. To be exact, Leo."

"Leo?" Copper was incredulous. "What on earth is he doing getting a phone call from an anonymous burner phone, I wonder."

Anna shrugged. "Can't tell you any more than that, inspector. Although, while we're on the subject of Leo Butler, Q.C., I've turned up a mention or two that you might be interested in."

"Oh yes?"

"Nothing scandalous, if that's what you're hoping for. Or criminal. Other than the sort of people he's dealing with in the course of his profession, of course," added Anna with a smile. "In fact, his whole C.V. looks pretty conventional – university, studying law, pupillage in a set of chambers, going on to get qualified and eventually taking silk and becoming a fully-fledged Queen's Counsel. It's all text-book stuff. And none of his cases have ever really hit the headlines particularly. What you might call run-of-the mill gangsters, as it were. The only thing is, over the last couple of years, there have been mentions of cases which he was expected to win, but which for some reason went sour."

"Do we know why?"

"No special reasons, as far as I can see. Sometimes there were unexpected flaws in the prosecution case, which turned up late and ended up with the whole thing being thrown out by the judge. Or there were missing pieces of evidence or gaps in the paperwork. Or witnesses vanishing. It varied."

"You'd think that people would take care to avoid that sort of sloppiness," remarked Copper.

150

"But doesn't that ring a bit of a bell, boss?" suggested Radley. "Don't you remember, when you told Leo he would have to hang around here and miss his court date, didn't Robin's missus suggest that he make up some sort of excuse to the judge to get things put off? So maybe he's not such a stickler for the rules as you'd hope."

"And that does tie in with Sir Lionel's remark about incompetence which Taff overheard," said the inspector. "More food for thought."

"Although when Sir Lionel was talking to Cordelia, she couldn't deny that her husband had had losses in court. She just tried to divert him towards Tyrone," observed Radley. "It sounds a bit like ferrets in a sack to me."

"Okay," said Copper. He paused in thought for a moment. "So, Anna, since we've mentioned Cordelia, have we anything interesting on her?"

"Actually, surprisingly little," replied Anna. "She's originally from New Zealand – I've got a record of the birth of Cordelia Lyne in Christchurch, and then she went on to study botany at university in Auckland."

"Wouldn't she have done better to go over to Sydney for that?" quipped Radley. He laughed. "Sorry, boss," he muttered, in response to the two blank faces turned towards him. "Aussie geography joke. Sydney? … Botany? … oh, never mind." He lapsed into silence.

"Anyway …" resumed Anna, after a hiatus which seemed to last forever. "After uni, I've got nothing. She seems to have vanished from the New Zealand records, but I found some mention of a row when one of their government's I.T. systems had a meltdown and lost a whole lot of data, so maybe her details got caught up in that. Don't forget, they had that earthquake in Christchurch. Maybe that was a factor. Then she appears in the U.K. a couple of years later."

151

"Gap years?" suggested the inspector. "Travelling? People do."

"They do. But you'd think there'd be some track of her somewhere. You don't meet many Cordelias, and Lyne isn't a very common surname, but no. So she came to the U.K., worked for a while for a garden design company, and then started her own firm a while after that. Very well thought of, according to her on-line reviews. She's won awards. I can't find much else."

"No guilty secrets?"

"Not that I've been able to track down, inspector. Sorry."

"So we'll move on. And since Cordelia seems to have wanted to point a finger at Tyrone for some reason, let's take a look at him."

"I will find him for you." Anna scrolled down her screen until she came to a fresh heading. "Here we are. Tyrone Butler. Youngest of the three sons, and something of a golden boy of the motor racing track. Although actually, not quite so golden lately, but I'll come on to that. So going back a bit, he didn't exactly have a misspent youth, but he seems to have been a bit of a party boy. You know, snapped by the paparazzi falling out of nightclubs, or photographed playing billiards in a Las Vegas hotel suite with a group of young ladies wearing very few clothes ..."

"Him or the young ladies?" queried Radley.

"Actually, all of them," replied Anna. "But nothing illegal alleged. But then there's his driving record. Nothing other than a couple of speeding tickets to his name, although there were a few occasions where his car was caught speeding on a traffic cam but Tyrone claimed to be sitting in the passenger seat at the time. His friend got the points. Eyebrows were raised, but nothing proved. But on the track, his talent for speed turned into a positive advantage. One or two wins, and quite a lot of high placings, but not so much lately. And that's even after a huge amount got spent re-engineering his car's cockpit, according to one magazine. In fact, there are reports of a couple of cases where he was all set to win a race but inexplicably slipped to second. Like his last race. Beaten at the last gasp by his great rival Miko von Staffen."

"That's the name Trey heard in Guernsey, boss," exclaimed Radley excitedly.

"He's one of the other racing drivers," said Anna. "Like Garcia – that's the other name you gave me, wasn't it? Again, with these results, one or two eyebrows were raised, but any enquiries came to nothing. And some of the soppier journalists in the celebrity magazines put it all down to him being distracted by his overwhelming love for his wife."

"Besotted by the lovely Jessica, is he?" mused Copper. "Well, she is rather lovely, I suppose, although maybe not the sharpest knife in the box."

"If that's so, it doesn't seem to have bothered Tyrone," observed Anna. "All the gossip mags are agreed that it's a love match, at least on his part. He pretty much fell head-over-heels at first sight. And the bad boy activity seems to have vanished from his dossier since their marriage, so there must be something in it."

"And that's testimony to the steadying influence of a good woman," said the inspector. "Wouldn't you say so, sergeant?"

"Well, maybe for some of us," muttered Radley under his breath. "I mean, yes, right, boss," he hastily added aloud.

"And while we're on the subject of Tyrone's wife," resumed Copper, turning back to Anna, "what do we know about her that might have a bearing on the case?"

"Not that much. Tons of photographs, which is only what you'd expect, but not very much in the way of facts.

Gossip column pictures of her in the company of older men when she started out, but that's not really a surprise. She was pretty young."

"I suppose," said Copper. "I imagine a lot of rich men like to be seen in public with a pretty girl on their arm. Lady Butler said much the same about Sir Lionel. They probably think it boosts their reputation, and it doesn't cost them anything. Anyway, do go on, Anna."

"She was spotted by a designer when she was in her late teens, and now she's with one of the biggest modelling agencies in the country. If you really wanted me to, I could probably put together a shoot-by-shoot diary for her covering the past three years, but I'm guessing that's not what you're looking for. All I can say is that she experienced a bit of an instant leap to fame, and I can't find that much about her before that, other than those photos. After she left school there's some mention of her being with some other small agency in London for models, but I can't find anything about it. Their web page has disappeared, and all the records seem to have been deleted for some reason. Maybe they went bust or changed their name or something, but I can't find anything. Which is odd." Anna looked puzzled.

"And there wouldn't seem to be an obvious link between the world of high fashion and the death of our murder victim," reflected Copper. "Unless Sir Lionel had fingers in the fashion industry pie."

"Not that have popped up here," said Anna.

"Oh well. So, we'll move on. Who haven't we covered?"

"There's just Robin and his wife, boss," pointed out Radley.

"Now we've heard a few snippets about Robin already," said Copper. "Murmurs about some financial iffyness surrounding his part of the Group. Butler Steels, to be precise. I wonder if you've got anything to back them up, Anna?"

"Financial iffyness is about as strong as it gets, inspector," replied Anna. "There seem to have been fluctuations in the valuation of the company which nobody can quite seem to account for, and nobody appears to have wanted to go on record as to why. The articles in the papers are quite vague – they talk about 'unnamed sources' and 'unverified rumours', but nobody seems to have been prepared to come out with anything definite."

"I wouldn't mind betting that Butler Steels retain some very expensive lawyers who would pounce on anyone who suggested anything that they couldn't prove," observed Copper.

"And don't forget, boss, Robin's wife is one of those lawyers," added Radley. "Or used to be. She was very firm in telling us that she was all about commercial law rather than criminal."

"Hmmm," said the inspector. "As long as the two never come too close to one another. But it must be very useful for Robin to have a source of professional advice sitting across the breakfast table. Should he need it, of course. So then we come on to the lady herself."

"Now Desdemona Butler seems to be the least interesting of the lot," said Anna. "I can't find any youthful indiscretions to lay at her door. She's not from a particularly wealthy background – just ordinary people from the suburbs – and she seems to have been a hard-working model student when she was just plain Desdemona Fender, and she got into the same law firm where Leo Butler worked without making any great waves."

"And presumably that's how she met his brother Robin."

Anna shrugged. "The internet does not tell, inspector," she smiled. "But what it does tell is that she

155

gave up her law work fairly soon, and she seems to have enjoyed moving in the moneyed circles frequented by the Butler family. Her name pops up a couple of times in the social columns of the gossip magazines, although not because of what she herself was doing. She just gets a mention as being one of the weekend house guests at Lady So-and-so's or the Countess of Whatnot's when there was a burglary. Although she seems to have been lucky. She wasn't on the list of people who had their jewellery stolen. But that omission seems to be her only claim to fame. Other than that, I've drawn a blank."

"Okay." Copper mused for a moment. "Just one thing more, Anna. Can you get hold of the details of Sir Lionel's will? In case it contains any startling revelations."

Anna raised an eyebrow. "And just how many regulations would you like me to break in order to do that, inspector?" she enquired with a grin.

"None at all, of course," responded Copper airily, suppressing an answering smile. "But I rely on your resourcefulness."

The researcher turned back to her keyboard with a sigh. "I'd best get on with it, then."

Chapter 15

"I hope you were making notes of all that, sergeant," remarked Dave Copper, as the two detectives made their way towards the police station car park.

"Oh, every last syllable, boss," responded Pete Radley with ironic cheeriness. "So you'll be pleased to hear that my writer's cramp is coming along beautifully."

"Glad you're enjoying yourself. Obviously, whoever suggested that a policeman's lot was not a happy one forgot all about the delights of copious note-taking." The inspector let out a sympathetic chuckle. "So you'll no doubt be pleased to hear that the day is only going to get better."

"Oh yes?" said Radley warily. "What's on the agenda now? Back to *Buck*?"

"Not just yet. We have a little trip to police H.Q. in Westchester in prospect. Surely you remember. There's a dead body lying there with questions hanging over it. I'm hoping that Una and Suzanne will have some nice clear-cut forensic findings on the subject of the late Sir Lionel Butler."

"Couldn't Una tell you anything last night?"

"We try our best not to talk shop when we're at home," said Copper. "We have much better things to do. Like, in my case, digging the garden." He stretched and gave a small groan in reminiscence. "Besides, the prospect of somebody's innards metaphorically spread across the dinner table would do nothing to sharpen the appetite for supper. Plus there wasn't anything to tell last night anyway."

"No? How come?"

"Una didn't get home until late, because she and Suzanne got delayed with the aftermath of this R.T.A. and drugs business yesterday. Fortunately, that's somebody else's pigeon. But it meant that she didn't have the

157

opportunity to get on to our case until first thing this morning, which is why she was up with the lark and away first thing before I was even out of the shower. So I'm hoping the early start means that she will have had a chance to get stuck into Sir Lionel. So to speak."

*

As he drove into the car park of the county headquarters in Westchester, Dave Copper couldn't help feeling just the tiniest pang of jealousy at the building's smart and stylish appearance, in contrast to the slightly scruffy state of his own police station. The ultra-modern block, sheathed in mirrored glass interspersed with cladding panels in bright red and gleaming steel, provided an impressive contrast to the county town's adjacent railway station, itself a statement of sombre Victorian terracotta magnificence. Crossing the car park, the detectives bounded up the steps to the entrance doors, flanked by their incongruous old-fashioned blue police lamps salvaged from the now-demolished old H.Q. building, and after a brief presentation of their warrant cards to the officer at the reception desk, strode across the cavernous marble-floored atrium in the direction of the bank of lifts.

"Six, isn't it, boss?" queried Pete Radley.

"Well remembered, sergeant." A ting as the lift doors opened on arrival at their destination. "And here we are."

At the end of the corridor, the detectives pushed open the doors to the Forensics Department, to be greeted by the customary faint aroma of chemicals with an overlying metallic tang. As they entered, Sergeant Una Singleton looked up from her desk, perfectly positioned to take advantage of the breath-taking views from the floor-to-ceiling windows at the end of the large room, while various of her lab-coated colleagues, after sparing a brief glance at the newcomers, returned to their tasks at their work-stations dotted about the department.

"Excellent timing, gentlemen," Una greeted her visitors, rising and advancing to meet them. "I was just writing up our first set of findings on your marina victim so that I could email them over to you, but as you're here, you can have them in person."

"That's good news," replied Copper. "I was afraid you might still be caught up in the throes of your assumed drug dealer."

"Not at all," smiled Una. "Some of us know how to delegate, so I have passed the mortal remains of that particular gentleman over to Darren to deal with, leaving Sooz and me free to concentrate on your murder mystery."

"So we are without doubt talking murder?"

"Oh yes. No question. And I suppose you and Peter would like to come through and take a look at our guest so that we can go over what we've found?"

"I can't think of anything more alluring," said Copper with a wry smile. "And Peter is particularly fond of examining corpses in a state of medical disarray. Isn't that right, sergeant?"

Radley gave a sickly grin. "Oh, absolutely, boss. Great fun. Just don't expect me to be able to face a full English breakfast for a few days."

"No? Not even the black pudding and sausages?"

"Stop it!" laughed Una. "Come on, you two. And don't worry, Peter. Sooz has completed all her work in the giblets department, and everything has been neatly tidied away."

"Thank goodness for that," murmured the sergeant, as he followed the other two through the frosted glass doors and into the department's inner sanctum. Here, the motif of bright fluorescent lighting, spotless white surfaces, and gleaming stainless steel of the main room was continued, backed by the faint whisper of air-conditioning which accounted for the noticeable drop in temperature. And in the centre of the space stood a structure reminiscent of the surgical table in an operating theatre, where Una's colleague Suzanne was just finishing draping a pale green sheet over a recumbent form.

Sooz Heming, a little older than Una, was a comfortably-proportioned motherly figure, whose unexpectedly impressive knowledge of the properties of decomposing human flesh, among her many other talents, made her an invaluable member of the forensics team. And since Copper had first met her in connection with a theatrically startling murder case before he and Una married, she had become a firm friend, and had acted as Una's matron of honour at the couple's wedding. She looked up with a welcoming smile.

"Good morning, chaps. Come to view the leading character in our latest production?"

Copper chuckled. "Well, I can't say much for the design of his current costume, Sooz," he remarked. "I'd have expected better from the wardrobe mistress of the Westwick Players."

"I haven't really had a lot of time to get my sewing machine out to create something more fetching," replied Suzanne with mock regret. "But don't worry – I've made sure that the hand-stitching on the gentleman himself is immaculate. I know how Peter worries about these things."

"Too kind, Sooz," grinned Radley.

"Anyway, enough of the frivolities," broke in Copper. "Let's not forget that we have a dead man here who is in need of some justice. So, love," he continued, feeling it safe to relax into informality while out of earshot of Una's departmental colleagues, "what do we know?"

Una stepped to the side of the table and drew back

the sheet to expose the top half of the body. "Sir Lionel Butler. Prominent businessman, I gather,"

"With, no doubt, a formidable business brain," interrupted Suzanne, chuckling wickedly. "I've got it in a bowl over there if Peter wants to take a look."

As her colleague continued to laugh at Radley's queasy look, Una raised her eyes heavenwards, before resuming with an indulgent sigh. "Well-nourished male in his late sixties, although with perhaps some faint indications that his young life wasn't lived in such a comfortable style as it appears it has been in later years."

"That sounds about right, from what his wife told us," said Copper.

"But no indications that the life of a rich man has taken a particular toll on him," continued Una. "No signs of heart disease, nothing to indicate exceptionally elevated levels of cholesterol, no damage to the liver which could be put down to an abnormally high intake of alcohol ..."

"Despite his apparent fondness for quite a fair old quantity of champagne," remarked Radley. "Or so we were told. Which, in a way, looks as if it ended up being the death of him."

Una shot him a look. "All in due course, Peter," she said. "Let's get the interior sorted out before we move on to the exterior."

Radley held his hands up in feigned surrender. "Sorry. Do go on."

"I shall. And as a special treat for you, I shall hand over to Sooz, who will regale you with details of the gentleman's stomach contents."

"Must you, Sooz?" winced the sergeant.

"I must," replied Suzanne with another wicked smile. "And you'll thank me in the end. And you're quite right, Peter. There had obviously been a certain consumption of champagne as the most recent addition

161

to the victim's intake. This was on top of a substantial meal, which consisted of smoked salmon and caviar, which we assume will have been the starter, followed by Lobster Thermidor with accompanying vegetables as a main course, and the whole was concluded with a portion of Eton Mess. There was also coffee and brandy."

"You know, in a weird way, that lot has made me feel hungry," said Radley, pulling a face. "Do you reckon I'm starting to get used to this?"

"And this is all very well," said the inspector. "We know Sir Lionel and the Butler family had a private dinner at the Porthampton Marina yacht club on the evening of Sunday. And if we'd wanted a menu, I dare say we could have easily got it from either the restaurant staff or the members of the family. I don't quite see what this tells us."

"And do we know what time this dinner took place?" enquired Suzanne.

"We do. And Sergeant Radley will correct me if I'm wrong, but we've been told that the party arrived at the yacht club a little after eight o'clock, and had finished dinner and left around ten."

"That sounds right, boss."

"In which case," said Una, "we will have a very clear answer to the question which was troubling me when I took a look at the victim while he was still *in situ* in his hot tub on the boat. I told you then that the time of death would be difficult to ascertain, because the normal processes of body cooling and onset of *rigor mortis* would have been compromised if the dead man was immersed in hot water. Parboiling a murder victim doesn't assist our post mortem procedures. But ... Sooz, back to you."

"But we do have a time window for you," said Suzanne. She darted across to a nearby computer terminal and studied the data on the screen. "Hold on a

162

second while I just do a little figuring out ..." She closed her eyes, evidently engaging in some swift mental arithmetic, before turning back to the detectives. "Your victim died between eleven-thirty on Sunday night and one o'clock on Monday morning. Give or take a little."

"And how do you come to that conclusion?" asked Copper, impressed.

"Digestion," replied Suzanne simply. "It's only decomposition by another name."

"Yuk," muttered Radley under his breath.

"And therefore," continued Suzanne, ignoring him, "because we can work out reasonably accurately the rate of digestion by the stomach acids of various foods, if we know when they were consumed, we can deduce the time of death by the stage the digestion had reached. It's not one hundred percent accurate, because the various chemical processes do continue to a certain extent after death ..."

"You know I said I was starting to feel hungry, boss?" murmured the sergeant to his superior. "Cancel that."

"... but not to the same degree," pressed on Suzanne, "because of the halted circulation of blood and the shutting down of the various other organs. But that's my best estimate."

"And it's a great deal better than nothing," remarked the inspector. "Thank you, Sooz. Now we can start looking at alibis and see if there are any cracks in anyone's story. Okay, Una. Back to you. What else do we need to know?"

"I don't think I've got any surprises for you when it comes to the cause of death," replied his wife. "A single blow from a champagne bottle, delivered from above and behind, presumably when the victim was seated in the hot tub in more or less the position you found him, although he had of course slipped down below the

163

water's surface after death. That's confirmed, by the way. There was no water in the lungs, so we can be positive that the blow didn't merely stun him, leading him to become submerged and drown."

"And we're also positive that it's the champagne bottle we found in the tub?" queried Copper. "No other candidates as the weapon?"

"Sometimes the most obvious explanation turns out to be true," said Una. "As I suspected, there weren't any forensic traces or prints to be gleaned from the bottle, on account of its presumed overnight immersion in the hot water. But as I think we saw when I first looked at the body, the victim's head had suffered a slight cranial depression during the course of the blunt force trauma ..."

"You mean the bash with the Bolly dented his bonce?" quipped Radley.

"You'll have to excuse the sergeant's fondness for layman's terms, ladies," smiled Copper. "It's his refuge in times of stress."

"And having checked the profile of the bottle," continued Una, in no way deflected, "we can confirm that the dimensions and the curvature correspond precisely."

"As you say, no surprises."

"Afraid not. Although ..."

"Although what?" asked Copper.

"The champagne," said Una. "There's a slight inconsistency. There wasn't enough in the victim's system to indicate that he'd consumed the entire bottle by himself. And an analysis of the water in the hot tub shows no traces of champagne, so the bottle hadn't been emptied into that. But there was only one champagne glass found in one of the glass-holding recesses of the tub. And that glass, not having been immersed, retained Sir Lionel's fingerprints. And nobody else's."

"So the question then became, who drank the rest

of the champagne?" wondered Copper. "What about that other glass I gave you? The one from the cupboard."

"Ah, now I don't know whether that's interesting or not," said Una. "Two sets of prints. Jessica's, overlaid with Tyrone's. The most likely explanation for that is that they'd been sharing a drink. But sadly, no indication as to when that might have been."

"Hmmm." Copper paused in thought for a moment. "So how about the water? Anything else to be gleaned from that? DNA traces? Any mileage there?"

"Afraid not," responded Una. "The chemicals added to the water for sterilisation purposes, even though they're in modest quantities, are there precisely to neutralise any bodily effluvia or excretions."

"And again, yuk," muttered Radley. "I've never fancied the idea of a hot tub anyway," he remarked aloud. "I mean, there you are, sat in a bath of warm water with other people, and you can't tell if they've washed properly around their ... er ... behind their ears, if you see what I mean. To my way of thinking, it's just 'people soup'. Whatever Una says about clever chemicals."

"What around the edges of the tub?" hazarded the inspector. "If somebody's getting in, they're bound to leave some trace, aren't they? Any mileage in that?"

"I took swabs," said Una. "We haven't got around to analysing them as yet. But if you want a top-of-my-head guess, I suspect there'll be either nothing at all, because of the spray resulting from the action of the tub or any cleaning that's been carried out, or else we'll have traces of anybody who's been in the tub over the course of the trip."

"Which could well be everybody in the Butler family. With an awful lot of cross-over DNA, I'd imagine, given that you've got father and the three brothers, although I don't really know what I'm talking about on that subject. No help there then."

165

"We'll run the tests," said Una, "but don't hold your breath. I can't promise anything."

The inspector held up his hand. "Just a sec. Can we go back to something you said earlier? It doesn't quite seem to make sense to me."

Una raised an eyebrow. "And here I was, thinking that our astonishing scientific expertise made everything crystal clear to you footsoldiers from the front line. What's the problem?"

"We're as sure as we can be that the champagne bottle was the weapon, right?"

"Correct."

"And you said that the blow was, in your opinion, delivered from above and behind."

"When, presumably, the victim was seated in the hot tub, at a lower level than his assailant, yes," explained Una patiently.

"Okay, I see that. Except that your famous cranial depression is on the left side of the forehead. So how does that work?"

Una smiled. "A small demonstration needed, I think. Sooz, could you pull that chair forward please. And Peter, why don't you take a seat? I'm about to murder you."

"Fine by me," grinned Radley. "Anything to help. But be gentle with me."

"Now, this is my champagne bottle," said Una, picking up an empty plastic chemical container from a nearby bench. "I go round behind my unsuspecting victim, bottle in hand. Perhaps I pour the remaining dregs into my victim's glass. Then, I change my grip and hold it by the neck, like this. And then, without warning, I swing the bottle, which passes round the side of the victim's head and connects with the left side of the forehead, with resultant calamitous consequences."

Light dawned. "So that's how ..."

166

"Precisely," said Una. "There's only one way to account for the precise combination of factors. Your murderer delivered the blow left-handed."

Chapter 16

Dave Copper maintained a reflective silence as the detectives rode down in the lift, crossed the H.Q. atrium, descended the entrance steps, and made their way towards the car, while Pete Radley watched him from the corner of his eye, unwilling to break his concentration.

Finally, as the inspector fumbled for his keys, his companion spoke up. "So what's the next move, boss?" he enquired. "Back to Porthampton and bash on?"

"That's precisely it," replied Copper. "Between them, I think Anna and Una have turned up quite a few questions, so we need to go looking for answers."

"Which will be found during the course of further chats with the members of the Butler family, I'm guessing," said Radley.

Copper gave a small dry smile. "How well you know me, sergeant. But I'm afraid that the bad news is that you're going to be needing to employ your calligraphic skills once more."

"You what, boss?"

"Your little notebook and pencil are going to be busy again, I have no doubt. And it's just as well that your handwriting is rather better than mine. My old guv'nor used to despair of my scrawl."

"No worries, boss," responded Radley cheerfully. "And you'll be pleased to know that I've almost completely recovered from my writer's cramp."

"Good." The inspector opened his car door. "Because I'm sure there's still plenty of scope to go searching for motives. So don't just stand there. Get in, and we'll get under way."

As the detectives once again drove into the marina car park, Radley was faintly surprised to see a marked police patrol car, placed so that its occupants could maintain surveillance of a silent *Red Buccaneer*, apparently deserted except for a single light shining in the wheelhouse.

"What's the score, boss?" enquired Radley, as the pair emerged from their vehicle. "There's a distinct lack of activity."

"That's deliberate," replied Copper. "Obviously the Butler family are still in the hotel. I wanted the crime scene to be kept as undisturbed by human traffic as possible, so I quietly suggested to Captain de Waters as we left last night that he might like to renew his offer of hospitality to his fellow crew members. He was quite happy to do that, so they've gone off to stay at his house once again. It's only just round the corner, so we can get them back at the drop of a hat if we need to. The captain himself has stayed on board with a sort of watching brief. But it meant that, if there was any further forensic examination of the crime scene required, there wouldn't be any contaminating factors, but as it turns out, Una didn't want to revisit. So no problem."

"And the wooden-tops?" asked Radley. "I'd forgotten about them. How come they just get to sit around doing nothing all day?"

"Our uniformed colleagues," said Copper, with determined emphasis and an expression of disapproval at Radley's disrespectful description of the patrol car's occupants, "are gainfully employed making sure that nobody, and least of all our suspects, makes any attempt to get back on board the yacht for who knows what purpose. So think yourself lucky. I could have detailed you to stand around on a draughty dockside keeping watch for hours on end."

"Right, boss. Sorry, boss," muttered a contrite sergeant.

The inspector made his way over to the patrol car, whose driver wound down his window as the senior officer approached. "Hello, sir. Something I can do for you?"

"And hello again to you, Constable Kapoor," replied Copper. "Anything to report?"

"Not a thing, sir," said P.C. Kapoor. "There's been virtually nothing going on at all. The captain of the yacht came ashore earlier on, and I had a quick word with him. He said he had your okay to stay on board, and he was just nipping over to the convenience store across the way for a paper. He was only gone a few minutes, and other than that, there hasn't been a soul anywhere near. Sorry about that."

"No, Kapoor," the inspector reassured him. "That's exactly what I hoped to hear. But what about your colleague from yesterday? Surely you haven't been sitting here on your own all the time?"

"Oh no, sir. Todd ... I mean P.C. Sweeney, sir ... he thought it might be a good idea to keep an eye on the people from the yacht, so he's trying to keep a low profile in the hotel foyer."

"Hiding behind potted palms, I presume," smiled Copper. "It sounds as if he's got the easier end of the deal."

"No, sir, it's been fine. We've been taking turns, an hour at a time."

"Essential if you need the loo, I should think. And no movement on that score?"

"No, sir. The family came down to breakfast at odd times, but none of them has left the hotel, as far as we know."

"Good. Well done. Which means that Sergeant Radley and I shouldn't have any difficulty tracking them down. We'll leave you on watch here." Copper turned back and beckoned Radley to follow him as he made his way in through the revolving door at the hotel's entrance. As the receptionist looked up with a well-practised bright smile of welcome, the inspector produced his warrant card. "I wonder if I might have a quiet word with the duty manager."

With a startled look, the receptionist scuttled into a rear office, to return moments later with a well-groomed man in his fifties, tall, suave, with iron-grey hair beautifully coiffed. His eyes held an expression of apprehension. "Good day, gentlemen." The accent was liquid and Italian. "My name is Angelo. I am the manager. How may I help you?"

Copper presented his card once again. "My name is Detective Inspector Copper, and my colleague here is Detective Sergeant Radley," he began.

The manager took a swift look around the area, and appeared relieved that there was nobody within earshot. Nevertheless, he lowered his voice to a discreet murmur. "I hope there is not a problem, inspector."

"None at all, as far as your hotel is concerned," replied Copper cheerfully.

"Because I was worried, on account of your officer there." Angelo nodded towards P.C. Kapoor's colleague, who seemed to be making himself as unobtrusive as possible behind a bank of telephones in a corner of the reception area. "He said he was waiting for somebody, but it does not look good for the hotel to have a policeman standing around where the guests can see him. They may think that there is something wrong."

"Which there isn't," Copper reassured him. "So please don't be concerned on that score. But some of your guests may be in a position to help me with a matter I'm investigating, and I was hoping that you might be able to let me use a room somewhere quiet, where I can have a chat with these people away from public notice."

"Of course." Angelo seemed eager to help. "Perhaps one of our small conference rooms? Just along that corridor there."

"I'm sure that would be perfect," smiled Copper in

171

appreciation. "That will keep us well out of the way of your other guests."

"Thank you so much, inspector." Angelo was positively gushing, but then the concerned expression returned. He nodded towards the uniformed officer hovering on the other side of the area. "And your policeman ...?"

"I think we can relieve you of his presence," said Copper. "Sergeant Radley, would you like to let the constable know that he can rejoin his colleague out in their car? But let him know that we may well need them later, so not to leave their post."

"Will do, boss." Radley made his way over to the young officer who, after a brief exchange of words, headed out of the hotel.

"Thank you, inspector," said a grateful Angelo. "Would you like to follow me, and I will show you your room." He led the way along the corridor at the side of Reception, Copper and Radley at his heels, and threw open a door, motioning the detectives inside. "I hope this will be satisfactory."

The room was small but tastefully furnished, with a long table in the centre and a set of eight upright armchairs ranged around it, all in pale wood in a Scandinavian style. Abstract pictures with hints of a vaguely nautical theme adorned the walls. "This will do very nicely," approved Copper. "Thank you."

"And I will arrange for a tray of coffee and refreshments to be sent through to you. And please let me know if there is anything else I can do to assist our police in any way." Angelo positively bowed himself out of the door, leaving the detectives looking at one another with faintly amused expressions.

"Our manager seems to be falling over himself to be helpful," remarked Radley. "Guilty conscience about something, do you reckon, boss?"

Copper chuckled. "Nothing of the sort, I suspect. He's probably just eager to keep us out of sight, and to get rid of us as soon as possible. As he said, it doesn't look good for the hotel to have a bunch of flatfoots cluttering up the place making people uneasy. So let's take advantage, and get under way. We'd better make a start by tracking down the Butler brigade."

"Do you want to start with any one in particular, boss?"

"I suppose we'd better begin with Robin, as he's the most senior. Otherwise he'll only get on his high horse and start harrumphing about the place."

"Not sure how I'm going to spell 'harrumph' in my notes," grinned Radley, "but I'll make an effort. So shall I pop out to Reception and see if they can tell me where to find the gentleman?"

"Doubtless in the best room in the place," observed Copper. "Right, off you go."

Moments after the sergeant's departure, there came a tap at the door.

'That was quick,' thought the inspector, and opened the door to find a waiter pushing a trolley with a tray bearing a coffee pot and cups, together with a large covered platter which, on investigation, proved to contain a selection of exquisite and delicious-looking canapés. 'Somebody's pulling out all the stops,' mused Copper to himself as, eyebrows raised, he surveyed the provisions. And as he expressed his thanks and the waiter made to depart, Radley reappeared in the doorway.

"You were right, boss," he reported. "Robin Butler and his wife are ensconced in the penthouse suite on the top floor. Very smart, according to Lenka on Reception. Anyway, she's phoned him to come down – I could hear from the squawking on the phone that he wasn't best pleased – so I'm just off to meet him at the lifts. I'll try to

173

pour some oil on troubled waters before I bring him in."

"Don't worry too much about that," responded the inspector. "I don't mind my suspects a little off-balance. In fact, I prefer it."

A few moments later, Radley escorted the burly businessman into the room. "Here's Mr. Butler, sir," he announced brightly. "In fact, Mrs. Robin has come down with him, but I asked her if she wouldn't mind waiting for a few minutes while you have a quiet chat with her husband. I believe she's popped to the bar. I hope that's all right."

"Very good thinking, sergeant," nodded Copper, wearing his blandest smile. "And I expect I'll be wanting a few words with her anyway, so it could all turn out to be very convenient." He gestured to Robin to take a seat at the table, while placing himself at its head, Radley at his side.

"Convenient for whom, may I ask?" barked Robin. "Certainly not me or my wife. May I ask how long we are expected to remain here at your beck and call?"

"Until I have made satisfactory progress in identifying your father's murderer, sir," replied the inspector forthrightly. "I'm assuming that you would have some interest in assisting me with that."

"Well, yes, of course," said Robin, taken aback slightly at Copper's bluntness. "So, what is it you wanted to say?"

"It's rather more what I want to ask, Mr. Butler. Because since we first spoke, I've come into possession of various pieces of information, and I'd be glad of your take on them."

"Such as what?" asked Robin, puzzled.

"Initially, some snippets of conversation between you and your father which don't quite accord with the account of your relationship which you gave me when we first spoke."

174

"Snippets of conversation?" growled Robin. "What, you mean somebody has been eavesdropping on private discussions, and then come running to you with bits and pieces of tittle-tattle?"

"I prefer to think of it as additional pieces of evidence which help me to construct a fuller picture, sir," responded Copper. "And when this evidence comes to me from more than one source, I tend to take it seriously."

"And what is this precious 'evidence' of yours, inspector?" sneered Robin.

"Talk that your company may not be as secure financially as you might wish," replied the inspector calmly. "Now I'm aware that the business world is probably awash with rumours of various kinds, but when these rumours tend to point in the same direction, they would have more force, I imagine. So if such doubts were raised as to the standing of Butler Steels, the company on which your father based his fortune, then I can easily see that he might have an opinion on the matter."

"This is mad!" blustered Robin. "Every company you've ever heard of has gone through peaks and troughs. And every family you've ever heard of has had its ups and downs. If you think that gives me some sort of motive to murder my father, you plainly don't know what you're talking about. Dad delegated the running of Butler Steels to me, and that's it. End of. How I run the company is my business."

"Your business indeed," said Copper, unmoved by the other's outburst. "And of course, there is the additional question of the gambling element."

"Oh, all business is a gamble," retorted Robin dismissively. And as the inspector gazed steadily at him, he stopped and cleared his throat. "What … what are you getting at, man?"

"I'm referring to the sort of gambling which takes place in a casino, sir. Which, if my witness reports accurately, was not entirely to your father's liking. There was mention, I believe, of it 'taxing your finances'. Any comment on that?"

"Oh, this is absurd," said Robin. "Just because I may have dropped a few quid at the tables and Dad made some sort of comment, that makes me a murderer? What next? That I killed my father because he disapproved of my taste in ties?" He stood. "If you've got nothing better than that, inspector, I think this conversation is over." He turned and strode from the room, leaving the door swinging wide in his wake.

*

"Oof!" said Pete Radley after a few moments' silence. "Well, there goes one very unhappy bunny. Our Robin's not exactly one to take things calmly if he reckons he's under attack, is he? How do we think that plays out if he and Sir Lionel had some sort of face-off?"

"I think it's a straw in the wind," replied Dave Copper, "but not necessarily any more than that. Is he one of those empty vessels who make a lot of noise? There's always the possibility that he's all bluster and no action."

"And he has changed his story, hasn't he, boss?" pointed out Radley. "First off, he said everything was hunky-dory between all the family. Now he's as good as admitted that he and his father weren't seeing eye-to-eye. And when somebody changes their story, we tend to look at things a bit differently, don't we?"

"We do," agreed the inspector. "However, there is one thing standing in the way. We can't place Robin, or any of them, in the right place at the right time. I can't put anyone at the murder scene. They all seem to be accounted for."

"Hang on, boss. That's not quite right. Don't forget about Jessica nipping off the boat for her sneaky ciggy. We've seen the video that proves that she was out and about."

"True." Copper gathered his thoughts. "Well, we'll get to her later. In the meantime, you'd better go and haul Robin's wife out of the bar, before she either gets too sozzled to speak, or more likely, before Robin has the chance to get her hackles raised against us in tune with his."

Radley got to his feet. "On my way, boss."

Chapter 17

Dee Butler entered the makeshift interview room exuding an atmosphere of calm. Once again, her outfit spoke of stylish understatement, consisting of a black silk blouse with full sleeves, tight at the cuffs, above a pair of black culottes. A triple row of substantial pearls, which Copper guessed might well have cost him a large part of a year's salary, gleamed softly at her throat, and they were matched by pearl earrings glimpsed as her hair swung aside, while one wrist bore a heavy bracelet, gold underlying an abstract pattern of black and white enamel. Pete Radley softly closed the door behind her as she gently subsided into the chair opposite Dave Copper and placed a half-full champagne flute on the table between them.

"Soda water, inspector," she said with a half-smile, in response to the detective's slightly raised eyebrows. "Were you under the impression that I might have been spending my time in the bar drowning my share of the Butler family sorrows?"

"By no means, Mrs. Butler," said Copper. "Although I imagine that, at a time of stress, some people might find that a drink could help to relax them. But evidently not yourself."

"No need," responded Dee dismissively. "Even though I appear to be the current target of your round of cross-examinations. Well, please proceed." She leaned back in her chair and crossed her legs in a pose of almost studied elegance, showing a brief flash of red from the soles of her black patent shoes.

"I'd scarcely call it cross-examination, madam," countered Copper, making an effort to sound as non-confrontational as possible. "We aren't in a court of law. I was simply hoping that we might have a friendly chat to resolve one or two queries which have arisen during my conversations with other people."

"The same sort of friendly chat which has just seen my husband storming into the lift with a face like thunder?" enquired Dee, a small smile of derision on her face. "I wonder what you've been asking him to set him off like that?"

"If I dare say so, Mrs. Butler," remarked the inspector, "the relatively little which I have seen of your husband so far leads me to believe that he angers fairly easily."

"My husband may have an irascible nature at times," agreed Dee. "That proves nothing. The world of business is fraught with tense situations. Not least in circumstances like the present ones."

"Indeed. And thank you for bringing us back to the matter in hand. Because I have to look into any tensions which may have arisen between the members of your family which could have caused someone – perhaps someone with an irascible nature – to bring about your father-in-law's death."

"Where is this leading, inspector?" asked Dee wearily. "I was under the impression that you wanted to ask questions concerning myself, not delve into philosophical theorising."

"I'll come to the point then, madam," said Copper. "Let's talk about the relationship between yourself and Sir Lionel. Would you describe him as a man with an irascible nature?"

Dee paused for a moment before replying. "He occasionally had forthright opinions, if that's what you mean," she said guardedly.

"You'd seek to avoid his disapproval?"

"Naturally."

"So if someone were to hear Sir Lionel in heated conversation with you, during which it appears there was some mention of Butler Steels and the undesirability of such a topic appearing in unfavourable newspaper headlines, what would your response be?"

Dee seemed to be taken aback for a moment. "I really can't recall ..." she began uncertainly, but then broke off. She gave the impression of someone desperately trying to marshal their thoughts, before taking a deep breath. "I would say," she said slowly, "that my father-in-law would naturally be concerned if there were any question of adverse publicity regarding a company with which he had a deep personal connection." She assayed a smile. "Other than that, I can't bring to mind what the occasion may have been. And anyway, if it concerned my husband's company, perhaps you should be directing your enquiry to him." Her look sharpened. "Or have you already done so? Was this sort of impertinent question the thing that annoyed him? In any event, Robin's business is Robin's business. I have no input."

"Well then, we'll leave that aside for the moment," said Copper mildly.

"So, was that all?" Dee prepared to stand, and in an unconscious movement, made to push one side of her bobbed hair behind her ear. As she did so, she let out a brief hiss of discomfort, as a strand of hair appeared to get caught in the catch of her bracelet, before she was able to disentangle it.

"Are you all right, Mrs. Butler?" enquired Copper.

"Perfectly fine," said Dee, and made to stand once again.

"That's a very impressive piece of jewellery," remarked the inspector. "I hope you haven't damaged it."

"Not at all," replied Dee shortly.

"May I see?" Copper held out a hand and Dee, with some reluctance, extended her wrist. "Hmmm – very stylish. I imagine my wife would be very envious of you." Dee regarded the inspector in silence. "And actually, that

180

reminds me of another little mystery which somebody mentioned to me. Oh, probably nothing at all to do with the case, but it just left one of your crew puzzled." Copper paused.

"How so?" asked Dee eventually, almost against her will.

"It was a small incident while you were in Guernsey," explained Copper. "Apparently you had been visiting a jeweller's shop, and after you left, the shopkeeper came out as if he was looking for you. One of your boat's crew was across the road, and he happened to notice you. But you had gone on your way, and the shopkeeper went back inside. According to my witness, the chap seemed upset in some way, so he went across to see if he could help, but he was assured that it was nothing. He was just a little puzzled, that's all."

"Oh, that!" Dee let out a light laugh. "Oh yes, I remember now. I went into a shop to look at one or two pieces that had caught my eye in the window, but eventually I decided that they weren't quite right for me. This was after the shop owner had tried to persuade me by offering me quite a substantial discount off the price, but I still said no. I expect he had second thoughts, and wanted to chase after me to offer me an even lower price. That must have been it. I dare say he was upset because he'd lost a sale."

"That must have been it," nodded Copper. "Another mystery solved. Well, I shan't keep you any longer, Mrs. Butler. Oh, except for one thing," he added, as Dee got to her feet and turned towards the door. "Can you just verify a small matter for me please. After you and your husband returned to *Red Buccaneer* after your meal at the yacht club on Sunday night, I just want to be certain that you didn't leave your cabin."

"No, I didn't."

Copper's attention was instantly alerted. "You say

'I'. What about your husband?"

"No. I mean ..."

"Yes?"

"Robin did go through to get a drink. Said he couldn't sleep, or some such feeble excuse."

"Really?" The inspector regarded Dee intently. "And what time would this have been?"

Dee shrugged. "I really can't be sure, inspector. Some time after we'd got into bed, obviously. Maybe some time around midnight. I wasn't paying that much attention." She sounded profoundly uninterested. "I was probably half-asleep myself."

"And can you recall how long your husband was absent from your cabin?"

"Not really," replied Dee with a shake of the head, but then appeared to rethink her answer. "Actually, I do remember now, because I was rather annoyed that he'd disturbed me just as I was relaxing. And I just wanted to get to sleep and forget all about ..." She broke off.

"About what?"

There was a pause. "Oh ... just about getting back to the daily grind after a lovely week's break," said Dee, with a guileless smile. "So, thinking about it, I suppose Robin must have been gone for about twenty minutes or so. I'm afraid I wasn't looking at the clock, inspector. Why? Is it important?"

"Oh, just trying to get a couple of things clear in my mind," said Copper. "But I think that will just about do for now."

"Good," said Dee. She stepped towards the door. "In that case, I shall go and find my husband. Perhaps I can manage to soothe those feathers you appear to have ruffled." With a patronising nod of the head to Radley as she passed, she swept from the room.

*

"Well, there's a turn-up, boss," remarked Pete

182

Radley, as he reached into his pocket and scribbled a brief entry in his notebook. "Two alibis potted with a single shot."

"You're right, sergeant," said Dave Copper, a hint of frustration in his voice. "And I'm not absolutely certain whether that's a good thing or a bad. It certainly gives us two more people with opportunity to carry out the crime."

"And spot on in the time window that Sooz gave us," agreed Radley.

"So that just leaves us to sort out motives. And if there isn't something amongst all the tales we've been told from various sources, I shall be very surprised. This will take some thinking about."

"What, now, boss? Do you want me to shove off and leave you to do the eyes-closed thing?"

Copper chuckled. "Not yet. We still have people to talk to. For a start, the other couple who can't be ruled out because of absence of alibi."

"Tyrone and Jessica, you mean?"

"I do. Do you want to pop out to your new friend in Reception and see if she's got any information as to where the golden couple may be."

"On it, boss." After only a few moments' absence, Radley returned with a broad grin on his face. "Guess what, boss. Wouldn't you know it? The lovely Jessica is enjoying the facilities of the hotel spa. Seems she felt in need of a pampering session. Reception gave her and her husband pass cards for the door about half an hour ago."

"In which case, I dare say we shall need the same."

"Ahead of you, boss." Radley brandished a credit-card-sized piece of plastic. "Lenka's a very helpful girl. And the entrance is just down at the end of this corridor."

"Then lead the way."

As the detectives entered the spa area, they were greeted by a gust of warm moist air, with a faint odour of chlorine mingled with lavender.

"Can I help you, gentlemen?" enquired the singlet-clad young man behind the reception desk.

Copper flashed his warrant card. "We're looking for Mr. and Mrs. Tyrone Butler. I understand that they're somewhere on your premises."

The receptionist consulted a computer monitor on the desk. "That's right, sir. Mrs. Butler had an appointment with one of our nail technicians ... oh no, she's finished that. So I believe she may be in our pool area. And Mr. Butler was in the gym the last time I saw him. Would you like me to fetch them?"

"No. I think we'll probably manage to track them down for ourselves," replied Copper. "Ladies first, I think. Perhaps you could point us in the direction of the pool." And in response to the receptionist's indication, the detectives made their way through a door, to be met by an even warmer and more humid atmosphere. And to one side of the gently-rippling pool, solitary on a padded lounger, wearing a bikini under a light chiffon wrap, lay Jessica Butler, eyes closed as she appeared to be listening to the soundtrack of soft whale-song emitted by the speakers in the ceiling.

At the sound of approaching footsteps Jessica, without opening her eyes, waved a languid hand towards an empty tumbler on the low table next to her. "Can you bring me another Sunrise Whatever-it-is," she murmured in her high-pitched voice.

Copper cleared his throat. "I'm afraid our duties do not include the provision of refreshments."

Jessica's eyes jerked open in surprise and, with the realisation of who her visitors were, she struggled rather inelegantly into a seated position. "Inspector! You made me jump. What are you doing here?"

"We're sorry to disturb you, Mrs. Butler," apologised Copper, "but we needed a further word. I hope that's not inconvenient." His tone made it clear that the model's convenience was the furthest thing from his mind. He turned to Radley. "Sergeant, perhaps you'd like to help the lady adjust the back of her bed. I'm sure she can't be comfortable sitting hunched like that." And as his junior colleague moved to alter the position of Jessica's lounger, the inspector pulled forward an upright chair from an adjacent table. "And I can just sit here, and then you won't need to move." The necessary arrangements completed, Copper sat and leaned forward, a friendly expression on his face, while Radley took a seat in the background.

"What is it you want?" asked Jessica uncertainly, evidently not reassured by the detective's demeanour.

"We're just trying to clear up a few details," responded Copper. "We've been chatting to people, and there are one or two things I'd like to clarify. Like, for instance, your precise relationship with Sir Lionel Butler."

The colour flooded Jessica's cheeks. "I ... I don't know what you mean. He was Ty's father."

"Yes, we're aware that Sir Lionel was your father-in-law," responded Copper gently. "I didn't mean that kind of relationship. I meant, how were relations between you and the gentleman? Would you describe them as, for instance, friendly?"

"Of course they were," replied Jessica. "He was ... he was always very nice to me."

'And that's something that's open to a variety of interpretations', thought Copper to himself, before choosing to leave the thought aside for the moment. "So there were never any tensions between the two of you? No arguments at all? Confrontations?"

"Why should there be?" said Jessica, now seeming more in command of herself.

"Now that's odd," said the inspector. "Because

185

we've had an account of an incident between yourself and Sir Lionel which sounded anything but non-confrontational. Can you recall what that might be?"

Jessica shook her head. "I don't understand."

"Perhaps it's slipped your mind," smiled Copper. "Let me refresh your memory. Do you recall a visit to the Dior Museum in France?" He turned his head. "Sergeant, remind me. Where and when would that have been?"

Radley flipped though the pages of his notebook. "That was in Granville, sir. On the Thursday. The day before St. Malo, and Guernsey was the day after that."

"So, almost a week ago," resumed Copper. "And after all the excitement since you returned, no wonder your memory is a little hazy. But it sounded as if it was quite the little spat. There seems to have been talk of secrets and betrayal. There were references to the past. I'm wondering if you'd like to tell me what that was all about."

"I ... I ..." Jessica was lost for words for several long seconds, before she managed to pull herself together. "Oh, I remember what it was," she declared bravely. "It was all about my modelling."

"Really?" The inspector frowned, puzzled. "In what way?"

"You see, what happened was," said Jessica, now getting more comfortably into her stride, "we were looking at all the fashions in the museum, and it reminded me of some of the girls I used to work with ... I mean, you know, model with. And a couple of them live in Jersey now, and I was saying it was a shame that we weren't going to visit them. But Lionel, he said that he'd heard enough stories about what some girls got up to, and he hoped I wasn't in with that group, because he didn't want me getting mixed up with that sort of thing. That was all." She gave a bright innocent smile.

"Secrets? Betrayal?" queried Copper. "How does

that tie in?"

"Oh, you always get affairs and divorces," said Jessica airily. "I expect that's what he meant. But I don't see those girls any more," she declared firmly.

"Ah." Copper elected to move on to another point. "So perhaps that all links up with something else that someone heard. This would have been when you were speaking with Mr. Robin Butler."

"I don't like to talk to him much," muttered Jessica.

"I can see why," sympathised Copper, "if the conversation which has been reported to us is typical. He sounded very critical of your career."

"He looks down on me."

"And disapproves of some of the people you used to know, by all accounts. In fact, didn't he threaten to go to Sir Lionel and your husband with some sort of tales of people you'd previously been connected with? What sort of tales were these, I wonder?"

"It's all nonsense," insisted Jessica, beginning to sound tearful. "I've done nothing wrong since I married Ty, and he can't prove that I did. And what's this all about anyway? Aren't you supposed to be trying to find out who killed Lionel? If what you think is right, shouldn't you be asking whether I had any reason to kill Robin? Which I haven't, however horrible he may be. I haven't done anything. So why don't you just go away and leave me alone?" She turned and fumbled with the supports for the back of her lounger, eventually succeeding in releasing it with a bang and settling back, eyes defiantly closed.

Chapter 18

"Well, that was a bit of a turnaround, wasn't it, boss?" remarked Pete Radley, as the detectives stood once more in the corridor outside the pool area. "Calm as you please when she thinks you're a waiter all set to bring her another drink, but point a few questions at her, and she's jumpy as a cat. What do you reckon all that was about? Guilty conscience?"

Dave Copper frowned. "Certainly something unsettled her. Talk about secrets from the past was clearly not at all to her liking. She was evasive, to say the least."

"Do you buy that explanation of hers about when Sir Lionel had a go at her in the Dior museum?"

"Not for a moment. There's no way that it accords with what Felicity Witcher described to us as the young lady's reaction. No, there's definitely something else, and I've got an odd itch just round the corner in my brain, but I can't quite focus on it. Something in her choice of words. Or maybe something someone else said to her." The inspector shook his head slightly. "Don't worry. It'll come to me eventually."

"In the meantime, boss, there's always the loving husband," pointed out Radley. "In the gym, wherever that is."

As if to answer his question, a loud metallic clank was audible from a door a little further down on the opposite side of the corridor. "Unless all my deductive skills have deserted me, I think that sounds like gym equipment," smiled Copper. "Let's investigate." He pushed open the door.

Tyrone Butler was seated on the bench of a formidable-looking piece of ironmongery, his arms stretched above his head as they pulled down a horizontal bar attached by cables to an impressive stack of weights. The close-fitting singlet he wore above a loose pair of jogging bottoms displayed a wiry but muscular physique. He flicked a glance towards the newcomers, registering their identity before unhurriedly completing his manoeuvre and lowering the weights to their resting place in a smooth and controlled movement, accompanied by a measured exhalation. He leaned down to pick up a towel from the floor alongside him, before wiping his face with it and swinging round to face the detectives. "Were you looking for me?" he enquired.

"I apologise for interrupting you in the middle of your training session, Mr. Butler," began Copper, "but we need to have a few words."

"Why not?" responded Tyrone unconcernedly. "Since you have us waiting around for no particular reason that I can see, I was just killing time putting in some weight training." He smiled. "I expect my team manager would give me some brownie points for actually doing something under my own initiative, instead of him having to badger me."

"I'd never really thought about it," admitted Copper, "but I imagine you must need to be quite physically fit to do your job. The strain of steering a car round a track, at speeds which would frankly terrify me, must take it out of you."

Tyrone shrugged. "It's all part of the buzz. And worth it when you win."

"Ah, now that reminds me about one of the things I wanted to speak to you about," said the inspector smoothly, seating himself on the bench of one of the gym's other machines. "Your record on the track. Because I've heard that, in some quarters, there has been some surprise that your results have been seen as something of a disappointment. Especially to your late father."

Tyrone sat up a little straighter, his brow creased

as if in puzzlement. "I don't follow you, inspector."

"That's the thing, Mr. Butler," said Copper. "I believe, from what I've heard, that Sir Lionel wasn't best pleased that you were following another driver over the finishing line a little too often, rather than being the first across. In fact, I've heard that he taxed you with it. It sounds as if he thought that perhaps his investment in your team wasn't well-placed. I think he asked, only a few days ago, if his money wasn't good enough for you."

Tyrone cleared his throat. "He may have said something of the sort. I really can't remember. But anybody would know that you can't buy race wins. There are too many things that can go wrong." He regarded the inspector with a touch of defiance in his eyes.

"Indeed. And I suppose it's entirely plausible that one or other of these things may have gone wrong during your recent races. For instance, one when the victory went unexpectedly to one of your close rivals. I don't follow motor racing myself, but wasn't it someone by the name of Von Staffen?" Copper turned to Radley. "Help me out, sergeant. I think that's right, isn't it?"

"I think it is, boss," replied his junior stolidly, a faint hint of a smile on his lips.

"Now that, Mr. Butler, is something of an odd coincidence."

"I don't know what you mean. What coincidence are you talking about?" There was unease evident in Tyrone's voice.

"The fact that, according to one of my witnesses, you actually encountered someone by the name of Von Staffen during your visit to Guernsey," stated Copper. "A German gentleman, I'm told."

"But who could have ...?" Tyrone tailed off before, after a pause which lasted far too long, giving an unconvincing laugh. "Oh, that!"

"Yes, that," said Copper implacably. "Perhaps you'd

like to tell me about that."

"Oh, it was nothing really," said Tyrone. "Just surprising. You see, I'd gone up to take a look at some old Nazi bunker above the beach where Jezza and I were spending some time, and this German guy appeared. And he happened to be my friend Miko Von Staffen's grandfather, would you believe? Turns out he was off the German cruise ship in the harbour, and he'd had the same thought as me and wanted to look over the old wartime relics. He recognised me, and we had a few words, and then he left. Was that what you meant?"

"It's certainly a very surprising story," remarked Copper, giving nothing away. "I'm sure not a lot of people would believe such an odd chance would occur. And of course, not all the information we receive from witnesses is one hundred percent accurate."

"So who ...?" began Tyrone, before biting off the question.

"So I think that will probably do for now, Mr. Butler," said Copper, rising. "I think you've given me plenty to think about, but now I'd better move on. I still have some of your relations to speak to, so we'll leave you to get on with your training session." He made his way back out into the corridor, Radley close behind him, leaving Tyrone sitting motionless, a look of apprehension in his eyes.

*

"So," said Dave Copper, seating himself once more behind the table in the small conference room, "where do you think we might find the last two of our ..." He paused with a chuckle. "What do you suppose the collective noun is for a group of Butlers?"

"Maybe a service, boss?" hazarded Pete Radley with a grin. "Or perhaps even a grovel?"

"Hmmm," retorted Copper. "Not a great deal of grovelling going on amongst this lot. Not to us, at least.

Anyway, let's go back to the old tried and tested. Nip out and ask your helpful friend in Reception if she can track down one or other of the Leo Butlers. In fact, let's start with Leo himself."

"Here we go again," murmured Radley, as he left the room, only to return a few moments later. "No mystery, boss. He was up in his room. Lenka's passed on the request for him to come down, and she's going to point him in our direction."

"You'd better hover in the corridor," instructed his superior, and within a minute or two, Radley was ushering Leo Butler into the room and holding the chair for him in silent invitation. Even dressed casually in an open-necked shirt and light corduroy trousers, the barrister managed to exude an air of courtroom formality. But as Leo took his place, the inspector couldn't help noticing that the confident good looks of the previous day were somewhat marred by dark circles under the eyes and a rather grim set to the mouth.

"Thank you for sparing the time to come and talk to me," began Copper.

"Did I have much choice?" retorted Leo grumpily. "Isn't it considered some sort of negative indication in our profession if a suspect refuses to talk to the police? Because you are viewing me as a suspect, aren't you?"

"One of several, Mr. Butler," replied Copper, surprised at the barrister's belligerence, and noting that the interviewee was seeking to place himself on the side of the angels. "But you needn't read anything particular into that. Certainly not before we've had a chance for a little chat. There are some queries which I hope you can help me resolve."

"Look, is this going to take long, inspector?" queried Leo. "Because I was sort of in the middle of something. In case you've forgotten, I'm in the throes of a court case, which you seem to have done your best to throw into disarray with these enquiries of yours. And I'm still trying to marshal my arguments from a whole lot of contradictory information, which I'd just finished spreading out all over the table in our suite upstairs when your summons came. And my wife had abandoned me to get on with it in peace, so I'd like to get back to it as soon as possible."

"Oh, I quite understand, Mr. Butler," sympathised Copper. "And I'm sorry if this investigation is disrupting your preparations. After all, we wouldn't want you to run the risk of losing any evidence, would we? At any cost?" He directed a meaningful look at the other.

Leo suddenly became very still. "I ... er ... I don't quite see what you're getting at, inspector."

"I'm just remembering what someone told me they heard you say during the course of a telephone conversation last week. Of course, I'm sure they didn't mean to eavesdrop, but you know how these things can happen when people are in close proximity."

"I suppose so," said Leo uneasily. "But I still don't understand what you're saying."

"I believe the call was from someone you were arranging to meet in Guernsey, Mr. Butler?"

"Was it? I'm not sure I recall ..."

"Let me see if I can jog your memory, sir," persisted Copper. "Because the gist of the conversation was that, if a certain piece of evidence were to be lost, it would cost a great deal. Of course, I have no idea what evidence that would refer to."

Leo screwed up his features as if trying to remember. Eventually, his expression cleared. "Of course!" He snapped his fingers and gave a light laugh which did not sound wholly convincing. "I can't think why I didn't twig straight away. Yes, that call. It was quite funny really. It came totally out of the blue. You see, an old contact of mine had seen reports about one of my

193

cases, and he just called up to offer his thoughts on the matter. And the whole thing hinged on a particular piece of evidence, and if that hadn't been presented correctly, the case would have gone completely awry. That would have resulted in some hefty court costs, all to no avail. Yes, that's what it was."

"And you met up with this caller?"

"Well," said Leo, "it's always good to touch base with old chums, isn't it?"

"You seem to have had quite a hectic time on Guernsey, don't you, sir?" observed Copper. "And the other conversation I've had reported to me doesn't sound as if it was quite so relaxed."

"Really?" Leo wore an intrigued expression. "You seem to be relying a great deal on hearsay, inspector. We tend not to do that too much in the courtroom," he added, with a touch of derision in his tone.

Copper refused to be nettled. "You were heard talking to your father, Mr. Butler," he said, "and the tenor of the conversation doesn't sound as if it was entirely friendly. In fact, Sir Lionel seems to have been taking you to task for some kind of failure on your part. And from what I've been told of Sir Lionel, he didn't view failure too kindly."

"And what kind of failure is this supposed to be, inspector?" demanded Leo. "Because I'm sure I don't need to tell you, losing the occasional criminal case in court is one of the hazards of my job. One has to take it on the chin."

"But why, I wonder," returned the inspector, "would that have occasioned a mention of your sister-in-law, Mrs. Desdemona Butler? Or rather, your former colleague under her maiden name, Miss Fender? Because when she was practising, she wasn't a criminal lawyer, was she? I gather her expertise lies more in the field of commercial law, perhaps dealing with more financial

194

matters. So why would her skills have been needed to 'extricate' you from a certain situation? Because that's how your father put it. So how, I ask myself, could there possibly be a link between the loss of a court case and the question of money? And what aspect of that would make Sir Lionel so hot under the collar?"

The barrister gazed silently at Copper for several long seconds. "Are you seriously attempting to put together a case against me, based on the fact that I may have had failures in court which led to such a bad atmosphere between my father and myself that I would wish to kill him?" he challenged. "On what you seem to be calling evidence, which is so flimsy that it would be laughed at by any self-respecting judge? If you want to talk about failures," he continued, growing more vehement, "I hope you're not forgetting to look in the direction of my brothers. Give a thought to Rob, with his thriving company which he seems to be managing to screw up, if what Dad said over dinner on Sunday is anything to go by. And while you're at it, take a glance at Tyrone, who's managing to lose races in a spectacular fashion, despite the ridiculous amount of Dad's money having been spent on that cack-handed revamp of all his cockpit controls. Just imagine how pleased my father was about that!"

"I'm simply considering the material which has come into my possession, sir," replied Copper calmly. "And if things can't be accounted for plausibly, then other conclusions may need to be drawn."

"Thank you for the seminar on the assessment of evidence, inspector," said Leo caustically, getting to his feet. "I shall be sure to bear everything you've said in mind during my review of the evidence in my current case. Which, may I remind you, continues to occupy my thoughts, so if you will excuse me, I think I shall go back to my suite and attempt to use my time more productively. Some of us have a living to earn." He turned and stalked from the room.

*

"Miaow!" grinned Pete Radley, as Leo's footsteps died away along the corridor. "Saucer of milk for our barrister friend. Do you reckon that's what he does in court, boss? Turn the attack back on his attacker? Or divert it away to other targets?"

"If there's one thing I've learned about barristers during the course of my career," replied Dave Copper with an answering dry smile, "it's that the more talented ones are very good at thinking on their feet. Especially when their backs are against the wall." He stopped and frowned. "If that's not too mixed a metaphor."

"So he's still in your sights?"

"More firmly than ever. When someone avoids answering a question, however craftily they try to do so, it only makes me think that the question is all the more important."

"So just the final Mrs. Butler to go?"

"Correct. I wonder where Cordelia went when she abandoned her husband."

"Let me go and see if Lenka has any suggestions." Radley trotted from the room, and mere seconds later his head appeared around the doorpost. "No need to ask, boss. She's sitting in some sort of conservatory lounge off the hotel foyer. And there doesn't seem to be anyone else around, so should we go and talk to her there?"

"Why not?" Copper rose. "This room isn't exactly luxurious."

"Although I quite approve of the nibbles," smiled Radley, grabbing a couple of the canapés and stuffing them into his mouth as he followed his superior in the direction of Reception.

Chapter 19

Cordelia Butler was seated on a thickly-cushioned wicker sofa, an open copy of a country- living magazine lying disregarded in her lap as she gazed unfocussed through the panes of the hotel's Garden Lounge in the direction of the moored *Red Buccaneer* outside in the marina. She looked up at the approach of the detectives, pulled the light cardigan she wore over a long flower-print summer dress a little more closely around her, and sat up a touch straighter. "So, the inquisition seems to have arrived at my door," she said, with a thin smile, laying aside the magazine.

"I'd hardly call it an inquisition," replied Copper mildly. "We're simply asking a few friendly questions."

"Not quite so friendly," observed Cordelia, "if my husband's reaction is anything to go by. Didn't I just see him go steaming past and into the lifts a few minutes ago? And to judge by the look on his face, 'steaming' is the appropriate word. Have you been accusing him of dastardly crimes?"

"I will admit that some of our enquiries weren't exactly to Mr. Butler's liking," admitted Copper. "Not that he was alone in that," he added. "But, as yet, nobody has been accused of anything specific. I'm still seeking clarification on certain items of information which have come my way."

"Well then, inspector, you'd better sit down and seek your clarification, hadn't you?" Cordelia waved towards the chairs flanking her sofa, and the detectives accepted her suggestion and sat. "Although I suppose you're not going to be forthcoming in the opposite direction and tell me what it was you said that Leo took exception to."

"Actually, Mrs. Butler, I believe I can do just that. In so far as there could be a plausible motive for Sir Lionel's murder contained within it."

"Oh?" Cordelia's eyebrows rose in enquiry.

"Indeed. Because it was all about the question of your husband's competence. Someone, I'd rather not say who, had heard a conversation between father and son, in which Sir Lionel had raised the question of how it was that Mr. Leo had contrived to lose in a number of important court cases. The charge of incompetence was levelled. Now the thing is, an entirely different witness had also heard Sir Lionel voice similar sentiments to yourself. And it's not beyond the realms of possibility to think that a loyal wife, in defence of her husband, might harbour a resentment against the accuser. Such a resentment might fester. It could lead to a confrontation. And during that confrontation, violence could occur."

Cordelia burst out laughing. "That really is one of the most far-fetched pieces of invention I've ever heard, inspector. You might just as well say that Dee or Jessica crept out in the middle of the night to murder Lionel because of what he said over dinner."

"And what did he say?" pounced the inspector.

The laughter was stilled abruptly as Cordelia was brought up short. "Hints, inspector. Hints. He went on about 'information received from certain sources', as if he had his own private army of investigators out there somewhere."

'I'm not too sure that he didn't,' thought Copper to himself.

"But everybody was a target," continued Cordelia. "Dee and her extravagance. Jessica and her dim-wittedness, although lord knows he didn't seem to mind that too much when the two of them were sitting together in that blasted hot tub of his, sipping champagne while she giggled at his least remark. If anybody was dim-witted, it was Tyrone for not seeing what was going on. And then there was the special venom reserved for Robin, the chief let-down, being the eldest son from whom Lionel expected so much. He kept talking about things that people thought were secrets, except that they weren't, but he wouldn't elaborate. So please don't think that Leo and I were the only ones to experience the rough edge of his tongue, because we were not."

"Except, of course, that none of you left your cabins during the period when Sir Lionel died," remarked Copper guilelessly.

"Who knows what the others were doing?" returned Cordelia. "And surely Leo wouldn't ..."

"Surely Leo wouldn't what?" asked the inspector sharply.

"He ... he was only gone a few minutes," said Cordelia haltingly.

"Gone where? And why?" insisted Copper.

"I was sure I'd heard something. It sounded as if there was somebody moving about on the deck above us. We'd only just put the light out."

"And this was when exactly?"

"Exactly?" Cordelia put her hand to her brow. "I couldn't say, inspector. About midnight, perhaps. I really wasn't in the mood to make a note. I was just ... well, frightened."

"Frightened?"

"Yes. I thought there might be an intruder on the boat. So I got Leo to go up and have a look. And when he came back, he said he'd been up to the wheelhouse to look, but there was nobody. Although he did say that the gate to the pontoon was open, which worried me even more. I could hardly get to sleep after that."

"And do you remember how long your husband was absent from your cabin?"

Cordelia thought. "It can't have been more than ten minutes. But he seemed very calm when he came back.

Reassuring. He said that now there was nothing to worry about, so we got back into bed."

"I see," mused Copper. He paused in reflection for a few moments. "Well then, there's just one thing I'd like to sort out in my mind, and that's an incident which occurred in Guernsey. It seemed to unsettle you."

"Guernsey?" Cordelia frowned. "I don't remember anything in particular. Other than the fact that the gardens I went to see turned out to be a total disappointment."

"No, this was before you even got to your destination, according to what I've been told," clarified Copper. "In fact, the incident happened just as you were coming ashore."

"I don't ..."

"Apparently there was a group of tourists landing on the quay from the cruise ship which was visiting the island at the same time as you. And one of the ladies, a New Zealander by all accounts, was heard to exclaim delightedly that she knew you, or rather, knew your mother-in-law from back home. And you, I gather, vehemently denied the suggestion. I hear that you virtually fled. It all seems a little odd to me."

"Oh, I remember now," said Cordelia with a feeble smile, after a brief moment when her face went totally blank, apart from a sideways flick of the eyes. "It happens sometimes. People come up to me and try to scrape acquaintance because they recognise my face from some magazine feature or other. And I was in something of a hurry, so I think I said she must be mistaking me for somebody else, and I managed to escape."

"And the remark about your mother-in-law? As far as we know, *Red Buccaneer* has never ventured that far. "

Cordelia, now calmer, shrugged. "How would I know? Why don't you quiz Sylvia about where she's been? She's a wealthy woman – surely there's no reason why she shouldn't have been to New Zealand. They do have planes, you know."

"Perhaps I'll do that," replied Copper comfortably. He rose to his feet. "Thank you for your time, Mrs. Butler. I'm sure that what you've told me will be very helpful. So the sergeant and I will get on, and leave you to continue reading your magazine. Or whatever it was that was occupying you. And perhaps we will speak again later." Without a backward glance, he headed back towards the hotel foyer with Radley, after a nod of farewell to Cordelia, in his wake.

*

Back in the interview room, Pete Radley threw himself untidily into one of the chairs, while Dave Copper prowled the room restlessly.

At length, the sergeant spoke up. "So what's the plan now, boss?" he enquired.

"Not sure," replied the inspector absently, before coming back to himself. "Sorry, Peter," he said. "Thoughts whirling around in my head at the moment. There are some answers in there, but I just need to get them into focus." He seated himself alongside his colleague. "It will probably help if I plough through all your notes from this morning. I assume you've got them written up?"

Radley looked slightly guilty. "Well, some of them, boss. But the problem was, I got a bit distracted when everybody started shooting their own alibis in the foot, so they're probably not as tidy as you'd wish." He grimaced. "Sorry."

"Right." Copper seemed to make a decision. "Then what is going to happen is this. You will stay here and complete your notes in your finest copperplate, to enable me to read them through without needing to screw my eyes up with the effort ..."

"Here, hang on, boss ..." Radley started to protest.

Copper chuckled. "Yes, I know. Your writing is

201

considerably tidier than mine ever was. D.I. Constable was always complaining that he could never decipher my drunken spider scrawl. Yours is immaculate by comparison. So, while you stay here and get on with that, I intend to go and have a mooch around our scene of crime."

"What's this then, boss?" grinned Radley. "Getting a feel for the '*locus in quo*'?"

The inspector gave an answering smile. "I see your training hasn't been totally wasted. Or is it that you've spent so much time in the last couple of days in the company of current and erstwhile lawyers, the Latin is starting to rub off? Whichever it is, you're absolutely right. I want to sort out a few of the mechanics of how this murder could have been carried out. Who could be where, and so on."

"The missing opportunity factor, eh?" said Radley. "Having no problem identifying the means, and with probably more motives than enough, once I've compiled my little dossier, you reckon you can weed out some of the family that way?" He grinned. "Well, good luck with that, boss. With that maze of rat-runs on that boat, I reckon anyone could be anywhere."

"Let's hope you're wrong," said Copper. "I shall have to pop across to see his lordship at the yacht club to get the gate passcode, so when you've finished your little exercise, why don't you come and find me on board, and we'll see if we can make any progress."

"Will do, boss." Radley settled to his task, as the inspector headed out of the hotel and strode in the direction of the Porthampton Ocean Racing Club building.

Red Buccaneer lay silent and oddly forlorn-looking, darkened except for the solitary light still burning in the wheelhouse. As Copper swung himself aboard, the slight noise he engendered brought a head popping out of the wheelhouse door in enquiry.

"Oh, it's you, inspector," was Bob de Waters' unsurprised greeting. "I wondered when you'd be back. Did you want me?"

"No, no need to disturb yourself, captain," replied Copper from the top of the gangway, as he looked up towards the yacht's skipper on the deck above. "I've just come to take another look around in order to get some thoughts straight, now that I've had a chance to speak further to the members of Sir Lionel's family."

"Anything I can help you with?"

"Not really. I need to familiarise myself a little more with your boat's layout. A question of how a person can get from one place to another. I can't think it'll take me long."

"Well, if you're sure. Mind you, you're going to need some light if you're poking about down below. We don't want you clouting your head or breaking a leg falling down a companionway, do we?"

"We do not, captain," smiled Copper in agreement. 'One severe clout on the head is quite enough to be going on with in this investigation,' he thought to himself.

"Hold on then, inspector. Leave it with me." Bob disappeared back into the wheelhouse, and a few seconds later, *Red Buccaneer* was transformed into the glamorous lady she was built to be, a brightly-lit floating palace, gleaming with reflections from glass, chrome, and polished wood in all corners. "How's that, inspector?" he called.

"Perfect, Mr. de Waters. Now ..." Copper glanced around him. "What's the quickest way up to where you are?"

Bob re-emerged. "Just pop straight up." And in response to Copper's slightly puzzled look, he continued, "See those recessed footholds in the cabin wall right in front of you? And the handrails alongside? Just shin up

203

there. Shortcut for the crew," he explained, as the inspector followed the suggestion and clambered up to the wheelhouse level. "It saves the crew from needing to go through the guest quarters to move around. Like the servants' stairs in a posh old house. It means the rich people don't have to look at the lower classes." He chuckled. "Not that there was anything like that with Sir. He was always the model of courtesy with his crew. Although you wouldn't be able to say the same with his family sometimes," he added.

"I'm learning something of the sort," said Copper drily. "By the way, how are your fellow crew-members?"

"Oh, they're bearing up, sir," said Bob. "Trey phoned me – he's been raiding my freezer and cooking for them all, so they're fine. Worried, of course. They're wondering what's going to happen, just like me."

"Well, captain," responded Copper, "I hope I won't have to keep you all waiting too long. My sergeant and I have been having some quite illuminating conversations, and he's tidying up his evidence notes as we speak. In fact, I expect him to be joining me shortly, but in the meantime, I'd like to take a look around."

Bob made an expansive gesture. "Help yourself, inspector. The boat's yours."

"Anywhere locked that I'm going to need keys for?"

"No, sir. Go anywhere you like. Like they say, *'Mi casa, su casa'*. Or in this case, *'Mi barco, su barco'*. We don't fuss too much about security once we're on *Buck*, because we make sure nobody gets aboard that isn't supposed to." He laughed. "I just growl in my best old sea-dog fashion at anyone who comes too close, and they soon clear off."

"Good to know," said Copper with an answering laugh. "Right. I must get on. May I call you if I need you?"

"Sure. I'm not going anywhere."

"But first, can I just check where everyone's cabin

was."

"Sir's suite was on this deck, but you already know that, don't you, inspector?" A nod. "And then one deck down, just under where we are now, that's the main guest suite where Mr. and Mrs. Robin were. Then you go down again, and you've got the other two guest cabins for Mr. and Mrs. Leo and Mr. and Mrs. Tyrone. And me and the other crew, we've got cubbyholes down in the bilges. With the rats." A chuckle.

"I'm sure no rat would dare to set paw aboard your boat, captain," smiled Copper. "So I'll start with Sir Lionel's own accommodation. Which is straight through here, isn't it?" A nod from the captain confirmed the inspector's statement, and Copper made his way from the wheelhouse, across the small lobby at the top of the stairs, and into the owner's suite. He looked around. Nothing seemed out of place – the room looked exactly as it had when the detectives had first entered it to interview Taff. And on the assumption that nobody else had entered the suite since the discovery of the body, mused Copper, it surely meant that Sir Lionel had, on his return to the yacht, neatly put his clothes away prior to changing into swimwear for his late-night session in the hot tub. Evidently a man of tidy habits, reflected the inspector. Not somebody who would lightly disregard something out of order. Such as misbehaviour amongst the members of his family.

Copper stepped through on to the open deck at the after end of the suite, overlooking the open deck below, where the hot tub was located. And now he noticed a set of steps, similar to those by which he had ascended to the wheelhouse, which gave access to the deck below. Which meant, he concluded, that Sir Lionel could have reached the hot tub from his suite without the need to pass through the yacht's saloon. Was that significant?

The inspector carefully made his way down the

steps to stand alongside the tub for a moment, before carrying on through the saloon to the forward end of the main deck, where the cabin occupied by Robin and Desdemona was located. So, from here, the access to the rear deck was quick and easy. Robin would have had no difficulty in reaching his father's location, should he wish to during that absence from the cabin which Dee had mentioned. Equally, if Robin had indeed gone to the bar for a drink at that point, Dee could easily have descended one deck and passed through one of the crew passages unobserved to get to the hot tub at the stern. Neither person could be ruled out. The opportunity was there for each.

With a sigh of frustration, Copper descended the staircase to the lower deck. Again, after what he and Radley had learned about the layout of *Red Buccaneer*, there was an easy route to the main deck from both cabins. If Jessica had gone ashore as she claimed, she could have gone via the main deck for whatever reason, and there encountered Sir Lionel. By the same token, Tyrone could have taken advantage of her absence and made his way to the hot tub's location, either directly or through one of the crew passages. And in similar fashion, if Leo had indeed gone up to the wheelhouse to check for the supposed intruder, he could have passed via the hot tub on the way, or else Cordelia, by a circuitous route, could also have managed to reach Sir Lionel's position while her husband was out of the way. With a wry smile, Copper climbed the stairs to the wheelhouse once again. Unfortunately, Radley's surmise had been correct. Opportunity was not going to be a determining factor.

As the inspector reached the wheelhouse, a thought struck him. "Just a couple of things, captain," he said, as Bob looked up enquiringly at his slightly breathless arrival. "When you and your colleagues came back on board first thing on Monday, were the curtains

206

across the rear windows of the saloon open or closed?"

Bob wrinkled his brow in thought. "They were closed, sir."

"So nobody could have seen out or in?"

"That's right, inspector. Does it matter?"

"It might very well, captain. And the other thing is, do you happen to know if any of the Butler family are left-handed? Does Trey, for instance, have to lay out anyone's cutlery in the opposite way to normal?"

Bob looked puzzled. "Oh, now you're asking. Let me think ..." He frowned again in recollection. "No, inspector. As far as I know, everyone's right-handed."

"Hmmm." Copper mused for a moment, before his attention was attracted by movement on the quayside. "And here comes my sergeant, looking rather pleased with himself. So if it's all right by you, I think he and I will use your saloon for a little conference."

Chapter 20

"Good news, boss," announced Pete Radley as he joined Dave Copper at the dining table in *Red Buccaneer*'s saloon. "I remembered I'd stashed a new notebook in the car, just in case I ran out of capacity in the old one." 'Which is more than likely, when the boss is asking questions,' was his unvoiced thought. "So I've transferred all my notes into the new one, nice and neatly like you said, and that's given me the chance to link the stuff that people have told us about each of our suspects all into one lump. I'm hoping that's going to be helpful."

"Very much so, I should think, sergeant," approved Copper. "Although you'd better let me have both notebooks, in case there happens to be a morsel tucked away in your original notes that I might want to check back on, just to make sure that your recollection coincides with mine. Not that I'm doubting your skills," he added. "But sometimes the odd word makes all the difference."

"Right. Well, there you go, boss," said Radley, placing the pristine new notebook on the table, together with its considerably more dog-eared predecessor. "The notes on this business start about halfway through the old one. Oh, and in the midst of all that, I had a phone call from Anna."

"And ...?"

"She'd succeeded in tracking down the details of Sir Lionel's will. And she told me to tell you that it wasn't too easy, and she'd had to wangle a few favours, and you owe her one. I told her not to hold her breath, and she'd probably get her reward in heaven."

Copper laughed. "I think I've lost count of the number of favours we owe that particular young lady. I'm sure we'll manage to figure out something appropriate to show our appreciation. In the meantime, what's the news on the will?"

"Actually, boss, it's a bit disappointing. Nothing too surprising. There are some odd charitable bequests, and quite a nice little legacy to Lady Butler. Obviously she told the truth when she said there weren't any hard feelings between them since the divorce. Other than that, it's fairly predictable. Robin gets his steel business and the yacht, Leo gets the freehold of an extremely smart set of buildings in the Inner Temple in London, and Tyrone gets outright ownership of the Barbarossa Formula One race team. And the three brothers each get an executive seat on the board of Sir Lionel's Pirate Group of companies, and the cash assets get divvied up equally three ways between Robin, Leo and Tyrone."

"Very equitable," remarked Copper. "And not really any particular help at all."

"Ah, but hold on, boss," grinned Radley. "There's more. Because that's the will as it stands."

"Oh yes?" The inspector was intrigued.

"According to Anna's sources, which she was very careful not to reveal, Sir Lionel had an appointment with his solicitor later this very week. And there was just one item on the agenda."

"Let me guess. A possible revision of the will?"

"Got it in one, boss!" declared Radley triumphantly. "So how does that stir up our mix of motives?"

"Quite beautifully," said Copper. "If the family dinner party gave an opportunity for Sir Lionel to state his reservations, to say the least, about the family's doings, then this appointment with his lawyer gave him the opportunity to take action."

"Which means that someone from the family could have decided to take their own action in order to forestall whatever was on his mind," concluded the sergeant.

"Precisely. So ..." Copper reached for the notebooks.

"Let's see what we can find in amongst this lot."

"Do you want my input, boss?" enquired Radley, suspecting that he already knew the answer.

Copper smiled. "Not at this juncture, I think, Peter. I'd rather mull things over quietly on my own, if you don't mind."

"Just like you usually do, boss. No surprise there," grinned the sergeant, in no way disheartened.

"Besides," continued his superior, "I've got another job for you. Our uniformed colleagues from the patrol car have been hanging about since goodness knows when, no doubt getting thoroughly bored, and probably starving into the bargain. And I wouldn't mind betting you're feeling the pangs yourself. So why don't you go and scoop Kapoor and Sweeney up and take them over to that pizza place by the marina entrance and stand them a bite to eat? On expenses. We'll put it through as surveillance costs. They'll need to be refuelled because, with a bit of luck, I may have something for them to do a little later, once I've digested all this lot." He gestured towards the notebooks.

"Digestion all round, eh, boss? I reckon I know which sort I prefer."

"Off you go then," said Copper. "And stand by for a call."

"How are you going to manage that, boss?" asked Radley. "You never have your phone with you when we're out on a case." He chuckled in remembrance. "Not that I blame you, ever since you told me about having 'The Laughing Policeman' as your ringtone."

"I'll think of something," replied Copper. "If all else fails, I'll get Captain Bob to sound off on the boat's siren. You leave me to worry about that. Go!" And as he regarded Radley's retreating back with a smile, he opened the first notebook.

At least, he thought to himself, it's something of an

advantage to have a restricted field of suspects. Because it was clear, from their own statements, together with the corroboration provided by the yacht club's surveillance footage, that nobody other than the members of the Butler family could have had access to *Red Buccaneer* during the crucial period. But, considering the question of opportunity, there had seemed to be an insurmountable problem, in that the three couples concerned all appeared to have alibis which put them out of consideration. Everyone originally declared that they had retired to their own cabins on the Sunday night, and not emerged until informed of Sir Lionel's murder on the Monday morning. But, as so often happened as the investigation proceeded, these alibis had unravelled one by one. The only problem was, that one person's unravelled alibi automatically negated the alibi of their partner.

Leo's fruitless search for an intruder had taken him away from his own cabin, and provided him with an opportunity to encounter his father, while at the same time, his absence gave Cordelia a perfect opportunity to seek out Sir Lionel. Was the tale of a supposed intruder manufactured by Cordelia in order to remove her husband from their cabin? Or did Leo take it as a godsend, which he could turn to his advantage? Likewise, Jessica's mission to enjoy a surreptitious cigarette may have been entirely plausible, but it took her out of sight of Tyrone for some considerable while. Plenty of time to make her way to the location of the hot tub if she had murder on her mind. She definitely went ashore – but was that before a possible encounter with her father-in-law? Likewise Tyrone, if he wished to seek a confrontation with his father, could well have seized the opportunity which Jessica's excursion ashore provided. And finally, Robin. His supposed visit to the yacht's bar brought him closest of all to the afterdeck where Sir

Lionel was found. It would have been a matter of a few yards and a few seconds to reach the hot tub. Was it significant that the curtains of the saloon were closed? Was that to conceal Robin's actions from anyone who came into the saloon? Or did it prevent Robin seeing what was happening outside? And where was Dee during Robin's time in the bar? She could have reached the area of the hot tub, albeit by a circuitous route, but if she wanted to remain unobserved for her own purpose, it was entirely possible. And with the curtains closed, Robin need never have known she was there.

Copper gave a small private smile. At least it seemed that there was one thing he could be sure of. None of the couples was working as a husband-and-wife team, conspiring to bring about Sir Lionel's death for whatever reason. Because if that had been the case, they would surely have backed each other's alibi to the hilt. Although ... the smile faded. There was always the possibility that some sort of plot could have been hatched between the husband of one couple and the wife of another. Was that plausible? The inspector considered the concept for several long seconds, before eventually discarding it with a shake of his head. He had detected nothing during the course of all his interviews to indicate any kind of closeness between the members of the different couples. Surely he would have formed some kind of intuition if there had been the slightest hint of such a thing. Far more evident was a smouldering hostility between the brothers and their respective wives. His instincts told him that this thought was one to be dismissed.

So consideration of the various suspects' opportunities to commit the murder was not proving fertile ground. Perhaps the question of motivation would be more productive. Copper smiled again, this time in reminiscence. Back to the old basic question which his former mentor Andy Constable had taught his inexperienced newly-promoted assistant in Copper's early days as a detective sergeant. *'Cui bono?'* Radley wasn't the only one who could quote Latin legal precepts. 'To whose benefit?' The inspector began to leaf through the notebooks lying open in front of him. First, the three brothers, those closest in blood to the dead man. Could the motivation be one of the oldest and most obvious – that of financial gain? Certainly the terms of Sir Lionel's will would leave the three sons considerably better off, on the face of it. Would that be enough? Ostensibly the three were already in an excellent position, with Robin at the helm of a major industrial enterprise, Leo moving in the upper echelons of the legal profession, and Tyrone pursuing a glamorous career in a well-financed and headline-grabbing field of sporting entertainment. Of course, the will seemed to have given the three wives no direct way to benefit financially from Sir Lionel's death, but would that concern them particularly? Jezza had her own successful modelling career as Jessica Bell, while Cordy appeared well set-up with her independent garden design business as Cordelia Lyne. Only Dee stood out as something of an appendage to her husband's career, having given up her own when she relinquished her place at the bar when she married and ceased to be Desdemona Fender. But then there arose the question of the presumed rewriting of the will. Were all the cards about to be thrown up into the air, and for what reason?

The answer to this clearly lay in Sir Lionel's apparent change of attitude towards his heirs and their wives. He had plainly come into possession of some facts which altered his intentions. He had his private sources of information, as Lady Butler had revealed. And there were surely facts which the rest of the family had sought to conceal from him and the world. Their guilty secrets, in short. And so often, in Copper's experience, the attempt to conceal a guilty secret was what had led to murder. So what potential secrets could be deduced from the series of interviews which the detectives had conducted? And how many of them might have come into Sir Lionel's possession?

Again, the inspector cast his mental eye down the list of family members. With Robin, there were the exchanges between him and Sir Lionel on the subject of finances, business and personal, to consider. As for Leo, what accounted for the mysterious phone call and the reference to Dee's skills? And what factors could explain Tyrone's lack of success which so irked his father? And when it came to the wives of the three brothers, all seemed to have gaps in their lives. Cordelia had vanished from the records of her native country for a significant period. Likewise, Jessica's early career didn't appear to form a constant narrative. And how did Desdemona, once she retired from the bar, manage to live such a stylish social life with no evident means to support it? As Copper turned the pages of the notebooks before him, snippets of information drew his eye. But what connected with what? Was a picture starting to form? As he reached the end of Radley's reiteration of the various interviews, he gave a sigh. It was in there somewhere. Only one thing to do. He moved to one of the armchairs in the saloon, pulled the lever to lower the back, and settled into a reclining position, his eyes closed. To those who did not know him, he might have appeared asleep. But the fluttering of his eyelids betrayed the busy activity taking place in his mind. And at length, with a sudden catch of breath, his eyes opened, and a slow smile stole across his face. Hauling himself upright, he headed towards the stairs which led up to Bob de Waters' eyrie in the wheelhouse.

"May I use your phone a moment?" he said without preamble, as the captain looked up, surprised, at his

214

arrival.

"Of course, inspector." Bob handed the mobile over.

After a few rings, a voice answered. "Hi, love ... no, still on the yacht, but I have hopes. Just one question. It's about that wine glass ..."

*

"*D.S. Radley.*" The phone was answered with a degree of reservation in the sergeant's voice.

"Sergeant. I wonder if you would be kind enough to rejoin me on board *Red Buccaneer*. We have work to do."

"*Righty-ho, boss,*" was Pete Radley's cheerful reply. "*Sorry, didn't realise it was you calling. My phone didn't recognise the number.*"

"And that's because Captain de Waters has very kindly let me use his phone."

"*Right. Be there in a jiffy, boss. Actually, you couldn't have timed it better. The guys and I were just finishing our puds ...*"

"I hadn't realised you were intending to indulge in a feast," remarked Dave Copper, amusement evident in his tone.

"*Oh, come on, boss. You can't come to an Italian restaurant and not have the ice cream, can you?*" responded Radley reasonably. "*Anyway, give us two ticks to pay the bill, and I'll be straight across.*"

"And you can bring your dining companions with you," instructed the inspector. "I think we owe them a little action in return for all the inactivity we've inflicted upon them. So I'd like them on board, standing by for a touch of official duty."

"*Will do, boss. I'll let them have the gate code. I'm guessing that all this means that you've got things figured out.*"

"I believe so. Which means that I'd also like you to call in to the hotel on the way over. I'm assuming that the members of the Butler family are still on the premises ..."

"*Unless someone's done a runner, in which case there may not be too much to do in the way of clever detecting,*" remarked the sergeant.

"Let's hope that's not the case," replied Copper. "So please ask them if they would join me in the yacht's saloon. If you like, you can hint to them that it's because I'm planning on releasing them from the restrictions on their movements."

"*So as not to give the game away, eh? I like it, boss. Leave it with me, and I'll get all that sorted.*"

A minute or two later, the two constables from the patrol car were climbing the gangway, to be greeted by Copper as he stood at the top. "Thank you for your help so far, gentlemen," said the inspector. "I have a little job for you."

"Anything to help, sir," responded P.C. Kapoor eagerly, while his companion nodded in agreement.

"Excellent," said Copper, concealing a smile at the pair's enthusiasm. "Constable Sweeney, I'd like you to station yourself by the pontoon security gate so as to let the Butler family through, and then come back on board to rejoin your colleague here. And you, Constable Kapoor, if you'd like to position yourself on the covered deck just outside the saloon doors, so that I can call on you when I need to."

"Of course, sir." The two young officers gave a smart salute, prompting Copper to control the impulse to smile once again, and then turned to their tasks, as Pete Radley could be seen making his way down the pontoon towards *Red Buccaneer*.

"They're on their way, boss," reported the sergeant.

"Then we'd better get to it," replied the inspector, a grim edge to his voice.

Chapter 21

"If you don't mind me saying so, inspector," said Robin Butler, as he led the family group into the yacht's saloon, "I think it's a damn cheek summoning us on board our own boat. Or, probably more accurately, my own boat." He bristled with irritation.

"I'm sorry if it strikes you that way, Mr. Butler," responded Copper in his most emollient tone. "But I thought you would all like to know the conclusions I have reached in my investigations, and I imagine that you would prefer that to happen away from the eyes and ears of others."

"If you say so," grumped Robin, not sounding at all convinced. "Well, I suppose we'd better hear what you've got to say, so that we can all get on with our lives."

As the members of the Butler family disposed themselves around the seats in the saloon, Copper took up a position towards the stern end of the room, his back to the glass doors leading to the open deck, with Radley stationed at the other end of the room next to the stairs. The inspector stood in silent thought for a few moments, before clearing his throat and preparing to speak.

"To judge from all appearances," began Copper, "Sir Lionel Butler was a highly successful man. He had, from relatively modest beginnings, built up a considerable business empire, and we only need to look around us to see how he enjoyed the fruits of that success. As an achiever, it is natural to assume that he valued achievement. But of course, the other side of that coin is that he expected high standards from those around him, in particular the members of his family, and when those high standards were not reached, in whatever field, it seems that Sir Lionel was not slow to express his dissatisfaction. And where this occurs, there will automatically be differences of opinion. Clashes. And in extreme cases, such clashes can lead to resentment, at the very least dislike, and possibly eventually hatred. A powerful desire to remove the source of the problem. A motive, in fact, for murder. And the tragic fact is that someone in this room, for their own particular reasons, took that course."

The inspector's audience shifted uneasily in their seats and exchanged covert glances. The charge had never yet been stated so baldly.

Robin Butler once again seemed to elect himself as spokesman for his relations. "Inspector Copper," he said, his tone a bluff contrast to the resentful note it had held before, "are you seriously suggesting that it could possibly have been one of us who was responsible for this atrocious crime? Surely you're mistaken. I can't see why you seem to be discounting the possibility that some deranged outsider, for whatever bizarre reason, gained access to *Red Buccaneer* while the rest of us were peacefully asleep, and committed this appalling deed. What other explanation could there be?"

"Ah, Mr. Butler," countered Copper, "I'm sure you wish that were so. Sadly, the evidence in our possession completely rules out your theory. We have absolute proof that nobody, other than you and your family, could have been on board this vessel at the time your father was attacked. I'm afraid that, unpalatable as it may be, Sir Lionel died at the hands of somebody present."

"You talk about evidence, inspector," challenged Leo. "I've yet to hear any. And you mention clashes. What clashes? Do you mean arguments? Everybody has words from time to time. It's human nature. It doesn't mean that a person is moved to murder."

"True, sir," agreed Copper. "But it depends on the nature of the clashes, doesn't it? And perhaps more important, what these clashes might lead to. Because murder occurs for many reasons. A person may feel threatened, and kill to protect themselves, or perhaps to protect another person. A person may be desperate to preserve a secret, and so kill to suppress the revelation of that secret. Often, the two combine. So, if you like, I shall move on to something a little more specific. Evidence, since that seems to be what you require. And during the course of my conversations with yourselves, as well as with the members of your crew, I have learnt a number of quite interesting things."

"You mean hearsay, do you?" unexpectedly spoke up Dee. "Now I would be the first to admit that my knowledge of court procedure may have grown a little rusty since I retired from the bar ..." She gave an icy smile of self-deprecation. "... but I'm sure I remember that any judge will give short shrift to hearsay when presented during a trial."

The inspector echoed Dee's mirthless smile. "We're not conducting a trial here, Mrs. Butler," he replied. "I'm simply presenting a number of thoughts which have resulted from information which has come into my possession. Perhaps, since you query the nature of the information I have, I might usefully start with yourself.

"The thought occurs to me that you, in company with some others here, might end up wishing that this yacht's call into Guernsey had never happened. Because if it hadn't, there would never have been a witness to your swift departure from a jeweller's shop in St. Peter Port, followed by the emergence from the shop of a somewhat distraught sales assistant. The witness offered their assistance to the shopkeeper, but was told that the matter was of no importance. I have to relate that my witness doubted that explanation and, visualising the scene, I must say that I tend to agree. Which may be nothing in itself, but from a totally different source, we have newspaper reports of society gatherings where significant pieces of jewellery have gone missing.

219

Occasions when you were present. Now that may well be the most bizarre coincidence, but it's not impossible that Sir Lionel may have had these reports brought to his attention by his own private investigation services. And he, like me, could not have failed to notice that you have a taste for some very impressive, and doubtless very expensive, items of jewellery. Could he have put two and two together and drawn a most unflattering conclusion about your own personal probity? Is that why he stated that a newspaper headline stating *'Butler Steals'* might be unwelcome?"

"Just a minute, inspector," said Robin. "Are you accusing my wife of being ...?"

"I'd stop right there if I were you, Rob," Leo swiftly interrupted. "If the inspector's going to be making any accusations, you'll want this handled formally."

"No accusations at this point, gentlemen," said Copper mildly. "Merely observations. Reasons why a person might kill to suppress the truth. So perhaps, Mr. Butler, I ought to move on from your wife to you yourself."

"What, so you want to say that I'm a thief too?" demanded Robin hotly, provoking a warning glare from Leo.

"It's more a case of what you feared Sir Lionel might be thinking," replied the inspector. "So yes, you might be concerned if that were the case."

"Are you trying to be deliberately offensive, Mr. Copper?" growled Robin.

"I'm seeking to establish why an investigating officer ... such as myself ... might see potential grounds for a suspect ... such as yourself, Mr. Butler ... to wish a murder victim dead, sir. Now again, there have been conversations, witnessed by people whose word I have no reason to doubt, that left your original description of the relationship between you and your father in tatters.

220

He was evidently concerned that Butler Steels, his original company, of which he was doubtless extremely proud, was in some financial distress. And the press reports he had seen, some of which I have been told about, must have troubled him greatly. He also made a remark about the situation 'taxing your finances'. That was in the context of your recent visit to a casino. So was he charging you with an uncontrolled gambling habit? Did he suspect that your inability to regulate your own finances had led to an inability to maintain control of your company's finances as well? Or worse still, did he suspect that the one might be supporting the other, and that you were subverting the funds of the business? Perhaps evading taxes? Was it another case of fearing a report stating that '*Butler Steals*'? A person might very well kill to remove that threat."

"You are aware, inspector, that you're treading on very dangerous ground," intervened Leo smoothly. "I hope your knowledge of the law is sufficient to keep you well away from the realms of slander."

"I hope so too, sir," replied Copper calmly, unruffled by the implied threat. "I'm sure a gentleman such as yourself, well versed in all the ways of the law, would make sure that I didn't stray off the straight and narrow. Of course," he continued, a steelier tone entering his voice, "I would hope that you would apply the same standards to yourself. And it does sound as if Sir Lionel felt that he was doomed to disappointment in that respect."

"I have no idea what you are talking about, inspector," declared Leo, the look in his eyes belying his words.

"Then let me refresh your memory concerning a conversation which took place between your father and yourself during that visit of yours to Guernsey. There was talk that you might need more than your sister-in-law

221

Dee's skills to extricate you from a particular situation. What skills? Well, of course, Mrs. Robin is a former lawyer, even if not in the field in which you practice. But two heads may be better than one in a particular situation. And what situation might that be? Again, we have clues relating to that visit to Guernsey. You were heard on a telephone call, arranging to meet a contact there. A call which came from an untraceable phone on the island of Jersey. And there was mention of the fact that it would cost more if a certain piece of evidence were to be lost. It's an odd mixture of facts, which could point in a very dangerous direction for you. Research into your case history shows a number of trials in which you unaccountably failed to secure a conviction. Sir Lionel was doubtless unimpressed and suspicious of the fact. And he was also in receipt of information from his own investigators, plus perhaps one other surprising source. That very same burner phone which called you from Jersey. Who would be anxious to conceal their identity? Someone with criminal connections, perhaps? Was your contact attempting to play two sides against one another? Or perhaps to extract money from both of you in order to keep silence about a matter which threatened your whole career? Had you, in short, been suppressing vital evidence in return for money? Did the shadow of corruption hang over you, did Sir Lionel present a threat to expose you, and might you have killed to remove that threat?"

The silence which settled over the room became even more profound and tense. It was eventually broken by Tyrone Butler's voice, lighter by contrast when compared with the heavier tones of his brothers. "This is becoming all very serious and doom-laden, inspector," he said. "I suppose you'd better give poor Rob and Leo a break, and move on to my supposed catalogue of sins."

"Since you invite me, I shall do just that, sir,"

responded Copper. "Here again, there seems to be a catalogue of failure which Sir Lionel found highly displeasing. Having poured what I assume would be considerable amounts of money into your motor-racing venture, the results you have been presenting to him of late have been extremely disappointing. He challenged you with that very fact. 'Is my money not enough?', he was heard to say to you. Could he have been thinking of pulling the plug on your career? Had he come to the conclusion that to continue would simply be throwing good money after bad? Perhaps so. But I wonder how to weigh that possibility, when I consider what happened in Guernsey." The inspector gave a dry smile. "The whole family seems to have had quite an eventful visit to that island. And you, sir, had an encounter which sounds as if it bears further study."

"But how do you know ...?" began Tyrone, before biting off the words.

"That you met up with someone else from the motor-racing world?" suggested Copper. "Is that what you were going to say, Mr. Butler? Because that meeting did occur, although whether by accident or design I can't say. My witness had no information on that point. But you did, I believe, have a conversation with the principal of one of your driving rivals."

Tyrone gave a not entirely convincing laugh. "Yes, inspector. Wasn't that a coincidence? Who'd have thought that Miko Von Staffen's grandfather would turn up at some old German gun-site? He must have had some family connection from the war, I suppose."

"That's as may be, sir, but it wasn't Guernsey's wartime history you were discussing, was it? That's not what my witness heard. It was rather more the immediate future of your motor-racing programme, wasn't it? And the subject of money arose once again. So was there something going on that you would have been most anxious to conceal from your father? Where, I wonder, was the emphasis in the question your father had asked you? Was it, in fact 'Is *my* money not enough?' You pointed out to me that money can't buy victory. But can it buy a defeat? If Sir Lionel had got wind of something untoward, might you have resorted to murder in order to suppress the truth?"

"Well, it's a very interesting theory, inspector," replied Tyrone, "but it all sounds very flimsy to me. Of course Von Staffen talked about money when I ran into him. It's what he's all about. Now if you want to talk about someone in the money world who might want to do a bad turn to Dad, maybe you should be looking in his direction for your murderer." He looked around the family group with the smile of one who thought he had put one over on the detective.

"I suppose one can never rule anything out, sir," said Copper. "But if Mr. Von Staffen had been in this vicinity on Sunday night, I'm sure I would have learnt of it by now. I prefer to deal with the actual facts before me, instead of considering fictitious possibilities. So for the moment, we'll move on from yourself, and consider your wife."

"Oh, you surely can't believe that Jezza had anything to do with this," protested Tyrone.

"Bear with me, sir," responded the inspector patiently. "Because one of the reasons I have to take a look at Miss Bell is the fact that you yourself told me that she had no alibi for the time of the crime."

"Ty, what did you tell him?" cried Jessica in panicked tones.

"Nothing, sweetheart, I swear," said Tyrone in an effort to sooth his distressed wife. "I just mentioned that you'd gone off for a ciggy. That's all."

"That's not quite all, Miss Bell," resumed Copper. "Because your absence from view at a significant moment is not the only reason I have to examine the facts surrounding you. There may well be reasons why your relationship with Sir Lionel was under some stress."

"But we always got on so well," sniffed Jessica. "Ask anyone. He was a sweet old boy."

"Not invariably sweet towards you, I'm afraid," contradicted Copper. "I've been told that, during your visit to the Dior museum in Granville, he spoke very harshly to you. You were left in tears, I think. He charged you with hiding something. Could that have been the same thing that Robin Butler was referring to when he made a remark about you earning a living? Because your early career as a model is shrouded in some mystery. Details are sketchy, apart from some surviving reports of you being seen in the company of older and wealthier men. As someone pointed out, there is more than one interpretation of the word 'model'. So might you wish to conceal a shameful past, whose details had come to Sir Lionel's notice? A man with his degree of power, and with his sources of information, could very easily have found the means to destroy you and your marriage."

As Jessica regarded the inspector with the eyes of a wounded animal, Copper decided to move on. "And so," he said, "we come to the final member of the Butler family, Mrs. Leo Butler, or to give her her professional name, Miss Cordelia Lyne." He turned to Cordy. "You do prefer to use your maiden name in your professional career, I believe, rather then your married name."

"That's true, inspector," replied Cordelia, sounding slightly puzzled. "Although I can't see the relevance here."

"The relevance is," explained Copper, "that we are still dealing with the subject of marriage. Now you, since your arrival in the U.K., have married into a very wealthy family."

"Isn't that a slightly unsavoury question,

inspector?" responded Cordelia. "I didn't think it was the British way to talk about people's personal wealth. And in any case, don't forget that I have my own very successful business. If you're implying that I married for money, you're barking up the wrong tree."

"You marrying for money is not the point, Mrs. ... Miss Lyne. Although your marital status is very much of interest to me. You see, I was very puzzled when I heard of the exchange between yourself and a fellow New Zealander on the quayside in Guernsey. She was adamant that she knew your mother-in-law well back home, although to the best of our knowledge, Lady Butler has never set foot in New Zealand. The two things didn't seem to fit together. And the records which my colleagues in our Intelligence department looked through were very little help. Cordelia Lyne seemed to have vanished from the New Zealand database for a while, but that became possibly easier to understand when I was reminded that the earthquake which occurred some years ago in Christchurch, your home town, had compromised some of the records. But that didn't explain this mysterious mother-in-law reference. That is, unless the woman in Guernsey spoke nothing but the truth, and she truly was a good friend of the lady in question. The lady to whose son, I deduce, you were married. Now again, there's no law against marrying twice. Provided, that is, you take the precaution of dissolving the first marriage before embarking on a second. Unfortunately, the gap in the records means that any trace of that divorce may have been lost. But why, then, would there be such a panicked reaction to the remarks by the woman in Guernsey? Why the flustered denials, when a brief explanation would have been so much simpler? There seems only one logical conclusion to be drawn. Your first marriage was still valid. Which therefore means that you are not legally Mrs. Leo Butler.

The revelation to Sir Lionel Butler of that information would have been highly destructive to your personal and financial prospects. And there we have a very sound motive for murder."

Chapter 22

"Cordy, is this true?" Leo Butler sounded aghast.

"What? No! Of course I didn't kill Lionel," replied Cordelia shakily.

"Not that!" responded Leo, almost dismissively. "I don't care about that. I mean, were you ... are you ... already married?" It seemed as if he could scarcely bring himself to ask the question.

Cordelia hung her head. "Oh Leo," she said, in a voice filled with tears. "I never meant to hurt you."

"You never meant ..." Leo's incredulity was plain to hear. "You never meant to *hurt* me? Is that the only thing you're concerned about? Not that you've committed bigamy? Not that you're about to make me a laughing stock? Not that the inspector here thinks you may well be a murderer into the bargain? The only thing you've got to say is that you never meant ..." He bit the words off, shaking his head.

"You want a confession?" snapped back Cordelia, roused. "All right. You can have a confession. I confess that I was married to Rick. I confess that I was young. We both were, and far too stupid to know what we were doing. But not so stupid that we didn't realise that we'd both made a terrible mistake. And one day, he just wasn't there any more. He got out. Nobody knew where he'd gone. Not his family, not anyone. And I went away to university, and while I was there, we had the earthquake in Christchurch. When I came home, there was nothing for me. My parents were already dead, the house was gone ... so I just tried to forget that the past had ever happened. I went back to my maiden name. I upped sticks and came over here ..." Her voice softened. "... and I met a man I fell in love with. I needed a new start. You were it."

"And that's your excuse, is it?" said Leo, apparently

unmoved. "That's your confession?"

"And you've got nothing to confess?" retorted Cordelia, aroused once more. "Haven't you been listening? Haven't you heard what the inspector's been saying? At least if I've committed a crime, some people might have a grain of sympathy for me. Whereas you ... well, I knew you were mixing with criminals. It's your job. But you're supposed to be staying on the right side of the law, or had you forgotten? Now it sounds as if you're mixed up with all sorts of corruption, and if that all turns out to be true, they'll break you into tiny pieces. So don't you dare lecture me!"

Leo took a deep breath and seemed to crumple. "You don't understand," he said, in a defeated voice. He sighed. "And I've nobody to blame but myself. There was a case a while back ... there was a gang in London ... not even a particularly important one, except that ... well, I screwed up. I let it slip that we had some evidence, and somebody on the other side tricked me into revealing what we had, only to see it suddenly evaporate. The whole case fell apart, and if my part in it had come out, my career would have been finished. But the accused were very grateful, and they had friends. Friends with money, and friends with muscle. I suddenly found myself with a large amount appearing in my bank account, and it was made clear to me that although it was untraceable, that could easily be changed if I didn't co-operate in future. I was also told in no uncertain terms that if I spoke to the authorities, my health would suffer. I was trapped. And frightened. So once in a while, when these so-called friends had one of their ... colleagues, you might say ... in trouble, I was enlisted to make that trouble go away. Don't think I was proud of myself. But for all that, whatever Dad might have known, I'd never have ..." His voice petered out.

"How can we know that?" said an implacable

229

Cordelia. "You know you left the cabin that night. It could have been you."

"Oh, he's not the only one who went wandering in the middle of the night, Cordy," suddenly interposed Desdemona. "Why don't you ask Rob whether he took advantage of his midnight stroll to go and do something that might put an end to the danger to him that the inspector's told us about? Well, Rob?" She turned to her husband. "While we're in the midst of all these confessions, why aren't you joining in?"

"I'm confessing nothing," snarled Robin in response. "I know I didn't kill Dad, and if you've got any evidence to prove that I did, inspector, you're welcome to present it. And you may well be a highly skilled accountant ..." His lip curled. "... which I doubt ... but unless you have any proof that my father was accusing me directly of embezzling money from the company, you have nothing. Newspaper gossip isn't evidence, and I have accountants who can tie you up in knots for years if they are so minded. So do your worst, Mr. Copper. Find a motive for me to commit murder if you can, but I think it may take you a while."

"I'm a patient man, Mr. Butler," replied Copper mildly. "Although it sounds to me as if your own wife may not be totally convinced of your innocence."

"Dee?" snorted Robin in derision. "She's fine one to talk, when she seems quite happy to point a finger at me to divert your attention away from herself. Tell me, darling," he said, addressing his wife, "just how much of your dazzling jewellery collection has been bought with my supposed ill-gotten gains, and how much have you acquired by more unconventional means?"

"You're raving," snapped Desdemona. "Can you hear yourself? Are you really calling me a common thief?"

"Oh, not common at all, by the sound of it," sneered Robin. "Very much the reverse. But why would you do it,

230

for goodness sake? It's not as if you've been living in grinding poverty. So why don't you tell Mr. Copper here about that wonderful sapphire necklace of yours? Exactly like the one belonging to Serena Buckingham that you'd so admired, and after she had it stolen while you were staying there, you had an exact copy made to remind you of it. Or at least, that was your explanation to me. Was I a total fool to believe you? Is that the kind of embarrassing coincidence that might put a little flesh on the bones of the inspector's deductions? How well would a close examination of that necklace stand up? Or maybe we should call this shopkeeper in Guernsey, and get him to trawl through the contents of your jewellery case to see if he recognises anything." A short sharp snort of contempt. "If Dad had got hold of information like that and the word had got about, I think you'd have found your social invitations drying up in very short order. And you wouldn't have liked that. So while I was in the bar, what was to stop you taking matters into your own hands?"

"You seriously think I did it for the money?" riposted Dee. "I mean, would have done," she swiftly corrected herself. "I'm not admitting anything. But can you imagine just how dull it is being married to you? I used to have a career, perhaps not the most exciting in the world, but at least I had some self-worth. And then I gave it all up when I married you. More fool me! Because while you were so full of yourself, being the grand boss, even with your stupid gambling habit and your little fiddles to finance it, what was there for me? Was I just supposed to be an accessory on your arm at business conferences? So yes, maybe I needed a little excitement in my life. Maybe the thrill of a little danger, like Raffles. But for the money? Never! Don't judge me by your own standards. And I don't think Lionel would have done either. He might have cut some corners in his time, but I don't think he'd have condemned me. He might even

231

have laughed, remembering that old buccaneer spirit of his that I don't think ever left him. So kill him to keep that secret? I don't think so."

"Oh dear, inspector," spoke up Tyrone, sprawled in the corner of one of the sofas. "You seem to have us all fighting like ferrets in a sack. Nothing like a few secrets emerging from the woodwork to liven up a family gathering. And here we all are, with alibis falling like dominoes. I expect you'll end up saying that we all did it."

"You may like to joke, Mr. Butler," said Copper grimly, "but in truth, you yourself are the one I have to thank for the steady fall of dominoes, as you put it. If you hadn't mentioned the fact that your wife left your cabin during the crucial period ..."

"But I really did go for that ciggy, inspector," stressed Jessica. "It wasn't till I came back on board that I ..." She broke off.

"Go on, Miss Bell," coaxed Copper softly.

"I came back on to *Buck*. And I was going to come straight back down to our cabin, when I saw Lionel coming down the back steps towards the hot tub. And he saw me, and called me up. He told me to go and get a bottle of champagne and a couple of glasses from in here, and when I got back, he was in the tub. And he wanted me to get in with him, but I said no, and he said that the least I could do was join him in a drink, so he opened the bottle and poured two glasses. And then he said he wondered why I was suddenly so reluctant. He said that reluctance wasn't exactly my trade-mark, was it? And I said I didn't know what he meant. And he laughed."

"Did he explain?" enquired the inspector quietly.

A deep sigh from Jessica. "He said he'd heard some stories that he hadn't much liked. He said that he'd thought I liked him for himself, because he was fun to be with but ... he asked me how many other men I'd told that they were fun to be with during my career. Because,

232

he said, it was a career, wasn't it? My profession. The oldest one, he said. And I didn't know what he meant, so he spelt it out for me. He said I'd been nothing less than a ..." Jessica couldn't bring herself to say the word. "And I never was," she insisted. "All right, my agency set me up with some rich men. Powerful. But I was young, and I was desperate to get somewhere with my modelling, and I thought that the more people I could make friends with, the more influence they might have ..." Her head drooped. "But I never did anything just for money. You have to believe me, inspector." She turned to her husband. "You believe me, Ty, don't you? And honestly, I didn't kill Lionel. You know that, right?"

"Of course I do, sweetheart," said Tyrone, moving to the side of her and clasping her hand tightly. "Don't worry about it."

"Your husband is right, Miss Bell," said Copper. "You shouldn't worry about being faced with a charge of murder. I know you weren't responsible for Sir Lionel's death. At least, not directly. And your husband knows that too." A pause. "Don't you, Mr. Butler?"

In the sudden frozen silence, Tyrone looked up sharply, to meet the detective's steady gaze. "I don't think I quite understand you, inspector," he said slowly.

"Oh, I think you do, Mr. Butler," responded Copper. "You see, there has been a lot of talk about evidence. Mostly, the people here alleging that I don't have any. And to a certain extent, that's true. Most of the information that's come my way is circumstantial evidence at best. A great deal of hearsay, as Mrs. Desdemona Butler has been so eager to point out. Mr. Leo Butler made a similar remark, and it's always good to be reminded by those with legal training of what is likely to carry most force when it comes to a trial. And I will grant you that circumstantial evidence is all very well when it comes to constructing the jigsaw which forms the solution to a case, but it's best not to rely on it entirely. So isn't it fortunate, at least for me, that I have one piece of solid concrete evidence which brings me to my conclusion?"

Pete Radley glanced quizzically at his superior. What was it, he wondered, that he wasn't aware of? Nothing, surely. The inspector wasn't in the habit of concealing facts from his colleague. So what had he missed?

"And it's something as simple as a wine glass," continued Copper, unconsciously answering the sergeant's query. "But if you'll forgive me, I shall resort to some deduction, and a little intuition, to reconstruct the circumstances surrounding Sir Lionel Butler's death. A great deal of what I've been told is the simple truth. Miss Jessica did leave this yacht to go for an unobserved cigarette. Sir Lionel did return in her absence, and evidently decided to enjoy one of the late-night sessions in his hot tub of which he was so fond. And on Miss Jessica's return, he invited her to join him. So far, so good. And this is where the guesswork comes in. Because I believe that, after a while, Jessica's husband began to wonder where she was. He came looking for her. How on earth," the inspector remarked, with a grim smile, "either she or he missed encountering any of the other members of the family, who seemed to be prowling around the yacht at a similar time, is beyond me, but since nobody has mentioned seeing anyone else, let's take it for a fact. But Tyrone did find Jessica. Perhaps he came upon the scene just as Sir Lionel was levelling his most damaging personal accusations against Tyrone's wife. I suspect that he must have intervened, on account of the fact that his wife was becoming upset at the charges. So, Mr. Butler, I think you suggested to your wife that she return to your cabin while you deal with your father. After her departure, I imagine that there was a heated exchange.

The conclusion of that argument was that you seized the bottle of champagne which the two had been sharing, went around behind your father, and delivered the final blow. You then returned to your cabin, and doubtless passed off the situation to your wife as having merely ended in angry words. But before you went back below decks, you did the one thing which gave you away. You took the champagne glass which Jessica had been using and returned it to its place in the glass cupboard in this saloon, in an attempt to disguise the fact that she had ever been at the scene of the murder. In essence, to protect her. And by your action, you proved that both she and you had been present. Because the fingerprints of both of you remained on that glass, yours on top of hers, proving that you were the last person to handle it. With your left hand. And if you had never been there, how could that be?"

"But that could have been from anywhen," blustered Tyrone. "Why should it have been then?"

"I think that Mr. Loader might well take offence at your suggestion, Mr. Butler," replied Copper. "From what I've learnt, he takes great pride in keeping everything on board in apple-pie order. I can't imagine him overlooking a dirty glass. In fact, he was the one who drew my attention to its condition. And although the glass is the main item of physical evidence we have, there are other indications of your responsibility for the crime. The fact that, according to our forensic team, the blow was delivered left-handedly, for example."

"But I'm right-handed," protested Tyrone. "Ask anyone."

"I have," responded the inspector simply. "And they confirm what you say. And I was puzzled for a while. But then I suddenly remembered a cousin of mine. He's right-handed in virtually everything – writing, playing golf, using cutlery. Except that he has one odd quirk.

When he's shuffling and dealing playing cards, he does it left-handed. And I was reminded of what your brother Leo told me about a very expensive modification to your racing car. A 'cack-handed' redesign of the cockpit, he called it. Cack-handed – an old term for left-handed. So I thought, if your left hand is dominant when you're driving your racing car, might it not also come into play when you're facing another extreme situation? Such as delivering a fatal blow to your father, for example."

There was a very long silence. Copper was content to wait, and eventually Tyrone drew a long shaky breath. "It wasn't for myself," he said.

"Ty, be careful what you say," warned Leo, but his brother waved him wearily aside.

"You know, everyone in his world respected Dad. They reckoned he was a strong man. Most people admired him for what he'd achieved, after starting out with a ratty little company in the East End, not much better than grandad's old scrap metal business. And most people liked him – that's those who never got on the wrong side of him." A mirthless chuckle. "I reckon those of us who were closest to him, his nearest and dearest ... we were just lucky. We got to see what he could be really like. He never suffered fools gladly. In fact, he didn't suffer them at all, and he thought anyone who failed to come up to his standards must be some kind of fool. I've heard him tearing a strip off my brothers more times than I care to remember, and it doesn't sound as if Dee and Cordy got off too lightly either. But when it came to my Jezza ..." He paused, blinking rapidly. "I don't really care what happens with my brothers and their wives. As far as I'm concerned, Dad could have thrown them under the bus, and it wouldn't bother me that much. But Jezza ..." He turned to gaze deeply into the young woman's eyes, and his voice softened. "She's my wife. I love her. I always have, since the second I first saw her. And if there

236

are some bits of her past that she's not too proud of, I don't care. That's all behind her. We're living in the now. But my father ... he wasn't what you'd call a forgiving man. You've heard what he was capable of. And I honestly don't know if he was trying to put pressure on Jezza to be ... more than a daughter-in-law to him."

"Oh Ty, you can't think that I would ever ..." Jessica's tearful denial petered out into silence.

"I was afraid," declared Ty, himself watery-eyed. "But when I heard him threatening you ... when he said that it was in his power to tell the world that you were nothing short of a tart ... I just couldn't let him do that to us. So after I'd sent you back down to our cabin, I told him that he'd better keep quiet about what he thought he knew. I told him I wouldn't stand for him ruining our lives. And he just laughed at me. Called me a ridiculous boy, and he'd do whatever he liked. He was still laughing when I got hold of the champagne bottle and ...." Ty broke off. "Inspector, can't we just put an end to this?" A look of appeal. "Can't you just take me away and do whatever it is you need to do?"

"I think that would be best, Mr. Butler," replied Copper gently. He turned to Pete Radley. "Sergeant, would you please take Mr. Butler here into custody."

Radley stepped forward. "Tyrone Butler, I am arresting you ..."

"Outside, I think, sergeant," Copper interrupted him. "There's no need for everyone to witness this. And then, would you ask Kapoor and Sweeney to take charge of the gentleman and deliver him into the care of the custody sergeant at our station. We can follow them shortly."

Tyrone Butler stood and reluctantly disengaged his hand from that of his wife, who kept her distraught gaze on him as, under Radley's escort, he made his way through the glass doors and out on to the afterdeck of

237

Red Buccaneer.

After watching their departure, Copper turned back to address the remaining members of the Butler family, still sitting silent and stunned. "Ladies and gentlemen, you are, for the moment, free to go. I shall be putting in a full report, and no doubt some of my colleagues will shortly be in touch with you. What happens after that is beyond my jurisdiction. But I would suggest that, whatever legal resources you have at your disposal, now would be a good time to marshal them." Receiving no response, he turned and left the yacht's saloon, following in the footsteps of the small party proceeding up the pontoon and out of the marina.

*

"Not planning on taking things any further tonight then, boss?" enquired Pete Radley, as the two detectives made their way back to their office after seeing Tyrone Butler safely installed in one of the station's custody cells.

"Sufficient unto the day, I think, sergeant," replied Dave Copper. "I don't know about you, but I think that'll do for me for today. We'll start fresh in the morning. I'm off home to shower praise on Una for the crucial part Forensics played in concluding matters. I doubt whether there's very much fresh to be gleaned from Tyrone Butler, although that may change, once he's got the benefit of a solicitor alongside him. And I know you'll have quite a lot to do bringing your notes up to date after this last session, and I shall have a very long report to write. There are going to be several of our colleagues who will want to follow up on what we've learnt."

"There are also going to be quite a few careers wrecked in the aftermath of all this, aren't there, boss?" mused Radley.

"True. Some people's lives are going to look very different."

"Although," said Radley, his usual irrepressible grin beginning to reassert itself, "once it's all over, Tyrone Butler may end up with some fresh opportunities."

"You reckon?" enquired Copper, baffled.

"Too right, boss," said Radley. The grin became a chuckle. "Think about it. He's more than likely to get banged up with a bunch of quite serious villains. Probably some of the unpleasant customers that Leo Butler counts among his friends. But also, maybe a few unreformed bank robbers."

"And ...?" The inspector still couldn't see his junior's point.

"Well, boss," gurgled Radley. "Once he's back out of the nick, with all his skills at the steering wheel, Tyrone could always land a new job as a getaway driver!"

After a moment's pause to absorb the suggestion, the inspector couldn't stop himself joining in his colleague's peals of laughter.

***

also by Roger Keevil

The Inspector Constable Murder Mysteries

Murderer's Fête
*Who could have foreseen the murder of a
clairvoyant at a country fête?*

Murder Unearthed
*Sun, sangria and suspects during a supposed holiday
in Spain*

Death Sails In The Sunset
*Murder ensues when a journalist won't let guilty
secrets be buried at sea*

Murder Comes To Call
*Three short stories to tax the talents of our
detectives*

Murder Most Frequent
*Another trilogy of intriguing cases for Constable and
Copper*

The Odds On Murder
*Who is riding for a fall when a prominent racehorse
trainer is killed?*

No Bar To Murder
*Complicated relationships make a potent and lethal
cocktail*

The Murder Cabinet
*A return to Dammett Hall leaves the nation's fate in
the team's hands*

The Game Of Murder

Sudden death at the TV studio as entertainment turns to murder;
PLUS a bonus short story, 'Exit A Murderer',
and a full index to all the Inspector Constable mysteries

The Copper & Co Murder Mysteries

Honeymooner's Murder

Even on an idyllic tropical island, murder never takes a holiday

Murder At Witch's Holt

Dark secrets lead to a strange death at a spooky manor house

***

Printed in Dunstable, United Kingdom